The Idiot of

Daniel C. Betts

Thanks for buying my book Radim!

DANIEL
C BETTS
29/06/20.

Dedication

In loving memory of Grandad.

Acknowledgements

Many thanks to those who have contributed to this, starting with the staff from Burgess Autistic Trust for their assistance with starting off the difficult publishing process. I also give my thanks to Heather Steed, James Wilson, Clare, Meghan, and members of my own family (hello Mum!). They were great people who had given up their spare time to help proof read early versions of the book.

And most importantly of all, many thanks to the author Mark Haddon, whose impeccable novel involving a certain curious incident helped highlight autistic people in a greater light and inspired myself to create a story of my own.

Before you read, here is a simple key:

This is the narrator, a character of a neutral background who overlooks the story from a third person view and gets an in-depth view of the world around Arnold.

But when you see this kind of text, you get to see the world through the eyes of the protagonist Arnold Holt, who is autistic.

Every now and then, you'll also see one of Arnold's visual representations as the story goes along.

Now enjoy!

1

Oddballs, misfits, deviants; the list could extend to negative proportions but these are words often conjured up by the neurotypical ones who dominate our society. If my assumptions are correct, you're also part of that group, but it's those that aren't that interest me the most.

The exteriors of these special individuals may look perfectly normal but their interiors highly distinguish themselves from the crowds, societies and communities that form up the general public. Unfortunately a fraction of these are highly puzzled as to why they exist and feel worried that they'll encroach on an aimless, solitary and unwanted future. We'll see Arnold, a genuine example trapped into an endless loop of routines, tries to better his life without the misery, regret and mishaps that were offered to him in his past years.

Aaron loved Everton mints. They were rectangular sweets that had zebra patterning and a toffee filling inside; he would absolutely pine for them. Back then a few individuals would often mistake them for mint humbugs while he was present and this would cause him to repeatedly correct them. Aaron lived in a partially suburban part of Kent where the main road was lined with trees on both sides whose leaves would shake in the breeze. Behind the trees was a hidden supply of yellow fields which Aaron never thought existed, which felt slightly ironic because the area he lived inside was known as Farnborough Village.

Nowadays every time I went to meet him, I promised myself to give him six Everton mints because the number six personally felt like a lucky number. If there were seven mints left in the packet for example, I would feel a jolt of discomfort in my stomach until I tossed away the remaining offender, whereas if the quantity of mints were 6 or under then I would simply purchase a new supply. I would then line up six Everton mints like a row of private cadets on guard duty holding their bayonets upright, bearing their stiff faces and lined up dead straight in front of his gravestone.

Out of all the scrapes and japes he had endured through his gaming life of virtual rifles and his joystick of justice (as he would call it), the online champion of *Unreal Championship* back in school four years ago, loses to cancer which was a foe he couldn't defeat. To be extra specific it struck him in his left leg but it was at that moment I was going to lose my best friend forever. Normally the default emotional response at a funeral or cemetery would be the woeful shedding of tears but I cannot bestow such sorrowful behaviour by passing tears and this would often give out dodgy looks from other visitors. But the passing away of an individual who had stood against your side, provided you with support and can understand if you're feeling sad by a split second glance. And furthermore-

'YOU!'

A brief bellow occurred from behind. A left-right visual search quickly reflexed.

'Hoi, you! So you're the one with the humbugs!'

'They are not humbugs. They're Everton mints,' I replied, correcting him but he did not stop to listen.

'I don't care! Those bloody squirrels are ruining my daughter's grave, all thanks to those blasted sweets you're leaving out!'

I turned around properly to face the man who was trying to disturb myself and Aaron. He wore a battered denim jacket with small holes where the front pocket would be and matching trousers that did not appear as abused as his jacket. But as he drew closer I could observe that his two of his teeth were missing and had red letters written on his knuckles; but worst of all the man appeared to be wearing a large hooped earring. After collecting his observations I knew that the next objective was to run from this dodgy denim individual and continue running until I knew that the man had given up chase, which happened when I passed the entrance to the cemetery but I still continued to run downhill, past the roundabout and the line of shops, until I managed to dart into the safe spot that I called home.

******

At the moment it was safe, safe until the "rush hour" began. 5:56pm, I am normally the first to arrive and it was roughly 33 minutes until the daily disruption of the silent, unscathed yet tranquil disposition I call home would occur, so I switched on the family television to take my mind off the unavoidable matter. Archived sitcoms had always been my choice of television viewing for numerous years, but living with those who'd rather watch the dirge off Channel 3 and see your programme genre as an anomaly can cause some conflict.

When time had passed the door sounded and the sound of high heels stomped quickly and grew louder towards the living room where I was sitting. The sound was coming from my older sister Rose, a 22 year old generic office worker who would indicate her presence in the household by shouting unnecessarily, drinking alcohol and giving out orders in a negative manner which was highly predictable.

'I want that crap off by the time I take my shoes off,' blasted her bossy feminine voice. 'You've been here all day, I haven't so it's MY time to watch the telly.'

'That is incorrect,' replied myself but she didn't seem to acknowledge my correction.

'Arnold,' she asked 'Why do you even watch this old rubbish?'

'I find it highly entertaining, there' is nothing wrong with watching classic comedy.'

'When it's an 18 year old watching *Last of the Summer Wine*, there is clearly something wrong with your brain and get your hand out of your armpit, it's making you even weirder. Don't run off when I'm speaking to you!'
By the time Rose said her last eight words, I passed through the door frame to the hall.

When the rush hour occurs, the pace quickens, tensions rise and the chances of a collision soar, just like in the family kitchen. The situation is nearly inescapable but only a knowledgeable few would attempt to avoid this by hiding inside the back roads which are often ignored by the general crowd because they are often tucked away and given a width restriction to scare off the motorists. The back garden was a decent alternative to facing the busy hassle in the kitchen, with the exterior of the house forming a near perfect soundproof barrier from the noises emitting from inside.

Of course there was another vital reason why I chose to enter the back garden other than avoiding traffic, something that provided myself with such content and fulfilment in my otherwise aimless life, which was the feeding of my beloved rabbit. Coincidentally most owners enjoy tending towards their pets when they feel as if they had been berated once again by mainframe society and that was another main reason I enjoyed tending towards my rabbit. With her hutch deliberately hidden behind the green side facing shed, it was invisible from those spying from the kitchen window as well as being the closest place of refuge where I would peacefully feed to my beloved pet and stroke her black and white fur, without being disturbed by my horrible sister or my idiotic brother.

Unlike humans (and Rose), rabbits cannot spout nasty or hateful comments at you for various reasons and they can't make fun out of your appearance or voice either, which I was almost subject to every day back in secondary school.

But during the honeymoon period of owning a new pet there was always the inevitable stage of naming the hapless animal. Naming a pet was rather different in my view because I am generally indecisive and if there was an incorrect amount of syllables or letters in the suggested name then I would reject it because the concept would feel unbalanced and this would sometimes give me a headache. The naming of my rabbit came from a suggestion from my sister Rose briefly after we brought the rabbit from an animal shelter. Here was an excerpt from that moment:

'Have you thought of a name yet?' asked my mother.
'Blacky?' responded myself with an answer-cum-question.
'One of my friends was called this at school and it made him cry.' replied my brother George.
'What about Black Shadow then?' I said.
'You might as well call it Condom then!' muttered my Dad in a slightly sarcastic manner.
'MILTH!' shouted Rose, holding a can of lager.
'That is a good suggestion,' I replied.
'Are you sure?' asked my mother looking slightly worried 'How about choosing another one?'
'No thank you, I like the name Milth, it suits her perfectly.'

And that was how the name of my beloved rabbit came to be. The spelling itself was my own assumption as it rhymed with "filth", which felt appropriate when my sister noticed the droppings Milth would leave on the ground; and when being asked by teachers to describe my pet they were amused at how it was spelt and commented on its uniqueness. My former helper also shared the same look as my mother when I told her about Milth until she read my homework describing pupils' pets and saw my explanation behind her name.

Then I jumped slightly when I heard the back door swung open and a voice calling from inside. Then from around the corner a bobbing clump of silver hair slid above the roof of the shed, somebody had discovered my secret refuge. This was my Dad, I knew this not just because of his hair colour but the only individual in the household to dwarf the garden shed at 6' 3".

'Hiding again as I thought,' he smiled, shaking his head. 'Are you alright Arnold?'

'Yes.'

'Are you sure?'

'…'

'Fine, we'll talk about it another time. There's a chicken 'n' mushroom pie in the freezer, would you like to share it?'

'Yes. Please.'

'OK then, aren't you going to come inside and read your book Arnold?' asked my Dad before returning to the kitchen.

'No thank you. It is too early.'

It was roughly 7:15pm that the 'rush hour' subsided and the opportunity to re-enter the kitchen but why they called it the rush hour was illogical because usually it either lasted from 37 minutes to an hour and a half the maximum but if the term hadn't existed, neither would that song I'd like to listen to every time whilst travelling with my Dad and his car outside Swanley.

2

It was 9:06am; and once again the cycle of daily objectives would begin. As soon as I woke up I was highly aware of how the daily loop of inevitable events would play out, albeit with some slight variations. Sadly no start-up music would accompany my awakening, duly because my alarm clock wasn't equipped with a radio but it was often the sound of the radiator clacking or the nearby pigeon singing outside that filled in for the silence. It appeared that my daily activities could be rearranged into a weekly TV schedule, closedowns and all, an example below:

9.00 AM Good Morning Arnold
9.15 Breakfast time
9.25 Feed Milth her breakfast [S/AD]
9.40 Watch a few TV repeats [S/AD]
10.30 Depart from home [AD]
10.50 Visit the library in Orpington [AD]
2.00 PM Return home for lunch [AD]
3.00 A weekly activity
6.30 Feed Milth her dinner [S/AD]
6.45 Supper time
7.30 Read *The Railway Series* and/or *The Curious Incident* books
10.30 Goodnight Arnold.

Key
[S]: Subtitles
[AD] Audio description

That of course was only a generic representation of my daily routine. The reasoning behind the audio description and the use of subtitles was it that provided my own comedic interpretation to the tasks which livened up the routine and increased the excitability, but there would be no "subtitles" used whilst eating and travelling, because the need to speak at those times was very minimal in my own view.

Normally I would recall the exact time in minutes when I either undertook a certain task or were asked how long the chicken escalopes were cooked in the oven but most generic TV guides round up the units to their nearest multiples of five and like myself are more familiar with a 12 hour display in their schedules.

A few slight exceptions were when schools programmes in the past used to be rounded up to their nearest minutes and that one moment back in July 2007 when the digital television system briefly malfunctioned and displayed the starting times for programmes in an honest and precise manner, avoiding the uses of fives and zeros. At the same time the Channel 3 station was briefly switched to Central but as usual I was the only one to notice such minor anomalies in the family household.

Sometimes I wished that I could sleep the entire day away to delete time like the brain-dead contestants on *Big Brother* but unfortunately that cannot happen, even lying in bed for the remainder of the day wasn't possible at all because boredom would quickly prevail and the chances of collecting peculiar markings on my skin would greatly increase. The worst possible case was the time I fell asleep after completing a jigsaw puzzle and woke up with the pieces benchmarked into my cheeks and wrists, I then tried to hide the marks with a bandage but the family soon noticed and laughed.

Or alternatively the option to fast forward through real time events like a VCR player would be a great benefit to myself as I won't have to spend half the day hopelessly trying to determine what my next stepping stone in life will be. Generally individuals would use the generic crossroads metaphor when they were at a staple in life where they can't decide what to do next or which decision to follow. For myself, the problem was far greater where all the fingerposts were blanked out and all I had to help me was an outdated road atlas where all the junctions were replaced by tiny dots and the pages either missing or mutilated by previous abuse and frustration.

******

In the next sequence, we'll discover another one of Arnold's everyday gripes. Of course we all have our flaws and individual quirks which make everyone truly unique in their own style; quite often we can override these bad qualities ourselves but for those similar to Arnold, these quirks are usually amplified in a way that can conflict with mainstream society. We don't know yet why he hates the following, it could be down to disliking change which is traditional, or that he just simply hates them.

Every time I would set foot in the town centre, this never-ending juncture would occur; of being surrounded by those disgusting youths that continuously thrive in the town centre with their pink striped shirts, oversized baseball caps and other hideous abnormalities. Their population would reach an annual peak every summer and it's at these periods that they increase drastically in numbers and try to obliterate the general public with foul language, empty drinks cans and rude questions; as if we were a shrinking minority. Wearing hardly anything above the belt, they would then expose their disgusting tattoos and belly button rings to the sweltering public, which metaphorically speaking had the same effects on myself as staring into the blinding sun, which could even start as soon as I stare out of the warm, simmering windows in my bedroom.

So far 8/11 of my objectives had been fulfilled for the day; and after taking Milth to the woods for a walk (she enjoyed it there today) the next task to undertake was feeding her. Yet for some reason I didn't have the urge to take cover from the upcoming "rush hour" and assumed that the reason why was because it was Thursday and my Dad would arrive home first on that particular day instead of my sister Rose. Soon after the sounds from the front door closing heavily and the jingle from his door keys were heard, my prediction was correct.

'Hello Arn,' said my Dad as he peered through the hall doorway. I refused to reply, as if he had insulted me.

'Sigh, evening Arnold,' he replied flatly, before he walked into the living room and stopped next to the fireplace. 'Are you alright?'

'Yes. Why?'

'Well I know by now there's something up with you and you always hide yourself from us outside in the back garden when something happens to you; and that's what happened yesterday evening, so what's wrong with you now?'

'Nothing,' I said.

'Is this about Aaron again?'

'No.'

'For god's sake Arnold I'm your father. Your helper is no longer around to solve your problems so please will you tell me what's up with yourself?'

He was right on his last sentence. Any more bouts of stubbornness from myself or he might turn sad, or even worse angry.

'I was at the cemetery yesterday at 4:01pm near Farnborough.'

'Oh yes, you like to visit your friend's grave every week, don't you?'

'Yes. I took the 358 bus there.'

'I know,' he said 'So what upset you at the cemetery then? Was it vandalised again? '

'No. I was visiting Aaron's grave when I was approached by a hideous man.' He sighed before speaking.

'Hideous? What do you mean by that?' he said, dropping in tone.

'He was wearing an earring, but he was shouting at me for little reason. I ran as fast as I could just incase he wanted to hurt me.'

'Oh Arnold, these things happen at least once in our lives, just leave it alone and move on. I know we always go down the same paths at times, but you can't let these things walk over you. You visit Aaron every Wednesday right?'

15

'That is correct,' I replied in a deliberately flat matter as the mood rose.

'Well change it to a Monday or a Saturday, that way you won't be likely to see the gentleman again, with the earring to be specific.'

'Thank you very much Dad.' were my final words in the conversation.

As he went off to the kitchen to arrange tonight's dinner, my mind had drifted off as I thought of another reality, one where Dad didn't confront me and start on the conversation which made me feel better. Although I decided to agree that the incident was only a minor issue which should be ignored, I did not agree on the idea on changing my visit to another day, let alone my Dad referring to the man with the earring as a "gentleman". Had the alternative event where I had never been confronted by Dad rolled out like that; I would've remained run down for the following week and earned my 4th mouth ulcer of this year.

3

A new day always presents a new challenge as they said, so let's glimpse at what Arnold was up to today.

It was depressing, shameful and worst of all, inescapable; it was not another rant on the delinquents that plague our streets, but stressing on the notoriously loathed local Jobcentre that generates these irregular creatures. One of the obvious reasons why I hate visiting those establishments are because of the sight of shady degenerates either queuing up or using the interactive search monitors; but the majority of them make short and stern stares at me as if I had done something wrong or don't fit in with 'their kind', nearly the same exact stares that Rose would often make towards myself at home.

The concept of visiting the Jobcentre was logically fracturing, to sign on literally required you to sign a sheet of paper every fortnight with your signature; before that the advisor (normally a bored individual with thoughts of suicide) would ask you if 1), are you looking for work? and/or, 2) Do you use the newspapers and job-points to help you look for work? The inevitable answers would follow as Yes and Yes (respectively).

And then they would simply let you free without further questioning yourself about the free payments. That was it, a plight of suspiciousness would build up every time I had to do this because the situation was equal to committing a robbery because in order to earn £47.85 a week you signed a sheet while the advisors sit motionless as if they've no control over the decision; either that or it was the easiest low-paid job in the country.

At least on the positive side it provided some variation to my metaphorical TV guide of routine, although one day a week was quite enough for my schedule. However, one negative aspect that I highly detested the most was being referenced as *unemployed* by others especially whilst relatives were visiting, such as my Uncle Tony for example who had asked if I had found a career when he visited three months ago. Here's another shrewd example from my own sister one evening:

'Here's a dessert I've brought especially for you Arn,' said Rose as she presented a dessert pot from the fridge, which upon viewing it caused a gauge of internal anger inside myself to fill up. It weren't just the silly shortening of my name that irritated me but the dessert was a miniature pot of Dole fruit, a crude reference to the Jobcentre. The disgust of being referenced

to being unemployed angered myself again to a point where I didn't want to eat the horrendously named snack; and four seconds later it was launched into Rose's face before it was thrown into the kitchen sink, as a side effect of rage with the contents slowly oozing out onto the, tea soaked basin.

******

In a previous chapter, we saw that Arnold had maintained a mental representation of his daily activities in the same style as a TV guide, including an entry called "A weekly activity", which he left unexplained. We'll some find out more about that missing activity.

Monday
Collect Giro Cheque from Downe Post Office
(Performed on Week 2)
Tuesday
DEA appointment with Elaine
(Week 1)
Wednesday
Visit Aaron Lockton at the cemetery
Thursday
Take Milth for her weekly walk around a park
Friday
Visit and/or sign on at the Jobcentre Plus

Above was a visual example of the activities that I would perform weekly in a table. I would often try to diversify my daily activities in a variable routine so that the tasks don't grow boring and repetitive after following them on a regular basis. These routinely rituals would take place in the afternoon around 3pm, which was the same time as visiting the Jobcentre on Friday. The weekly appointments with Elaine, the advisor from the Disability Employment Agency were exempt from this rule as they took place on the early afternoons of Tuesday but not on the same week as signing on at the Jobcentre.

Visiting the grave of my late best friend always occurred every Wednesday because that was the same day that his funeral occurred. Unfortunately I will have to change that to another day to lower the risk of being spotted by the hideous man with the earring who may attack myself if he saw me the second time. One of my favourite methods of deleting time was by taking Milth for a weekly walk around the local parkland inside her plastic pet carrier which doubled as her exercise, as well as one of my preferred objectives. Roundabout Wood* was one of her favourite locations to visit because it contained a long white footpath that would sliver into a wide forest consisting of tall trees that pointed towards the leafy roof like upright pencils that helped support this special retreat.

The local park was also another visiting place, though I don't enjoy going there due to the countless visitors that often disturb us such as young children who would frighten Milth by poking their slimy fingers through the plastic mesh door on her carrier and older individuals who would distract both of us with swear words, therefore tampering with the objective.

*A long forest located north west of Orpington.

I thought Dad's suggestion of rescheduling it on Monday felt uncomfortably viable because there was little to do on that particular day during the first week and Tuesday was my second choice despite the clash with the DEA appointment which took place every two weeks and besides there were a few possible reasons as to why Mondays were preferable to Tuesdays:

* There were 6 letters in a Monday whereas Tuesday had only 7.
* I prefer Mondays despite sayings from individuals that it should be universally loathed.
 * I am often depressed on Tuesday for unexplainable reasons, probably because after meeting Elaine from the DEA, I have to wait another week to see

her again.
* Today was Monday.

Monday	Tuesday	Wednesday
Visit Aaron at the cemetery. (Week 1) Collect Giro cheque at Downe PO (Week 2)	DEA appointment with Elaine (Week 1)	N/A

Thursday	Friday
Take Milth for her weekly walk	Sign on at the Jobcentre Plus (Week 2)

This was how the list of activities appeared inside my head now. The advantage was that every Monday from today I would be constantly occupied with alternating events. But then I immediately realised there were already something wrong with the table, if I were going to visit Aaron on a Monday, then it meant that on Wednesday I was going to undertake a degrading task that thousands of disgraceful teenagers across Orpington are excellent at doing, nothing.

Doing nothing wasn't an objective at all; it was actually the opposite of an objective because it generated boredom, to the extent that the only way to counteract it was by performing tasks. The problem with visiting Aaron on another day was that it felt uncomfortable when minor alterations and/or rescheduling disrupt the familiar flow of the ritual to the point that a lump at the back of the throat or a sickly taste in my mouth would be felt if it were announced.

I was already on the bus; essentially it was all going to be the same routine, the minor difference being that it was Monday instead of Wednesday. Unfortunately I recognised it to be a major difference because the familiar passengers that exist on the sparsely populated bus like extras on a television soap weren't there. The Chinese female with the mole on her upper lip (who always got off outside Shire Lane) was not there and the bald, grey bearded

20

man who wore a criss-crossed jumper wasn't sitting behind the bus driver as predicted. But the old man who would always carry a plastic bag with a map of Central London along with him was there today. He would sit three rows of seats ahead of myself on the left (so that I could get a good look of his white bag with the colourful lines) but this time he was sitting two rows back on the right hand side, meaning that his custom A-Z was out of view today.

Something still didn't feel right on the bus; and it didn't belong to the current passengers. Two bus stops later and a couple more passengers would board and/or alight. One of them who boarded was a hideous looking man, unlike the one from the cemetery who were tall and thin, this one was short and wide, wore a loose florescent jacket that hung off him due to being unzipped and the uncovered part of his jacket revealed an aged, grey t shirt that was terrible at hiding his hairy stomach. It was these features that made him resemble a cowboy builder.

Mainly these types of individuals don't bother me whilst on the bus because they mostly sit at the back just like the obnoxious schoolchildren who would do the same. But something else was not right and that was the newcomer's choice of seats. There was an empty radius of seats in the front row and behind myself; and a sense of coldness could be felt going through my mid-section. Instead of sitting at the back of the bus as predicted, the "cowboy builder" was actually sitting right next to me, which meant I was trapped.

'Oh lordy it's freezing outside,' he said to nobody in particular. Who was he talking to? The concept of him speaking started a chill that spread straight to my limbs the moment he tried to communicate. 'What's your name?' he said again. I remained silent, not because I couldn't speak from my teeth chattering, it were because this genuine stranger who had sat next to myself for a few minutes, was trying to talk to me as if I had known him for several years.
'We've a quiet one here,' he continued, talking as if he brought a sidekick along to witness the event but nobody else had boarded. I still remained silent, looking out from the window, to be distracted by better sights outside other than that man's unshaven face. Take for example, the double-sided sign plate for Osgood Avenue that would stand alone in the green clearing (making it unique) and a blonde pedestrian wearing a dark jacket trying to walk on the damp grass with her narrow high-heeled shoes. 'See any birds outside?'
The coldness in my heart disappeared when I saw the oddities through the bus window but when the man sitting next to me reared his head again to

talk; I quickly began to feel warm, the radius of heat spreading out from my chest. 'She's a tasty lady, don't you think?' What is he talking about; the blonde woman outside? If I tried to taste her I would have vomited, purely because of the disgusting silver necklace she was wearing that resembled a bicycle chain. 'Well say something then.' The heat then gradually shot up into my mouth and I could taste the warmth; and then it began to pinch my throat painfully to the point where I decided to say something back to him to release it.

'GO AWAY!' I bellowed angrily towards him, before jumping over the vacant seats in front (lucky nobody was sitting in them) before darting off towards the red reclining doors of the bus.

******

'Somebody had got out of the wrong side of bed today,' replied the stranger right after Arnold left the bus. But he didn't get to hear the stranger because Arnold was hiding behind a bush in a cul-de-sac, waiting for the bus to disappear from view.

4

Once every fortnight, Arnold would visit a typical village post office in order to retrieve the money from the giro cheque; which also acted as a temporary refuge for our young misanthrope. The repetition of signing the cheque didn't bother him at all; but it still saddened him due to reminding him of the times back in school when his signature was regularly defaced to read a rude sentence.

Instead of visiting Aaron as newly devised on the schedule, today I had to visit the post office in order to receive my Jobseeker's allowance. Without it I am unable to purchase the items to maintain Milth's hutch such as straw bedding, let alone Everton mints to maintain Aaron's gravestone. After arriving home after 4pm a chill rattled my backbone when I saw the family car in the driveway, it meant something wasn't right.

'Is that you Arnold?'

It was my mother, she had left work early.

'Well? Is there something you'd like to tell me?' she demanded.

'Why?' I asked

'For example, what were you doing in Downe today?'

There was silence. She had discovered one of my other secret places.

'I was visiting the post office.'

'What were you doing there?'

'I was retrieving the money from the giro cheque.' I replied.

'Why would you do that?' she asked again. Confused, I decided to reflect back her question instead, for a more accurate response.

'What were you doing in Downe today?' I asked curiously.

'You bloody know I sell properties for a living around the area,' she exclaimed 'but the question is why would YOU go to the post office there when there is already one in Orpington which is much closer?'

I pretended to crack like an imaginary windscreen when she said this.

'It's because I do not like looking at the staff there.'

'Why? Is it because they're black or Indian?'

'No,' I replied unhesitant. 'Two of the workers there have disgusting nose rings.'

'Pardon!?' bellowed my mother 'Are you pulling my leg again?' A quick shake of the head indicated no.

'Oh grow up Arnold; we've already dealt with this crap before. If you don't change this, then you're going to end up as a miserable old man for the rest of your life. You're 18 years old now, I can't see why I need to keep telling you to grow up in the first place!' she paused for breath 'And finally stop putting you hand under your armpit, we don't want the neighbours thinking you're Napoleon, not to mention the stench on your hand.'

And then she marched off to the kitchen to put the kettle on for her coffee. Out of curiosity I sniffed my right hand to detect some sort of odour before examining the moist sweat patch on my green chequered shirt. She was right, although the sweat patch wasn't there before my mother spoke to me.

******

The "Golden Idiot" was a nickname given to George Aston Holt, the younger brother of Arnold Holt. In his spare time he likes to deliberately annoy his brother by blurting out nonexistent words in front of him, so he could distract Arnold from his state of calm and tranquillity.

Despite being one of the neurotypicals at 11, George had the strangest ability to detect whenever his brother was approaching, probably due to a strong scent of mints combined with TCP.

As the result of my mother's ordeal, I decided to hide in the dining room, whilst fondling a navy pillow for extra comfort. But this cushion weren't an ordinary pillow stuffed with wool and feathers. Inside the casing was Milth's dark unwanted fur, which I had kept accidentally for over two years after an unwanted argument with my mother.

She had originally complained about the amount of fur that my rabbit would moult off outside her hutch and spread around the garden like autumn leaves. When gathered together I then realised that the mound of fur felt like touching Milth, albeit twice as soft and the urge to store this new texture was immediate and a pillowcase was the only object I could find for collecting her remains for future perusal.

Usually when I am in this disposition, the "Golden Idiot", better known as my younger brother George would start his inevitable attack. He would appear by spouting out meaningless phrases like "Poopaloomps" as an attempt to distract myself from my activities before sprinting off to another family member to take refuge.

Sometimes he would also perform disturbingly vile stunts such as

24

spreading butter onto his corn flakes before tasting it, as well as mooning "back to front" by revealing his tiny penis towards myself. I have little idea where the "Golden Idiot" originated from, although I presume it was Aaron who created it because when I visited his house, one of his console games we used to play there contained a final boss which was an enormous golden robot who would dispense smaller and colourless copies of itself out of its stomach to attack the player. This had created the theory that the golden idiot was the king of all known idiots, the master idiot; therefore it was the most appropriate name for my brother.

'HA HA! Mummy told you off!' It was George, the golden idiot. 'That means you are stupid!'

'No I am not,' I replied, countering his idiotic quote.

'Yes you are!' he said again. I decided not to counteract his last response as an attempt to avoid entering another infinite loop of discussion. Inevitably George then made his way to the doorway before throwing last minute insults. Giving chase to the golden idiot would cause him to flee and take cover next to the nearest parent available which was an unwise solution to follow.

'Guess what Arnold?' said George, starting his getaway.

'...'

'GOTBALLZONMAHCHIN!' he said unprompted; and he finally left the room before bashing the stairs with his feet, causing peace to resume once again.

******

Today, there was a sudden urge inside myself to read one of my past school reports from secondary school* again. The school reports were stored in a short red container underneath my bed that had cracks around the handles from overuse and the reports were stacked with the most recent academic year facing the top of the pile and the subjects in alphabetical order to make it feel more comfortable to read.

I've little idea where these urges come from but perhaps it were because references to my abysmal time back in secondary school were mentioned by accident from a previous conversation by a family member. The majority of the content on the reports appear loosely unreadable, except the box above the signatures where the teacher's feedback can be found, as well as their unique handwriting. There is little reason why these reports require themselves to be re-read continuously because over 75% of them all state the same message.

Inside the Year 11 school reports, the first report on the pile, which was mathematics, read "Arnold is a very hardworking pupil, but often lacking in self-confidence..." The second page in the same school report, which was geography (my favourite subject because it involved reading intricate diagrams); read this, "Overall, Arnold Holt is a star to teach but he just needs more confidence..." And then inside the P.S.H.E. report of the same year, the last sentence is "...needs to be more confident in the classroom."

Unfortunately these consecutive sentences continue to appear on the remaining unnamed subjects on the same school reports I were holding. However there was one exception to the previous comments displayed was from a P.E. report from Year 10 that was face down because I refused it and stated this: "Arnold is a loner who likes to stand on his own and not talk to anyone, he also quite weak..." It seemed illogical why this rogue report was still hiding inside my bedroom, because it should have been incinerated (along with all the bullies from that time period) but if I were to actually destroy the document; then every school report from the five secondary years who need to be eliminated as well for unexplainable reasons, probably because removing it would've bartered my archives and reduced my accurate review of how terrible it was in secondary school at the time; as well as developing an upset stomach as a result.

*From years 7-11.

After some logical thinking, I promptly realised where the reference had originated. Prior to my last discussion with Dad, he referenced my former helper Mrs Rita-Ann Leslie not being there to deal with my own problems. The earliest I had known of Mrs Leslie was on an October back in Year 3 when the teachers called her to assist me in the classroom by trying to help fix my attention to the letters and numbers presented on the blackboard.

To be highly honest, I found the posters of the colourful flags taped between the classroom windows more amusing to stare at but Mrs Leslie managed to encourage me to pay attention to the information on the blackboard through a number of clever schemes such as using illustrations from the *Railway Series* to pull my attention away from the flags; but my most favourite of them all is that she used to put raspberry jam in my sandwiches before lunchtime as a reward for hard work and listening to everything mentioned inside the classroom.

This routine grew less frequent in Year 6 but it ended forever during entry into secondary school after my mother shouted at me whenever I wanted to continue eating the jam sandwiches back then, couldn't remember why. When I joined secondary school, Mrs Leslie also joined to help me focus properly during the main lessons after I had a difficult moment with another support assistant; but then she also helped another pupil during an English lesson that had difficulties with his reading and writing. That was when I had first encountered Aaron.

It was a dark and wet Monday afternoon when I first met Aaron, the classroom window had been left ajar by accident, causing the heavy rain to slide onto the glass panel, causing a miniature waterfall outside. Mrs Leslie had arrived into the classroom four minutes late with her brown duffle coat on and she was also using it to shelter a pupil with a birthmark on his right cheek and hair so short that his scalp was visible when huddled inside the dark interior of my helper's coat. I felt rather upset and betrayed when I saw the pair drying off, because the only individual I knew who was authorised to huddle up to Mrs Leslie, feel her coat brushing against my face and admire her older charm and perseverance was myself. Along with the stunted stranger, she trudged slowly around the desks trying not to touch the seated pupils by accident, before she sat down and placed a transparent folder next to my desk which felt slimy from the wet weather.

'Hello Arnold, sorry I'm late,' said Mrs Leslie.
'...'
'Are you alright?'
'Who is that person?' I asked, offended.
'This is Aaron,' she gestured at the stranger 'We will be working with him as well from now on.'
'Oh,' I replied sadly 'Does that mean I am going to leave?'
'No, no, of course not Arnold,' she exclaimed 'the teachers decided to move Aaron from another class because he has trouble reading and focusing on things as much as you have. Also I still know you and your tricks quite well Arnold, for now can you just give him a hello for me please?'
'OK miss. Hello Aaron.'
'Hi Arnie,' spoke Aaron for the first time.
'What?' I said, offended by the silly nickname.
'Aaron, he doesn't like having his name shortened, I've no idea why,' interrupted Mrs Leslie.
'That's fine by me, replied Aaron 'Hello Arnold, my name's Aaron.

Glad to be your new classmate.'
    'Thank you and welcome to your new lesson Aaron.' I replied, before
reaching across Mrs Leslie in order to shake his hand.

With Mrs Leslie's support, he would eventually become my first permanent best friend for several years until his unplanned death. This regime of being assisted by Mrs Leslie would continue until we finished Year 11; and unfortunately I was not aware that it would also be the last time I'd see Mrs Leslie before she decided to leave secondary school three months later and move away to the north of England to work at another school inside a 'special village'.

She now lived near the 'special village' and occasionally sends letters to myself asking about my current status, as well as her own with much amusement. Her previous letter was sent before my 18th birthday, which included her book *The Curious Incident* as a bonus present. She left Orpington at least two years ago but back in secondary school Mrs Leslie used to be my preferred choice of staff to consult when something bad had happened like being bullied to myself (or Aaron); and when she wasn't there she gave me a small notepad and pen to record these mishaps (although this would get full very easily), but whenever I felt something wrong had happened, I found it very comfortable to talk to my helper instead of the staff or the school prefects.

Infact, the last time I refused to talk to Mrs. Leslie was back in Year 10 after I had a horrible dream where she was sitting in a black hole and she wrote on my IEP*, describing myself as moronic.

*Individual Education Plan: a rare target sheet which was kept inside my school journal.

5

Today I had an apparent urge to photograph the contents inside my bedroom again, using my trusty 35mm camera. The routine would start by taking multiple camera shots from the corners closest to the door before working my way towards the window and finishing by taking a photograph of the view outside the bedroom window. This was done occasionally so that I had an annual timeline of my bedroom, before I would compare identical perspectives of my bedroom and observe the differences in between. More importantly if I were to leave home abruptly, never to return than I would have visual evidence of what my bedroom used to look like. Luckily the only person who knew about this was my Dad, which was ironic because he caught me at least four times taking photographs and never complained.

'Morning Arnold,' He roared 'Is it that time of year already?'

'Yes,' I replied bluntly before watching him leave. Then my next sudden urge was to fall straight asleep on the bed, in an apparent attempt to delete time but that was soon foiled fourteen minutes later thanks to a younger sibling.

'Arnold, come quickly!' said George as he grabbed my left hand and tried to pull me out of the hallway. George would often attract my attention for a variety of meagre reasons such as a dead housefly on the windowsill or the computer would not function properly because one of the sockets had loosened. It was when he would continuously pull me around the house that it would be a serious matter that included the entire family. But the last time I recalled him pulling myself around was when I was too nervous to greet Uncle Tony who had popped over for a brief visit, because he would inevitably ask questions about my jobless disposition as usual.

The physical sign of being tugged by your younger sibling would result in a surprise at the end of the journey but after slowing down to close the door connecting the kitchen to the garden, George then released himself of my hand before walking down to the concrete path towards the sideways shed where my mother, father and sister were standing; where my brother then said 'He's here Dad.' before turning his back to join them.

After making my way round the imaginary crescent caused by my family standing around, I saw an untidy flurry of twizzled hairs of the black and white kind accompanied by random puddles of blood inside the concave gap. Outside the vandalised hutch and lying at an angle I'd never seen before were the remains of my rabbit Milth. She was dead.

'Oh dear.' was my sole reaction to this tragedy.

******

Whilst I was supposed to show tears, I did not. It had to happen at one point, after all rabbits had an average lifespan of ten years and to be honest, Milth's passing away had to be inevitable. That was simply my own opinion that I said inside my head, if I were to say that in front of somebody they would either patronise myself in a naïve voice (George) or interpret that as offensive dialogue and insult me (Rose).

The remainder of the late afternoon was spent in my living room, with my arms crossed and looking at the random scribbles and etches on the ceiling; that looked as if it were created by a cowboy builder but in fact originally intended to adorn the ceiling. And yet these sparsely random lines brought enjoyment to myself for reasons that cannot be verbally interpreted, but up until recently my brain processed a suitable answer, as it was no more than just a meaningless distraction.

Ordinary individuals see a distraction as a negative value because they automatically divert them from paying attention from something else so that they pay attention to them instead, when they really shouldn't. In a way I actually like positive distractions but in general found it more plausible that they should be divided into two sectors, good distractions and bad distractions. An example here:

Good distractions
* A 1974 OS map of York on display at the local *Oxfam*.
* An aquamarine Vauxhall Corsa passing by that had an upside down number plate.
* The spontaneous patterns on the living room ceiling (at this very minute)

Bad distractions
* A plague of hideous youths congregating outside the Jobcentre.
* The Golden Idiot trying to catch my attention by being cross-eyed.
* The *Channel 5* logo.

My reasoning behind these bad distractions are that they were general eyesores that attempt to pull my attention towards them when I don't want them to and sometimes they either make myself angry or sick. The Channel 5 example (as stated) was initially referring to the logo that would perpetually appear on the top left hand of the television screen. It was the sight of it that almost made me physically sick. A logo appearing on a terrestrial channel!? That was just absurd! Back in those days you only saw unnecessary clutter like that on inferior satellite channels with programmes of a lower quality, on a mainstream channel the concept alone was just sickening. And the most saddening part of this ordeal was that nobody else knew about it, because if I were to say that they would make myself sick, they would laugh, jeer and insult me with hurtful comments.

Good distractions on the other hand would immediately pull my attention when I had temporarily run out of actions to undertake and an interlude would be required in order to fill in gaps of extra time before I've realised what my next objective would've been.

It was also handy to keep yourself occupied in a nasty situation where you are temporarily exiled inside a waiting room with a stranger sitting next to you, especially if it were a dense youth trying to communicate with you in their abysmal native language, often by using made up words and slurred suffixes that sound like questions to a minority like myself.

'Arnold!' it was my mother whom called me this time 'I've told you several times not to stare at the flipping ceiling when someone's talking to you. Now would you like some French bread or not?'

'Yes please.'

'Good, hopefully next time you'll actually listen when I call you to collect it.'

Eighteen minutes later (after the French bread was consumed), I was inside the dining room, sitting against the pine table and wondering what my next action would be. Eating the French bread would count as a friendly interlude because it helped delete a small fraction of time; as well as help decide on what my next action would be. But promptly after the interlude had finished, my mother stepped into the dining room. 'You alright Arnold?' she said. There was silence before my mother broke it again with a sigh. 'What's wrong with you now? I should know because you didn't say thank you when I gave you your French bread so what is it?' I remained silent. 'Come on, you know there's a problem with yourself again. Don't do this to me!' I still decided to remain silent. She sighed before speaking again. 'Have I said something nasty to you again?'

'Yes.'

'What have I done to upset you this time Arnold?'

'...'

'Well? Was it because you failed to respond to my call and now you've got the hump with me?'

'No.'

'Then what is it?'

'It was when you accidentally found myself in Downe village and this caused yourself to say rather nasty comments towards me.'

'Arnold that was over two weeks ago!' exclaimed my mother. 'God, you're always keeping these little things bottled up don't you? I've told you a thousand times before that you must stop doing this you silly sod. I know we have trouble getting on together, especially with your condition but so does the whole family; and you should know by now I lose my temper from time to time with everyone after failing to sell a single house but overall that doesn't mean I'm evil or anything. Do you agree with me?'

'Yes.' I said slowly.

'Now let's say we put this in the past and have a nice big cuddle instead.'

And then we cuddled together.

******

Later on that day, it was an estimated 3.5 hours until dinnertime and I tried to delete time by counting how many single floral patterns there were on a horizontal stretch of wallpaper in the living room, when George disturbingly snaked in as if he were suffering from epilepsy (or that was how Rose described it). That was catalogued as a bad distraction although I was pertaining some eye contact, not at his stupid dance but at the distinctive blue book he was clutching while he danced.

'Turtle willies!' squealed the Golden Idiot, crossing his eyes in the process. 'I know who killed your rabbit!' he boomed without warning.

'That is mine,' I replied, referencing the book he was holding.

'You and me are going to find the killer, like the boy did in your book!' replied George, still holding the novel.

'That is my book,' said myself again.

'Yeah, that's the only one in your room that doesn't have *Thomas the Tank Engine* in them,' he replied back.

'Actually they are called *The Railway Series* and they are not the only books that-'

'Poopaloomps!' rasped George idiotically before sprinting off to find my mother.

The obnoxious twit, it mentally burns me when I hear that idiotic catchphrase instead of finishing my own sentence but the concept of accompanying him in his stupid fantasy sounded laughable. However the golden idiot may have had a valid point after all. The chunky paperback might be the first novel I had actually read from cover to cover (37 times to be precise); but the fact that it used pictures and numbers throughout the book may explain why I continued to read it.

Overall, trying to read an extensive novel felt comparable to dyslexia. I am not saying that I had the condition myself but Aaron would sometimes struggle when reading out a random sonnet back in our English lesson at school; this was when his brain would involuntary shuffle the words into awkward positions that his eyes can't understand. But I don't have dyslexia; the letters are in their correct places as well as their size and font. The overall problem was that they're too perfect.

One viable example was the time I failed my English test in Year 9 where I thought Link and Shelter were the same person from a novel I was forced to read, which was part of an essay where the class had to write about homelessness in general. My test result was 9/38. Now if the words were spaced further and highlighted in a distinguishable colour; or contained an image depicting a scene from a random paragraph, the score would have been drastically bettered.

6

It was the following Sunday and it was one of those boring Sundays when my dad preferred to stay at home and zip through the pages of old motoring magazines that were stacked next to the living room sofa, just to ensure he hadn't missed out on any articles he read previously before discarding it and purchasing a fresh issue. There was also a small interval I had discovered myself where every fortnight on a Sunday, Dad would take myself and George on a mysterious car journey to a random location where we would walk aimlessly to explore the surroundings before returning home to a Sunday dinner served on a white plate with a brown ring as the circumference, the 'good china' as my mother called it 11 years ago. Last week, we visited Leeds Castle.

My schedule was exempt on Sundays for a couple of good reasons the first one being that Sunday was traditionally the day of rest and as previously mentioned, we had a day out every 2 weeks on that particular day which greatly used up the morning and early afternoon while spending the rest of the afternoon recuperating and watching repeats of *Top Gear* and *Antiques Roadshow*. Unfortunately most of the time when reminiscing, I would be disrupted by a member of family which in this case was George.

'Poopaloomps!' he blared.
'Go away,' I said for the fourth time towards him this week.
'Nope, Mummy said you have to go next door with me!'
'Why?' I asked bluntly.
'To find out how Milth died.'
'Why?' myself asking again.
'We're going to solve a murder mystery!'
'Why?'

This was illogical, purely illogical. An obnoxious 11 year old who cannot tell an orange from a tangerine and thought bird flu was nonexistent was going to kettle me in as his sidekick which would have meant zigzagging from door to door like vigilantes in hats from a cheesy American children's drama. These ordeals would be easily avoided if I simply said "No", one of my most uttered words in my vocabulary of speech. Why I agreed to opt into this unnecessary juncture was questionable (even without verbal movement) but certain that the reasons I did were probably because:

1) The boy was an idiotic twit who would squeal and/or moan inexplicably if I had disagreed with him.
2) Worst of all he would tell my mother and then she would shout at me.
3) I had nothing else to do.

Oh well, it would be genuinely funny if George really tried to turn Milth's unrequited death into a murder case as if it were a parody of that particular book I was currently reading. For example, a parody is an event that was copied from another event albeit displaying an alternate tangent from the original which is intended to be funny. In the end, I went off to seek the parody by joining him on his ill-fated mission, in silence.

******

The fun had started as soon as George had opened the front door. The dancing buffoon was clutching a flip up notebook with both hands and wagging a HB pencil towards his face like a deluded cartoon character, trying to make himself look superior. It appeared that from this point I was the reluctant sidekick, but instead of being smaller and less intelligent, I was more or less the hyper competent and savant like version of a sidekick like that cat from the cartoon about a dog that fights crime with kung fu.

The first suspect came in the form of our next door neighbour's house. The neighbour can be perceived as a reoccurring acquaintance, like a minor character in a generic soap. Often I did not like being spotted by neighbours in the garden for unknown reasons but if they were pre-occupied in routine garden work (e.g. cutting hedges), their awareness of yourself would be a lesser frequency, depending on how high the fences bordering the two are.

'Hi sorry to disturb you,' said George 'but can we look in your garden for 5 minutes?'

'We?' she replied 'You're a bit young to be on your own aren't you?'

'No, my brother is around here, I think.'

At certain situations unknown to his brother and everybody else, a mini-game called "Where's Arnold?" would often occur, where Arnold's shyness would get the better of him. The advantage with shrubbery in front gardens was that they made perfect hiding places as well as porches (if available) but then again for Arnold, the sweat inducing act of "facing the music" was always inevitable when George soon spots him hiding behind a bush.

'Popping up around bushes then Arnold?' said the neighbour in a cheery tone 'I think your brother has kicked a football over the fence again.'
'No,' I replied, taking off my shoes (unlike the idiotic boy whom trundled inside with his red trainers on)
'Oh, then what has he kicked over this time?'
'He apparently thinks there is a carcass of my dead rabbit in your back garden and he wants to investigate.'
I was already thorough faring through the neighbour's hallway when I said this before trying to reunite my left foot with my shoe while leaning next to the back door.

Back outside George walked down the neighbour's crazy paved footpath, stared to the left of the path and paused again, albeit the pause was longer. He then moved back towards me and started tugging me again like he usually does every time he had a little dilemma he could not work out himself. It appeared that his dilemma turned out to be the only untidy section of garden, a mountain of mud, which was actually a compost heap. It created a disgusting smell caused by the fumes of dead flowers and rotten mushrooms rising from the bottom of the heap up towards the clean air.
'Can you see if she's behind that pile of mud?' he asked.
'Why?' I responded curiously.
'Because there are worms in there and my feet will get muddy."
A stifling, bone crunching jolt rattled through my body again since the incident with the hideous stranger on the bus, except that this time my joints had locked together instead of warming up and I could only move my mouth by an inch. Why would George, whom was oblivious to the side effects of wearing his shoes indoors, suddenly pay attention to the wellbeing of his feet? 'Do it for the sake of your own bunny!' continued George. His voice sounded more rigid as if he was cross but I was still grinding my teeth at the overall concept of surrendering to the Golden Idiot. 'Do it Arn!' he demanded again loudly. Then something rare had happened to myself, my inside voice became my outside voice.
'MY NAME IS NOT ARN!' I bellowed angrily as I broke free of my stifling pose and lashed out towards his direction.

George was now situated on top of the compost heap face up. I found his accident to be very comical yet justified as the idiot was oblivious to the dangers of shortening my name to Arn or Arnie, which I strongly dislike because it makes me sound like one of his obnoxious teenagers with feminine haircuts and speak as if there was a question mark on each end like this (?).

The challenge of sealing my lips shut (which I'm rather good at) was now impossible. *(laughs uncontrollably)* A compost heap, he fell straight backwards onto the compost heap, you will only see something similar happen to Compo in an episode of *Last of the Summer Wine*. For something comic like that to occur in real life, it would've been at least 30% funnier; and I was right.

He was still lying on the compost heap, waiting for somebody to pull him out as if he were afraid of touching the muck. I decided to remain static, savouring the moment and picturing an image in my mind of him trying to create a snow-angel using compost instead of snow. Soon he managed to pick himself up coincidentally when the neighbour confronted us, clutching a mug with her little finger.

'Is everything alright? I heard some shouting going on outside.'
'He fell,' I replied, pointing to his body print in the compost.
'So did you find your rabbit then?' the neighbour asked again.
'No,' I said joyfully.
'Ah, sorry I couldn't help much,' she said. 'You'll find her again in the meantime. For now, good luck to you and your brother with the search.'
'Yes and goodbye,' I said, talking back to the neighbour.
After the next-door neighbour closed the front door behind us, I found George standing a few feet away, distanced by the strong smell of compost. We took a while to decide which house to investigate next. I still had the giggles after pushing him into the compost and it affected my thinking because the laughter had made our next objective sound like a competition for example:

Q) Which house should Arnold and George visit next?

A: The one on the other side of their house.
B: The next one along
C: Or the one across the road

I was tempted to choose C because it would have created a zigzag pattern but George had correctly answered B and already made his way there.

He did not appear to be making ludicrous faces and he did not mention any of his idiotic quotes, but on the pavement I overtook him deliberately, so I could get a closer look at his face. I drew a huge grin when I saw that his face turned into a crumpled pout because the last time I saw him make that face was back at a family outing where we played piggy in the middle with my cousin Raymond for three hours (and George was the piggy throughout).

I had no intention of hiding away from the neighbours again; perhaps this time his scowl will swallow his face inwards like a crumbling wall. Instead I rang the bell and stared through the distorted glass on the door until a movement appeared behind it.

'I'll answer it. It's only the oddball who lives two doors away,' said a voice behind the door.

Hmm… must be referring to George. Finally the door swung open, revealing the voice as an aged blonde woman who shared the same height as my brother. 'Hello?'

'Greetings, my younger brother and I are searching for our pet rabbit, which we believe is missing inside your garden?'

'What?'

'Can we look in your garden please?' said George, whom spoke since lying on the compost heap next door.

'Yeah, come in.' And so we did, shoes off obviously. 'Can I just ask the name of your bunny? Perhaps it'd be easier if we call it, that way it might come to us.'

'Milth,' I replied immediately.

'Come again?'

'Milth,' I replied again.

'Are you having a laugh or something?' Eh?

'It was my sister whom named her,' I said innocently.

'Right, you're asking for it,' she replied again, this time snatching a purple broom off the wall.

'Asking for what?' I asked him, before my brother tugged my shirt and propelled our way out through their front door, of course holding our shoes by their shoelaces. I did not understand why the homeowner would want to attack myself after mentioning Milth's name and why George would want to save me after being pushed into the compost heap but at least he didn't say anything on the way home.

******

Once we arrived home, I remained inside my bedroom until my mother had called me downstairs. Something did not add up at all whilst on the fool's detective outing. The anticlimax of the event happened when we visited the second house to gather more clues about Milth's disappearance. There was nothing foul about the house that disgusted myself whatsoever and the neighbour who lived there appeared innocent (i.e. no tattoos or noserings). What I found wrong about it was the anticlimax should've happened inside the third house, that myself and my brother were going to visit and NOT the second house that we visited, which felt severely uncomfortable.

It was actually an intriguing observation that I picked up since primary school. It was a theory that appeared in a fictional story where a character was subject to perform a series of identical tasks in a consecutive manner. But the third time he/she performed it, it either deviated slightly from the previous two that he/she performed or it goes completely wrong as much to their dismay. Take the story of the 3 little pigs for example; the big bad wolf manages to blow down the first two houses successfully but fails to blow down the third house and gets eaten as a result of falling down a chimney (in which I find disgusting because wolves are hairy and filthy).

'Arnold. ARNOLD!' called my mother from downstairs. In the kitchen, she looked angry judging by the way she was holding the telephone cord. I wanted to stand near the doorway, but the Golden Idiot was already there.

'Apparently those tosspots two doors away claimed that you and George were insulting them earlier.'

'?'

'What I'd like to know is what the hell were you two doing there?'

'We were going on a murder mystery to find out about Milth's disappearance,' I paused 'as you approved.'

'I did not approve any of this,' she rebutted 'Besides you should've known that bloody rabbit wouldn't survive the attack at all so why were you over there asking the neighbours in the first place?'

'It's because,' I replied, trying to be honest 'If I did not, then you would have shouted at me.'

'What a load of bollocks, as if the rabbit would die here and then jump into next door's garden to die again! Where do you get these ideas from?' asked my mother.

'It was George who claimed that I had to search for my rabbit.'

'Arnold,' she paused while inhaling air. 'You should know I won't ask

you to do anything as stupid as that, now thanks to you I have to go over there to reason it out, next time use your common sense for god's sake!'
And then she waved me out of the kitchen, which was a sign that she didn't want me in her sights but unfortunately George had disappeared when this happened.

******

I returned to my bedroom again, this time trying to remember the time when I first bought Milth as well as the last letter I had received from Mrs Leslie.

Mrs R Leslie
Xx xxxxxxxx Close
Xxxxx xxxxxxxx
Xxxx xxx
(Address obscured for personal reasons)

Dear Arnold

I hope you've been well since we last made contact, but overall I can't believe that you're now 18! Wow, three more years before you'll become a young adult, my how the time flies!

I also sympathise with your lack of luck on the job front, apparently people from the centre are pointing to the upcoming recession as the blame, but I've met a few clients on a local work prep course who have defied this so I'm hoping this problem will soon blow over. You ought to make a visit over here one day; the centre is in a lovely part of Yorkshire and I'm sure the residents will be nice to you, after all on an average day, it's sometimes like working with you times fifteen!

Also I hope you enjoy your new present. It's a popular novel about a boy who is quite similar to you and the story revolves around him trying to figure out who murdered his dog. I can still remember your weakness towards reading long stories back in school but this book is filled with lots of clever images and fonts which will greatly help you out but overall my favourite feature has to be the chapters which are marked in a clever sequence, don't you think?

Before I go, don't forget to tell your family that I said hello and of course, send my love to Milth as well.

Best wishes,
Mrs R Leslie.

That was approximately seven months ago. Unfortunately I have not had the chance to visit her, presumably due to a circle of disapproval from my parents. For example, if I were to ask my mother that very question she would reply with 'Not now Arnold, try asking me later.' But if I tried to ask the question again to Dad he would say 'I'm not sure on that one, have you tried asking your mum yet?' which would then turn into an infinite loop. Then again I consider it a paradox because Dad used to regularly visit several regions of the country, only to compare his car with several identical versions and I used to travel with him (along with an atlas), solely for entertainment reasons.

If I were invited the opportunity to visit Mrs Leslie, I would have to turn down the offer because Milth would have been left behind, with nobody suitable to look after her at home. But what interested myself the most was that my parents thought she were dead, despite her missing body. George almost bypassed this statement, until he forced me to go outside to find out if she had died in someone else's garden.

In detective novels, they used the term "red herring" to label a person or item that lead to a dead end. In this case George's "murder mystery" would've been one, but what was more surprising were that the real red herring was actually the incident that started it. For it wasn't a fox that mauled Milth to death; and alternatively it weren't my dad who tried to murder her either, it was Arnold Holt.

7

This doesn't add up at all. Why would he want to kill his beloved rabbit, the only entity that he cherishes more than his siblings and even converses with her without any lack of confidence whatsoever? The cause or motif was unquestionable but perhaps if we let him continue, the answer will be revealed.

Like nearly every generic detective novel the culprit was always the one you would least expect. The reader would obviously expect that the miscreant were the butler, the swimming pool attendant or a shady character that disappears unexpectedly most of the time. In this case the culprit was the one who would've been most disheartened by the 'murder', myself.

Now here came the next alarming surprise (mostly situated at the end of a chapter), Milth was in a better place, albeit instead of it being in heaven, she was at Roundabout Wood. No, I am not using any silly metaphors to describe her soul resting in peace; Milth is still very much ALIVE.

I thought it would be very appropriate to send my final greetings to Milth in this location because this was her favourite area and coincidentally it was rather close to Petts Wood, which was where Mrs Leslie bought her and the first part of the place name was a vague reference towards her relation to myself at the time as my pet rabbit. Milth can now be located wandering the undisturbed grassy heaths outside the forest for hours on end and resting in the patches of sunlight, lying down in that abstract furry sausage shape that rabbits usually do whenever they want to sunbathe.

But the most difficult aspect of all was faking the visual evidence of Milth's death. The pillow crammed with her moulted fur which lay underneath my bed was the so-called "base" for this evidence and felt easy to apply. But with generic animal murders there had to be blood soaking the corpse; but I didn't want to extract any blood from my beloved rabbit. Luckily there was a bush inside my back garden which grew berries that contained a liquid similar to blood, so very carefully I picked 29 berries off this bush and with my fingertips squeezed them slowly over the dry rabbit fur. But it felt unfinished; it needed a third ingredient, a topping. I carefully entered my sister's bedroom (luckily Rose was away at work) and searched every used fast food container that was lying on her floor until I found my third ingredient, bones.

They were then generously scattered onto the fur and "blood" on the ground. Satisifed, I then collected Milth and travelled towards Roundabout Wood where we said our goodbyes.

But the ultimate question as to why I would wish to part with my furry companion, someone who had been so close to me all these years (literally), a brush of insanity? That seemed like the obvious option but the reasoning was far more logical and tear inducing as I didn't do it for the better of myself, I did it for the better of her.

******

It happened one Tuesday night at roughly 11:54pm (that was the time I left the kitchen) and I was outside in the back garden tending to Milth who used to conjure up a racket with her hind legs whenever she was harassed by a fox or a cat. Generally she did this at least every week but it was only when the thumping continued for over a minute which indicated that intervention would be required.

Every time this happened it appeared that I was the only one who can hear her but up to that point the kitchen light immediately flickered on and two figures shuffled in sight of the window overlooking the garden. Out of curiosity I quietly snuck up to the side of the window within earshot but out of sight just incase I didn't startle anybody, like I did back in 2005 where I was locked outside by accident (for the 5th time) and Rose screamed when she saw me waiting from the darkness, causing her to swear at me.

Normally I would return inside once the kitchen is clear but this time my parents' voices filled the room, which caused my legs to promptly tremble.

'The kettle's on.' That was my mother's voice. 'Guess who I saw yesterday while I was working?'

'Who?' replied my Dad. 'Was it Chris from down the road?'

'No, Arnold. In Downe village.'

'So? Perhaps he went there for the fresh air, or the countryside.'

'No Geoff, I spoke to him last night about it and believe me, what he said was vile.'

'Is this about the man with an earring at the cemetery?'

'What? NO! - but he was having a strop over a semi-related issue at the post office.'

44

'Oh well, it can't be as awful as the time he was thrown out of *WHSmith* can't it?' Their volume increased but the kettle then started bubbling loudly, making my parents' voice even more difficult to hear until it finished boiling.

'Right stop it; you're being as difficult as your two sons.'

'Difficult? But there's nothing wrong with having him here, infact I asked George about him the other day and he enjoys his company.'

'It's draining our resources as well as our family time and besides, it's driving us apart.'

'It's a "he", not an "it"!'

'For Christ's sake Geoff, you're doing it again!'

'Okay, okay, he'll be gone by the end of the month.'

'No, I want it rid of immediately, the sooner the better or you'll be the one leaving!'

The conversation my parents were having inside was critically awful, infact I recalled a previous situation where they had an inferior argument concerning Rose but now it was myself they were arguing about and the volume of furore was greater than before and they both collaborated that I should be promptly expelled from the house! I was too unconfident and depressed to go inside, where I would most likely enter the crossfire so I decided to bypass them by camping out on the wooden board underneath Milth's hutch (as I've done before) and sleep on a sack of clean straw for possibly the final time until the following morning where I should have enough to think out new objectives to suit the ordeal given out by my parents.

So it appeared that his motif behind the faked murder of his rabbit was down to listening to his parents, whom were apparently plotting to kick him out of the house; presumably resulting in Arnold having to part with Milth.

It sounded like a plausible strategy, but perhaps Arnold easily misinterpreted the conversation by taking the place of one of his father's valued possessions with vastly devastating results.

8

The phrase "getting out of the wrong side of bed" had always riddled me for various reasons. From overheard conversions it was supposedly a slang word used towards someone who was in a bad mood. I cannot understand why it was invented because:
1) I have displayed a variety of moods from one side of my bedstead.
2) My bed was positioned next to the wall, therefore making it impossible to get out of the other side of the bed.

Whatever emotion was displaying inside my mind certainly seemed to be a negative one. Infact it felt like a *Super Black Day* would occur (a reference to the book from Mrs Leslie) although the main difference is that there did not appear to be any yellow parked vehicles on Sevenoaks Way, just a silver car with a *Superman* symbol on the filler cap and a few other parked cars in the distance. And unfortunately because summer was almost approaching, every day would feel like a *Super Black Day*. The disgusting youths in the town centre would be more prominent at this time of year; and what's worse would be that the hot weather will make them more idiotic and start losing their clothes, exposing their deformed bodies. The increased insects and cigarette smoke would make the atmosphere horrific (would had been more horrific for Aaron because he used to be asthmatic) but the most depressing reason of them all was that summer was when the leaflet distributors visit Orpington.

The leaflet distributors would lie in the tube of pathway facing the supermarket, close to the Jobcentre which was my initial destination. A quick diagram that I had illustrated and signed revealed the formation they were positioned in, as well as a zigzag, my avoiding path which resembled a mountainous route.

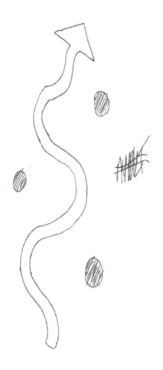

The dots were to represent the dreaded leaflet distributors whilst the arrow was there to represent myself. Oh and the summer holidays, I almost left that out. Today was Friday and because it was the second week of the bi-weekly routine, it meant I had to visit the Jobcentre again in order to sign on. I don't like travelling there but if I refused, then I wouldn't have the funds for the Everton mints that I would regularly purchase for Aaron as well as the equipment to maintain Milth such as bedding and yoghurt drops; but the worse part would be the consequences of my mother finding out. If she did she would shout even louder than she did that certain evening with my Dad, droning that the jobseeker's allowance could be stored for a future use to purchase valuable items, according to her last discussion on that topic.

Whilst visiting I would often see Elaine sitting at her desk and she would respond back if I made eye contact, but today she wasn't there which made the place feel uneasy because she was the only person that I would communicate with at the centre. She was the only person I knew inside the building who would smile automatically whenever I approached her, which was reminiscent of how Mrs Leslie would react every time I met her outside the classroom before the first lesson began.

Whenever I signed on, I could hear a clock gradually ticking louder inside my head, until I manage to escape from the awful establishment. I then continued to rush home (from the town centre), but an unexpected figure thwarted my plan to do so by blocking my route.

'Whoawhoawhoa, look who it is!' barged in a voice that made me jump. My mouth dropped even further in horror when I looked up to see the culprit, it was the "cowboy builder", the same one who approached me on the bus. 'Fancy seeing you here, I'm Vincent by the way. Heard the news over there?'

'Pardon?' I don't recall them discussing anything relevant over there.

'Ooh, looks like we have a posh boy here on the dole! Anyway the big news is that the Jobcentre is closing down.'

'Why?' I asked, looking at the doomed building instead of him.

'Because of the credit crunch. But we're going to be moved somewhere else that's better,' he replied.

'Where?' I asked

'Bromley, you'll like it there. There are more pound shops over there than Orpington and I heard that there's gonna be another one where the *Woolworths* used to be!'

I felt rather uncomfortable listening to that.

'I don't want to travel there,' I said, revealing my dislike.

'Oh yes you will,' he nodded. 'And next time, don't jump when you see me, OK?' finished Vincent as he turned away and left. Thanks to his presence, I was in an even more negative mood but I wasn't focusing on where my feet were going.

And inevitably Arnold strayed off his special path and onto the nearest fundraiser, who took the opportunity to pounce on him.

'How would you like to see the light?' asked the man, waving a card alongside him. Arnold, who was not willing to communicate in a bad mood, continued to walk past him but was not anticipating a second appearance from the fundraiser. 'Last chance before you-'

WHACK!

He hit him. It wasn't a punch, or a slap but more like a strike which blew the fundraiser back a few inches and left him temporarily stunned. All he could do was turn glum from the attack and watch the falsely indestructible force that was Arnold storm off home.

******

This day was awful. Not only did I have an encounter with the stranger from the bus but realising that the Jobcentre was moving to Bromley at the same time made it at least four times as worse. At least I could see my house in the upcoming distance, but I hope Rose hadn't arrived yet because I do not intend to interact with her whilst in a negative mood.

And unluckily it appeared that his sister was already home, he can often tell when a letter to "Mr A Holt" had already been opened with the contents intact and also when her bag is present, slouching across the stairway.

'I guess you're shaken at having to change your silly little routine,' she said nastily.

Nothing came of my mouth until I found a suitable sentence to say.

'Why did you open my letter?' I asked her.

'Because I thought it was your P45,' Rose replied, this time drinking from a glass bottle.

'You are not allowed to do that,' I said 'Our parents disapprove of it.'

49

'Well, guess what disapprover?' she hissed 'It isn't my fault you treat your life like a fricking mystery Arn.'

'My name is not Arn.' I said stiffly.

'I can call you whatever I bloody want! Arnie, Artie, Mary Sue. Oi, no walking off when I'm talking to you!'

Once I left her vicious clasp, my mind was knee deep in thought. These apparent changes she was alluding, what was it precisely and did it concern my earlier list of daily objectives? Or even worse, did she automatically know that Milth didn't pass away and that it was entirely my doing? And then she would tell the family and as a result my mother would tell me off and I would be exiled to a mental home where individuals who don't align properly with today's society stay and spend their remaining lives wearing a white jacket with the sleeves tied up inside a knot.

I tried to fall asleep on my bed again to remove these pestering thoughts about change, but that was foiled when Rose ordered me downstairs to be harassed later on. 'He's here Mum, time for you to face the music.'

'What's this all about again?' asked my mother.

'It's about the Jobcentre down the road closing down,' Rose replied. 'He's going into sulk about it Mum, I can see it in his eyes and besides,' she said turning towards myself 'you should've known about it anyway; it was mentioned in the local paper last week.'

'I do not read the articles in that newspaper,' I replied.

'Then what do you read in there then?'

'The sub-section featuring the cars,' I said.

'Oh, is that all you read then Arnold?'

'So?' entered my Dad 'There's nothing wrong with reading the motoring pages, I read them too.'

'What's wrong is that,' Rose pauses 'this person does not work and admits that he doesn't take a single glance at the jobs section! And at the same time didn't know that the Jobcentre is closing down. How ironic is that?'

'I think it's flown past your head that there's a big recession on that the moment,' warned my mother.

'Yes and you shouldn't be hard on your brother Rose, besides 2009 hasn't been a good year so far to find work, unemployment and all that.'

I had already snuck out of the scene and could faintly hear the last sentence from my Dad. But I could hear louder indistinct noises coming from Rose before she left the living room and passed me.

'As for you, sticking your hand up your armpit like that, who do you think are you are anyway, the idiot of Lord Nelson!?'

******

        I decided to go to bed earlier (than my planned schedule) after accepting the tragic news about the Jobcentre moving to Bromley. My reasons for disliking it were identical to Orpington, the difference being that they're more intense, my vague hypothesis being that it was closer to Central London in terms of radius and therefore more degenerative. For example, the dreaded leaflet distributors that thrived in Bromley town centre were greater and took several formations that were unpredictable but could be easily bypassed like this for example:

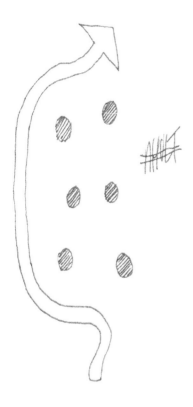

I also discovered what a P45 was and essentially, it was a pink form that appeared when jobseekers allowance payments were permanently finished. That would be bad for several reasons stated earlier, particularly the mints. But with the money I've saved up from this (roughly £413.90) and the maps that I collected from the local library, I have decided to create a brand new objective: find Mrs Leslie. The steps were here:

Plot
Step 1: Orpington to London Victoria
Step 2: London Victoria to Kings Cross
Step 3: Kings Cross to York
Step 4: ?

The reason why Step 4 was unconfirmed is because I don't have the exact location of the "special village" where Mrs Leslie works. The only clue I have was that it was situated somewhere NE of York but once I arrive at that area, additional information should follow. I've also currently packed these items to take on the journey.

Items
* 35mm Camera
* My pocket A-Z dated 2004
* A cushion containing Milth's moulted fur
* My box of drawing pins (to help myself make decisions)
* *Henry the Green Engine* (my favourite *Railway Series* book)
* *The Curious Incident* (the book from Mrs Leslie)

I haven't confirmed a precise day to carry out this objective; although Thursday appeared suitable because Milth was no longer around to take for a walk (she now had a forest to herself). It also gave myself enough time for a farewell to Aaron by presenting him with a complete bag of Everton mints for the final time (and not the basic *Sainsburys* brand).

I was also intending to bring my trusty 35mm camera along as well, not just to photograph the thrilling highlights that the objective would bring, but most importantly the film also contained the images of my bedroom that I had wisely photographed before Milth's unofficial departure.

9

It was already Wednesday. To commemorate my final day in Orpington I decided to visit the cemetery for the last time to see Aaron before going towards the "special village" the next day. It had been approximately five weeks since I last visited the cemetery because of the two hideous strangers that previously appeared and corrupted the visits. If I had continued to visit Aaron on a Wednesday, the first stranger, the man with the earring would have assaulted myself and if I had tried to visit him again outside Wednesday, it was likely that the second stranger called Vincent would've appeared.

But I decided to visit the cemetery on Wednesday anyway, purely because I wanted to see Aaron for the final time without taking any regard for the dodgy obstructions that are likely to occur upon visiting on that particular day. The journey on the bus earlier felt rather positive because I did not see a single degenerate on board so presumably there must be a low chance that either one or both (which is very unlikely) of the hideous strangers will make an appearance today. Entering the gates past the church, there were no signs of Vincent or the man standing around, so it was safe to proceed to where Aaron's grave was located.

As soon as I lined up against his gravestone, the mints were already out of the pocket. On a generic day I would line six of them at the front of the grave in a neat pattern so that it would resemble a neat zebra-coloured snake. This time the whole bag was going to adorn the grave; but before this happened I noticed that four Evertons whom appeared to have aged due to the absent white stripes were already there. A thought occurred. Picking up the old mints I decided to place them around that object on the grave that resembled a showerhead before laying down the rest of the mints.

But as the first handful lined the front of the grave, something familiar was watching this event. Was it Milth? But it wasn't my former pet at all; it was a grey squirrel. Perhaps the reason behind the confusion was because of its reflecting dark eyes (which Milth had) and it also imitated her movements because it then started to make tiny bounces towards myself as Milth would during feeding time. Out of interest I tried to do an experiment by offering the squirrel an Everton mint to find out if it'll accept it as food (unlike Milth who hated them). It continued to bounce even further towards myself, which felt rather positive but this swiftly increased when the squirrel finally reached feeding distance. After crouching down, it slowly craned its tiny head and when it grabbed the mint out of my hold with its teeth, the climax had been reached.

The crunching from the squirrel's mouth felt loud and then I decided to give it a rabbit stroke by reaching out my hand once again. It accepted the stroke. Could this animal become a new replacement for my former rabbit? I thought before a voice caused me to spring out of my crouch.

'I knew it! I KNEW IT!' the call sounded as if it was directly calling me and it felt familiar. Standing still, my mind was busy trying to come up with a suitable response. Had the stranger with the earring returned? I refused to turn around to see the answer. Instead my feet decided to step sideways from the grave (so that I wouldn't face the entrance where the anomaly was standing) and ran in a straight line off the tarmac path. Presuming that the exit was blocked I hastily tried to discover a new exit alongside the borders of the cemetery. Running between parallel gravestones (and carefully avoiding them) I noticed that a few of the bars on the black iron fence protecting the graves from the trees were missing and once the final tombstone was passed, I quickly crouched and painfully dived into the hole in the fence where one of the branches from the hostile trees whacked me in the face upon entering, knocking my glasses off. I lay down on the ground after I had finished stumbling from the hole and continued to lie there for three minutes; the dirty leaves felt far more comfortable than underneath Milth's wooden hutch.

As Arnold lay back in the concealed forest he eventually forgot about the apparent dangers that caused him to get there in the first place; and he felt slightly conceited in his temporary refuge because he had succeeded in hiding from the dangers.

Meanwhile, the only 'danger' that was lurking back in the cemetery was a bald, middle aged man wearing sunglasses, who was speaking so loudly on his mobile phone that he disturbed a large flock of pigeons grazing several feet away.

* * * * * *

It was 6:24pm when I arrived home from the cemetery. It would've been an ideal timing because there were only 6 minutes left before Milth's feeding took place but as she longer lives in the back garden, the task had been cancelled which had left a slight discomfort inside my stomach. Instead the rest of the evening was to be spent on preparing the suitcase with essential items before the special journey tomorrow (as listed in the 2nd last chapter). All I had heard when I entered the house were peculiar noises from upstairs so I decided to curiously walk up to the landing to investigate the sounds. Oh dear, it appeared that my sister has left her television on unoccupied as usual, best to leave before she notices me. But as soon as I tried to retreat to my bedroom, Rose spotted me.

'What were you doing in my room?' she asked.

'I wasn't in your room.'

'Bloody hell, I saw you just LEAVING my bedroom, now what were you doing in there?'

'I thought I heard a familiar sound on your television.'

'That's fine, but next time,' she paused frigidly 'don't lie about it OK?'

'I weren't in your room, only my left foot was.'

'Oh Jesus,' said Rose 'Can I ask this,' she paused again, glancing at the images on my bedroom door. 'Why on earth do you read maps?'

'They help me sleep during the night.'

'Oh, in that case I've no interest in what you're looking at Arnie.'

'Arnold.'

'What?'

'My name is not Arnie,' I said, correcting her error.

She said nothing next, instead she fully scrunched her face and gently pushed past me as she entered her bedroom and closed the door where the audio from the television dropped to near silence. Despite her abrupt exit, that was to be my sister's last appearance. Forgetting our encounter, a thought occurred. Using the surplus time from Milth's feeding, I grabbed my 35mm camera and absent-mindedly walked down the stairs and outside the front door onto the pavement, as if an invisible version of George was pushing myself from behind as if there was a task that had to be completed. Then clutching my camera, I pointed it towards the house and began taking several photos of the building from different angles. This continued for a few minutes until a car horn sounded from behind, which indicated that my Dad had arrived home from work.

'Taking photos again Arnold?' roared Dad as he left his car. 'Are you going to follow in your Mum's footsteps and put our house on the market? Hehe, that'll please her,' said Dad as he gave a gentle pat on my shoulder before entering the house to take off his shoes. I chuckled slightly at what he had said because he was oblivious towards the reason I were taking photos of the house from outside. Like the interior of my bedroom, I wanted to possess visual evidence of what my house would have looked like if I had to leave home abruptly; and that was tomorrow morning.

10

After giving out a long goodbye to the house, I managed to successfully enter Orpington station without facing any obstacles on the way such as dodgy individuals for example, but in order to activate step one of my mission, I have to purchase a ticket and find the platform on time. Back then, every time I went on an occasional train journey with my family or a school group, it would either be Mrs. Leslie or my parents who would encounter the ticket provider at the manned booths to collect our train tickets. Now it was only myself, alone at the train station and there's only me who can purchase the tickets. I always saw the interface of the ticket seller as a 50/50 concept. The reasoning for this is that after clearing the queue, the likeliness that the ticket seller is or is not a rude rogue covered in profanities is half chance in my opinion. 50 years ago, I might've faced the same dilemma and if I faced the bad consequences of the probability, it would've foiled my mission completely (which was very unlikely) but luckily not today because there appeared to be a self-service ticketing machine standing idle alongside the barriers.

Purchasing a ticket alone turned out to be less stressful than I had intended. Feeding the £10 notes into the machine wasn't troublesome whatsoever, the only worries I had were the chances of the notes disappearing as soon as they left my pocket, which didn't happen at all. This used to happen frequently back in secondary school and Mrs Leslie warned that I should not bring any form of money into school, regardless of amount. The next step was to find the platform in order to board the correct train.

There it was, the 10:53 to London Victoria platform 8 with four minutes remaining, plenty of time to disembark. It also gave me a minute to look back through the metal fence and down the station approach as an honorary "last glance at Orpington", before photographing the tarmac slope with my 35mm camera. But when I finished glancing I noticed there was something wrong on the platform, an unplanned obstacle was rushing between the platforms like a ball trapped in a pinball machine, it was Vincent. I immediately hid behind a roof pillar when I saw him, as I wasn't expecting his appearance at the station. Also I didn't want him to see me because any form of interaction with him could possibly destroy my planned ambition to find Mrs Leslie. And then my throat began to scrape itself, which often happens if I'm about to cry because of a dilemma that I had just realised.

If I had continued forward, Vincent would see me and attempt to disrupt my boarding of the train at the time. But if I stayed behind the pillar, Vincent wouldn't see me but then train would be missed. There were 39 seconds left (according to the station clock) and I felt as if I was going to drown if I ran out of time, similarly to a fictional blue hedgehog. I then heard a countdown tune being played inside my head so without thinking, I dragged my suitcase awkwardly to the next pillar, before launching it towards the entrance of a train carriage and catapulting myself also. At the point I weren't worrying whether Vincent had seen me or not, but felt relieved that the countdown inside my head had stopped.

******

As soon as the train for London Victoria left (with myself inside obviously) my first objective had kicked off. Presumably nothing critically bad should happen, likewise with the observation concerning the "three little pigs" theory. But the theory appeared to be flawed over a week ago whence approaching the second house to pretend that my rabbit had died and/or gone missing in their garden my request was rejected. However this was the first step of the one-way journey and I specifically chose to take an off peak service where hopefully less individuals will board so there should be nothing overly drastic that would rapidly avert the original plan, causing distress to myself and the entire train.

But as soon as the train passed Bickley, the doors hissed off sight and my insides began to clench again. Why was it? It was because the passenger sitting opposite myself, turned out to be a disgusting goth. It was a generic one which had dark features, it's face painted to resemble a deformed everton mint but worst of all it appeared to have a key ring painfully hanging out of his nose as if he were a crazed bull. There he was giving me an ominous stare like a bull readying to charge and the urge to flight was starting to kick in but what's strange is that it wasn't my brain giving the order to flee, it was my stomach. The clenching sensation that I felt back on the bus trip had returned and it felt even worse than before. I sprang out of my seat and swiftly fled onto the aisle that lay behind me and tried to search for a safe place for the pain to subside – the toilet. My throat began to feel more compressed as I became more desperate to find an area where I could let it out inconspicuously but as time ran out my options drew short.

Disaster! There weren't any toilets on this carriage. Instead I checked the next carriage for a toilet and all that was present was an empty bin hanging next to the doors with a plastic liner messily protruding from it. A left to right search to check if any passengers were around, luckily the carriage was empty apart from myself. And without fail, I quickly vomited into the slanting bin, tugging ferociously onto the plastic liner to prevent any of the remnants of today's breakfast spill onto the floor of the carriage where it would be noticed easily. The taste of hot acid continued to bleach my tongue as I folded the liner inside the bin and returned to the next carriage, this time closing my right eye in order not to see the disgusting goth.

But as soon as Arnold readied himself to sit down, he peeked at the two connecting doors along the far end of the carriage behind the goth and did a double take. He couldn't determine what was more unusual; the presence of a toilet, or the passenger emerging from it holding a red lampshade that contrasted with the horribly grey décor of the train.

******

Once I had alighted from the train carriage, phase 2 of my newest objective, which involved taking the London Underground Victoria line had automatically started. It felt quite relieving that I had completed phase 1, but my head felt as if it were to overheat because I could not properly predict the dangers that might follow for the next steps since the bad luck that occurred outside Orpington at the time. Honestly the mishap involving the vomiting back on the train only accounted as a minor fault, but the sudden disruption on the final portion of the adventure like a cancellation of a train service would account as a dangerous fault, capable of ruining the entire journey and warping myself back in Orpington to start over again.

It felt very uncomfortable sitting on the seats of the London Underground. It wasn't the temperature that I found discouraging, it was the seating arrangement. The buses back in Orpington were positioned so that every passenger (apart from the front two) all faced in the same direction whilst travelling. Here the seats were placed so that every passenger could stare at each other. I was nervous at the consequences, any minute now a goth, 2x as hideous as the one I saw on the train might sit opposite me but it shouldn't happen. The three little pigs theory, if it were true then nothing disastrous should happen during this part of the journey. I tried to diffuse the thoughts by looking at the map above the windows, to avert the inevitable gazes from the other passengers.

All I saw was a blue line very similar to a single carriageway motorway, with several junctions indicating the stops. Most of the stops such as Warren Street looked like roundabout junctions whilst my preferred exit, Kings Cross St Pancras resembled an overblown free flowing junction. Apart from the stop that completed phase 2, only one station greatly absorbed my attention. Hmm... it appeared that Pimlico was the only stop on the Victoria Line that did not interchange with any underground or railway lines. How interesting, that fact could come into use one day. For example:

'Arnold for tonight's mystery prize just answer the following question: Which station has no interchange on the Victoria Tube Line? You've got five seconds.'
'Pimlico'
'That is...the correct answer! Well done Mr Holt, you'll be walking home tonight with £10,000 cash prize and a year's supply of Everton mints!'

That would've been a splendid turning point in my life if it happened, but it was as likely as Aaron being resurrected from the dead. But the concept of removing my sight away from the passengers that sat opposite myself was becoming slowly impossible. After realising that the inevitability was strong I tried to remove these urges by staring at least one passenger opposite. It was a middle aged, blonde haired woman with purple trousers whom resembled a generic *Barbie* doll. But fortunately before I saw her face the underground carriage left Euston station, meaning that it was time to alight from the Victoria Line and prepare to run out of the carriage and dash up the escalator like a generic commuter would have done.

******

At 11.58am, I made it onto the next train, which initiated phase 3 of my newest phase: Kings Cross to York station. The journey should last exactly two hours, which gave me plenty of time to confirm phase 4 of my next objective once the destination is reached.

The difficulty with arranging phase 4 was that my preferred mode of transport had not been confirmed and I felt I need to alight at York station in order to find the "special village" as referenced on Mrs Leslie's letter. I could try hitchhiking from York to the "special village" like they do several times on television, but then again I have little idea on who would accept myself, as it could even be a dodgy driver who wears rings on their thumbs and has awful breath, but mother said that I should never hitchhike at all, not even at the last resort.

According to the "three little pigs" theory, something critically wrong was due to supposedly happen on this phase of the journey. But the theory had almost been defied by the vomiting back in phase 1, which should not have happened at all; and my notes also contained the mysterious phase 4 of the journey which does not fit with the number of lead characters in the theory's origin, which are the three pigs. I decided to withdraw from this problem on fear that it would override my next problem, which had greater priority.

And the "special village" formed my third problem. I had no idea of its exact location on a map, only by vague suggestions on my helper's letters as well as photographs of the region. I roughly assumed that it was near a road called the A64, but it could also be close to another road that lay north called the A170. It was wise that I brought an atlas along to aid this, but the primary reason why I brought it because it was also a clever way of deleting time. If I fell bored, I used to select two random locations out of the glossary before linking the two places with a driveable route using road numbers. There were less than two hours before the train reached York so I decided to provide an example.

I selected Sheerness as the start so after randomly pointing at a page, my finger had decided on Frome as its finish. My mind said ready, Go! A249, M20, M26, M25, M3, A303, A36. Oh and the A362, almost forgot. I cannot explain how the numbers stay inside my head, especially because I found it difficult to absorb plain and chalky text scribbled onto the blackboard back then; but it was more interesting than watching putrid youths dancing on television. Let's try another one, Gloucester to Fakenham: M5, A46, M69, M6, A14, A605, A47 and A148. Sigh, that one only took six seconds to work out.

Apart from the atlas, *The Railway Series* and *The Curious Incident* (which I've read approximately 38 times before), there was nothing else interesting to view on step 3 of the journey. Looking outside the window was not comparable to that of the car, mainly because the stationary objects that I would like to stare at were over 3x faster, which felt highly frustrating because I could not pinpoint the precise location on this train, as I would had done back home when travelling around the countryside with Dad. And then a marvellous idea occurred inside my head. The atlas was out again and I realised a new challenge, Maldon to Edenbridge: A414, A12, M25, A282, M25, M22 and B2026. After giving out the correct answer, I noticed that something wasn't right about the atlas at all; the M22 was a new motorway.

The train then immediately stopped, launching myself forward and smacking onto the plastic desk from the seat in front. I woke up. After quickly accepting that the M22 did not exist at all, I noticed that a young bearded man wearing a black waistcoat and a brown pouch with the *British Rail* logo on was staring at myself, positioned as if he were to touch me.

'Come on, come on now,' he called

'?'

'This train ends here.' Pardon?

'Why?' I asked, realising that we reached York sinisterly early.

'Can you please leave the carriage, the train has stopped.'

'Where we are?' I asked him with suspicion.

'In Kansas,' He replied calmly.

'But Kansas isn't in Yorkshire,' I said correcting him.

'Christ, see for yourself then,' He snapped before pointing a finger towards the window with his hand and walked into the next carriage grumbling quietly. There was something suspicious about arriving at York station too early and a gaze at the plaque next to the waiting room already provided the answer because it didn't read York, it read Selby instead.

Oh no.

This was not good.

Something wasn't right, this was far too illogical. Several hours of intricate planning, only to be postponed by a sudden delay outside the target destination! No, no, no! This was too unfair, my rejected "three little pigs" theory turned out to be accurate all this time and most importantly; I had fallen the third hurdle and failed in the newfound quest to find Mrs Leslie and confirm my future in the special village permanently.

******

Instead of remaining static on the platform, Arnold did the opposite. He flailed his arms angrily, stamped his feet as hard as he could and he emitted a chainsaw like noise from his mouth all at once, taking it out on the station platform. He was no longer taking account of his surroundings because he was too engaged in having a meltdown. He enjoyed stamping his feet the most because the ground effortlessly absorbed it whilst the surrounding passengers whom were at the platform were watching in confusion and curiosity.

A plain-clothes officer, who was watching the furore, decided to leave the crowd to approach the ballistic man in an attempt to diffuse him. But because the officer was wearing rings on both ears in a symmetrical fashion and a kingfisher tattoo on one of his muscular forearms, instead of diffusing Arnold he unknowingly detonated him.

11

I felt rather light when I awoke. Ahead lay a rectangular building, similar to the entrance to the 'special village' featured on the photographs in Mrs Leslie's letters. Perhaps Mrs Leslie is inside, anticipating my debut or even making jam sandwiches. I circled the building to search for an entrance, ducking past every window (just incase she saw me, thus spoiling the introduction) until I found a doormat shaped like a two-headed fish that read "Entrance" which revealed the doorway.

'I don't believe it!' that voice didn't belong to me, it belonged to Mrs Leslie. I was overjoyed at her positive appearance, so much that I became speechless. 'Your timing is splendid Arnold,' said Mrs Leslie. 'We were just about to have ice cream in a minute. Why not take a seat next to the others.' And so I cheerfully obeyed her and skipped into a classroom where the banquet took place. While searching for a clean chair to sit on, this particular one made myself scream continuously in absolute horror, but soundlessly because I was still mute. Peering down at the highly fluorescent chair, a black hole was already sitting there. Sigh, not again.

I actually woke up this time, but instead of feeling light, my face felt as if it were pressed against a jigsaw puzzle due to feeling the newly made marks. Something wasn't right, firstly my suitcase had disappeared, like those reoccurring nightmares I had where I left it behind whilst going on holiday; and secondly the room, which contained obscured glass windows and distinctly brown radiators that were opposite each other, resembled the interior of a mental home. What was going on? Was this an elaborate trap arranged by my parents to be sealed inside a cushioned room forever or as mentioned, simply a deluded dream? I was about to react angrily when a stranger conveniently interrupted by opening the door.

'Out of the nod are you then?' he asked before closing the door. 'Not to worry, you're not doing time, but I'll need some of yours instead. My name's Doctor Bradbury, I'm a psychiatrist but you can call me Ian if you like.'

'Where is my suitcase?' I asked as he grabbed a chair to sit on.

'Your belongings are being kept safe in the other room for the time being, but enough about that. I'm here to explore your mind from the inside and scoop it out, but instead I'm going to have a chat with you which should be less painful than that,' he laughed. 'I'm actually an amateur at this, but my colleague Terry is in the bog at the moment so he'll be joining us shortly.'

But four seconds later the door knocked, but it wasn't the colleague. Instead walking towards myself, was the horror that I faced previously, the individual from Selby station, the one with earrings on both ears, was a policeman. Upon his sight I immediately tried to form my right hand into a facial shield, not only as a botched attempt to hide oneself, but to avert my gaze on the visual profanities he was bearing.

'Alright doc?' he asked.

'Yep, all things are fine here, won't you agree?' said Doctor Bradbury, staring at me.

'Well he behaved well during the trip from Selby.'

'Really?' asked the doctor again.

'Yeah, but that was because he was unconscious the whole time. Don't know why the constable wanted to take him to York when there was already a police station next to the railway.'

Pardon? I almost dropped my shield in horror.

'You shouldn't have said that,' replied the doctor. 'He was just coming round.'

'I'll try not too next time, has he been giving you any aggro too? I thought the constable called for two spin doctors, not one.'

'Terry, the other "spin doctor" is in the toilet as we speak. He then has to go back to the van to fish out some paperwork but I've got enough here to conduct a brief diagnosis.'

'So,' said the policeman, nodding towards myself. 'Has he got the asperger's then?'

'I can't automatically declare the level of his condition …yet. But once Terry checks the data and gives it a once over, you should get that golden answer, OK?

'Fine, but we also did a search on his belongings and we've found some strange stuff. A handful of sharp objects and what appears to be black contraband sealed inside a cushion.'

'?'

'Well I'm quite sure there's a back-story behind everything,' said Ian.

'Alright then,' said the policeman 'But my senses will be on high alert so give me a shout if you see him thrashing out again.'

'We'll be OK,' replied the doctor. Soon as I saw the policeman close the door behind himself, it indicated that it was safe to retract my facial shield.

'He's gone now; cops are like marmite these days. You either love them or hate them.' I breathed out, trying to display my relief although I couldn't.

'Where am I?' I asked, so that I could hear the location again.

'You're inside York police station. But don't worry, you're not under arrest. I am just going to take a note of your name, address and most importantly find out the reason behind your meltdown back in Selby station. Given your specific condition as well as your behaviour towards the policeman, they decided it would be better to call us down to here so we could have a chat with you and minimise the risk of another accident. Do you understand what I'm saying?'

'Yes.' I replied quietly.

'OK. Ooh I just forgot; do you have a name?' I froze, whilst making the decision to answer back or not. 'Take your time, you have all day,' he said again.

'Arnold Bentley Holt,' I replied.

'Nice name that. Mind if I shorten it to Arnie?'

'Yes.'

'Okay, Arnold it is. Where have you come from Arnold?'

'Orpington.'

'Ooh that's a long way, that's in London isn't it?'

'Kent,' I replied, correcting him.

'Really, I never knew that. Got any brothers and sisters back home?'

'One brother, one sister,' I replied again.

'And I'm guessing they bug you out right?'

'Yes.'

'I see. Do you know why you're here in the first place?'

'I am searching for a "special village" inside North Yorkshire where my helper currently lives.'

'There are a few I know around here, are you talking about the one near Danby Botton?'

'No,' I said confidently.

'Are you sure?' he asked 'That place is famous for disabled people looking for a fresh start; the village even appeared on TV once.'

'Danby Botton is situated above the A170 in North Yorkshire. The "special village" I am referring to lies below the A170.'

'What is the A170?' he asked

'It is a road.'

'Okay, okay, I'll look into it,' said Ian, displaying both of his hands. He then rose from his seat and exited the room, which meant I was alone once again. The silence lasted for exactly 2.5 minutes, at which time I closed my mouth even further shut in anticipation that Ian would return which the correct answer.

'Yeah you're right Arnold, there is a similar place that lies south of the dales,' he replied. 'I've barely heard of it because I don't think it is part of Camphill, but I'm sure Terry knows more about it.' Hooray, how positive that had felt.

'Is there a lady who works there called Mrs Leslie?' I asked with excitement.

'Whoa, whoa there, I've just heard of the place. Why are you after that particular person anyway?'

'I want to visit Mrs Leslie,' I said.

'You came all the way from Orpington just to see her?' I shook my head sideways.

'I want to live inside the "special village" with her, which is the reason I left Orpington.' Ian paused, presumably thinking because he put as hand over his face.

'Hold on a second,' replied Ian. He paused again, as if he had forgotten what to say next. The silence was then abruptly broken when the door handle turned and opened the door, revealing another stranger. Assuming that it was the policeman, my face had already covered by my hand in anticipation of his return.

'Hello there! Is everything alright in here?' called a female voice.

'Yeah, long day today, that's all,' said Ian

'Is he alright over there?' called the lady again, presumably referring to myself.

'Yeah he's fine, thinks you're the bloke with the tattoos.'

'You mean Colin? Anyway can I get you a drink?'

'I'll have coffee with two sugars please. Would you like a drink Arnold?'

'No, thank you,' I replied, removing my hand in the process.

'Right, I'll have your coffee in five minutes doc.'

'Cheers.'

The lady left, closing the door after herself. I did not actually see her at all, only the tip of her face sliding backwards behind the door as it closed shut. 'OK, where was I? Right Arnold,' Ian paused for the third time. 'I can understand that you would travel this far to see your school helper; and start a new life with her right?' I nodded back in agreement. 'Well unfortunately, these kind of things aren't that simple nowadays.' The room fell silent. 'Do you understand what I'm getting at?'

'Pardon?' I replied randomly, trying to prevent the silence.

'What I mean is that you can't just turn up at the centre willy-nilly and expect to instantly get a new home in the countryside and live there for good. The situation's a bit like trying to get a council flat, have you tried to get social housing in the past?'

'…' I replied with nothing.

'Well it's a bit like that. There are tens or even hundreds of people similar to you who want to move to a "special village" where they could start afresh, get the support they really need as well as learning to become totally independent, something that they would find hard achieving back where they live. You on the other hand are an exception. Nearly all the clients from the special centres were accepted from the wishes of families and local social services, who beg for us to take them in and care for them; you've come all this way hoping to find one of these centres as if it were a mission. I've heard cases of disabled adults making these types of journeys for reasons that escape me but your reason just intrigues me.' He pauses again to inhale a handful of air. 'But then again if you hadn't flipped out back in Selby, then I wouldn't be here listening to your adventure.' The door knocked again.

'He-llooh!' The lady had returned.

'Ah, just on time,' said Ian

'Your coffee and two sugars doc, as you asked.'

'Lovely, thanks,' replied Ian as the lady left the room again. He then quickly sampled his mug of coffee before speaking again. 'As I was saying, you are a special exception Arnold. You're a bit like errr…, like the Hulk or *Superman*! Mild-mannered Arnold minding his own business one day, when suddenly he transforms into his alter ego, causing havoc all around him!' He then stared at me in a peculiar manner, as if he wanted me to laugh at him; but I could not understand the reason as to why Ian would compare myself to *Superman.* He then grabbed his mug to take a heavy mouthful before speaking again. 'Sorry about that, couldn't think of anything else to say. What I really meant to say is that whilst you appear plain and average on the outside, your "insides" are like a vivid jungle of mystery which nobody else can navigate through except yourself and part of my job requires building a door into this jungle to be explored. Do you understand now?'

'Yes,' I replied back, hoping that he would stop using obscure sentences.

'…I never said you can't get a place there, but if possible there is a way of "jumping the queue" which would boost your chances and find out if you're fully eligible to move to where you're going.'

Then Ian fished his left hand underneath the table before pulling out a flat yellow sheet of paper. It was littered with text of different sizes and featured illustrations of pink pieces of *Meccano* as well as individuals in various poses; the bottom left corner (top right to Ian) appeared to contain the *NHS* logo. 'This is basically a watered down version of the classic diagnosis tests that we would use for somebody of your "special disposition".' He then raised two fingers from both hands up. 'Ahem, excuse the brackets silly me. But don't worry though; I'm not going to attach wires to your head or anything, think of it like doing your SATs again.'

'…'

'Now if you bear with me, I'll get the rest of the test below.' He then disappeared from my view underneath the table again where a zip fastener was briefly heard. He reappeared again, but this time holding a thick wedge of annotated paper which looked unattractive, to a point that it had caused that lump in my throat to return once again.

'Are you alright Arnold?'

'Yes.'

'Don't worry about it, there's no right or wrong answers in the test. In the end of the day it's just a little exercise that helps with our research and it may help with your dream of finding your helper too you know. Oh! And don't forget to take your time as well, that's very important.'

Ian was nearly accurate in stating the comparison of the diagnosis test to an examination paper; the only main difference was that I was currently completing the test in a blue biro instead of the generic black and yellow pencils that we were forced to use back then in secondary school. It had taken 43 minutes to complete and consisted of questions that were quite hard to answer due to varying levels of difficulty. Here was an example:

12) Do you sometimes hear voices inside your head?

Yes ☐ *No* ☐

13) Can you carry out the following unassisted (without help)?

- *Getting dressed/undressed*
- *Having a bath/shower*
- *Preparing your own meals*
- *Travelling by public transport (e.g. bus/train)*

- *Following directions*
- *Asking for help*
- *Going to the supermarket*

9) From a scale of 1 to 5, state how you would react to meeting new people:

But overall the most difficult questions on the diagnosis test were these ones

3) Do you have autism?

Yes ☐ *No* ☐

20) Do you think you are autistic?

```



```

      The first question stated was fairly hard because I had not been officially confirmed that I generically had autism, the last known reference being of the time my mother wrote a letter to *WHSmith* concerning an incident over a year ago and left it exposed inside the hallway by accident. The second felt difficult because it required an open answer (one that did not want Yes/No as the main answer); and the wording was too vague to the point that I could not remember correctly if that particular task would have been carried out on a daily basis. If it were a closed question (the opposite of open question), the answer would be easier to obtain for example:

20) Do you think you are autistic?

Yes ☐ *No* ☐

Instead I wrote down "N/A" inside the blank box below the question before moving onto the next one.

'Right, thank you for filling this in Arnold,' said Ian, holding the test paper. 'Now all we have to do is get Terry to check it through before we get your results ready.'

      'Pardon?'

12

Eight minutes later, a knock occurred. 'Ah, it seems that my colleague is off the bog now!' smiled Ian as he stared at the door, revealing a vague shadow of a head behind the bumpy and distorted glass, similar to the neighbours' door back in Orpington. 'If you don't mind, I'm off to have a valuable word with my colleague for five minutes before we discuss your results if that's fine with you Arnold.' I nodded.

And he left the room, which meant being alone once again. Behind the obscured glass there appeared to be two figures vibrating as they spoke, one of them presumably Ian. I rather disliked it when this situation was encountered because it would inevitably result in something negative happening to me; such as my parents approving my disappearance which explained my presence here. I tried to overhear the conversation, as I would often back at home, but I could only pick up vague sentences.

'...yep, another autistic lad....wears odd shoes..... carries pins around...'

'could do with a good chat...'

The obscured conversation lasted for roughly 1.5 minutes before the figures behind the glass grew disturbingly large which meant they had finished.

'We're back now,' called a voice.

Returning to the room was Ian, along with the individual that he was talking to. He appeared old, thin and had hairy eyebrows which looked frightening.

'Ah you must be Arnold, let me introduce myself, I'm Doctor Terence Campbell,' said the individual, reaching over the table to shake my own hand. 'I hear that you're looking for Welbourne Mills.'

'Pardon?' I replied.

'From what I gathered from Ian, that's the centre you're trying to find. Anyway, we've just finished up the analysis from the papers you filled in earlier and unfortunately, we may have some news that you won't like.'

'Pardon?'

'Basically, we think your autism is too mild to grant a permanent stay at the refuge.'

'Mild?' I asked curiously.

'Would you like a further explanation Arnold?'

'No, but the first time I heard the word "mild" was in 1997 in an advertisement for *Anchor* butter.'

'Right; and how exactly do you know the year may I ask?' he asked again

'It's also my helper's PIN number!' I said gleefully.

'It's smashing to hear that,' Said Ian 'But I think you should pause and listen to the results again for a thorough understanding.'

'You see Arnold,' said Dr Campbell 'this refuge that you're trying to access, has only a limited number of spaces and it caters more towards those who are less able and require more support. Do you understand?'

'Oh,' I responded.

'Well I tried to warn him earlier Tel,' said Ian 'You should have heard how far he had come to make it here; I doubt that the other clients at the centre would've travelled a great distance on their own.'

'Hmm… really?' replied the other doctor. 'It reminds me of a similar scenario I read before; a novel about a boy who runs away on the train to London to find his mother, Mrs Shears. No wait, that's not her name…'

'That's his neighbour you're thinking of but leave that for later Tel,' answered Ian. 'Arnold, I know it's hard for you to hear this but I realised that whilst you're up here, down there your family must be missing you by now.' No, this predicament cannot commence at all.

'Oh well, do you have a mobile phone on you Arnold?'

'…'

'Do you know your parents' phone number off by heart?' asked Terry.

'NO!' I shouted 'I DO NOT PERMIT YOU TO CONTACT MY PARENTS!'

'Eh?' responded Ian.

'THAT ACTION WOULD RESULT IN MY PARENTS FACING MYSELF BACK HOME WHERE I WOULD BE SHOUTED AT AND EVENTUALLY DISPOSED INTO A MENTAL HOME.'

'Ok no need to shout! Anything else you'd like to tell us?'

'MY NEWEST PURPOSE TO FIND MRS LESLIE WHERE SHE'LL GIVE ME A NEW DISPOSITION!'

'Disposition?' asked Dr Campbell.

'OBJECTIVE OR TASK, IT IS THE SOLE REASON FOR MY SPECIFIC TRAVEL TO THIS REGION. I EVEN HOAXED THE DEATH OF MY BELOVED RABBIT TO BEGIN THIS JOURNEY AND I DO NOT INTEND TO BE WARPED BACK TO ORPINGTON WHERE I WOULD REFACE THE PERENNIAL LOOP OF MY OLD DISPOSITION!'

They sat there silently, but strangely instead of attempting to restrain Arnold, they both left the office and stood a few feet away from the door. Arnold thought they were talking about him because he could see their hands swinging at each other and their mouths moving through the frosted glass but he couldn't understand a word. *Should I listen or not?* he thought as he slowly jerked his ear towards the door.

'…but it's more notable when he's angry,' said a voice,
'At least he didn't attack anyone this time…notice how his vocabulary changes in conjunction with his mood?' I tried to listen but the buzzing from the lights made it difficult to hear.
'…would be better if they took him in for the time being.'
'?' My hands had stopped sweating when this was mentioned. I tried to listen further again but their figures both advanced towards the door again, which meant they were finished speaking.
'We've had another chat and thought very carefully about this,' said Terry. 'And we've decided that after witnessing your "meltdown" as we call them, to provide you a place over at Welbourne Mills, albeit on a temporary basis. I know it's not what you're after but the time you spend there should do yourself better and give you time to recover from what you've experienced.'
'As Tel had mentioned,' responded Ian 'You're in, but remember what we talked about Arnold. Everybody falls out with their family at least once in their lives, but soon enough you'll be missing them and they'll be missing you. I bet that after two weeks in the centre, you'll be crying to see your parents again; won't he Terry?'
'Yeah, but he needs his suitcase before he does.' Terry then placed his hand in front of another doorway outside onto the next room, presumably where my grey suitcase was hiding. He was correct. When I opened it, the suitcase appeared intact except that one notable item was missing; the pillowcase of Milth's fur. I began to feel upset.
'Oh and one last thing' said Dr Bradbury, unhanding Milth's fur 'Here's your special stuff; and don't go sniffing it.' Pardon? What did he mean by that?

13

'It's over there on the right Arnold,' noted Ian.

He pointed towards the white minibus which had black and yellow industrial striping on the rear. I felt rather unwary with the concept of travelling inside one with two strangers, until I noticed that the yellow and orange chevron patterning on the seats were identical to the seats on another coach that I used during a school trip back in Year 7, where myself and Aaron spent the day running around a dockyard like hooligan children. The minibus was one of the generic types which had three seats at the front, making it appear uncomfortable to sit on, so I decided to sit on one of the seats located in the middle, closest to the window. The two doctors promptly sat in the front of the minibus, started it and were talking to each other again, minus the obscured glass in my sightline.

'Yeah Terry, the place has been going strong for four years, but why aren't they part of Camphill then?'

'No idea,' responded Terry. 'Perhaps the guests over there don't want to; maybe they don't like the change at all.' And the two doctors quietly laughed at each other.
How rare.

'We once had a chap a few years back called Paul who was quite a celebrity, as he could effortlessly speak nine languages without fail.'

'Yeah I remember him,' said Terry 'the only irony was that he wasn't very fluent his first language which of course, was English. He works somewhere in Bangkok, last time I heard.'

'Yeah, loves it over there.'

The minibus continued to plough through several unclassified country roads before turning suddenly onto a new one, making them difficult to identify on my atlas.

'Not to worry, we're nearly here!' replied one of the doctors, although it did not help with my search at all. Then the minibus made another sudden turn, this time onto a grassy tramline which lasted for half a minute. Afterwards it passed through a long maroon gate before the wheels started to crunch the gravel underneath as the vehicle spun around in front of the surrounding buildings, as if it were searching for a suitable method to park itself.

'Well, it looks like we're here.'

The entrance to the "special village" appeared different from my dream. The front building resembled a turquoise rectangle with three neat windows on the side; and its doormat was a hedgehog instead of a two-headed fish. It felt quite disappointing but then again, this layout was to become the front door to my new home.

'The reception is through there,' pointed Terry 'Once we're finished with the van we can get your stuff sorted out inside.'

'Yes thank you,' I replied although I wasn't focusing on going towards the reception at all, I was actually facing away from it.

'Changed your mind already?' asked Ian, standing outside the reception.

'No,' I said back to him.

I was busy recalling the hazardous journey I had taken to reach the 'special village' and found it appropriate to stand facing away from the entrance and outside the gates to make it easier to remember what I had encountered along the route. But creating a mental tribute to the overall journey felt extremely difficult. If one was not created then the journey itself would be branded as incomplete and then a nasty stomach ache would occur as a result. Suddenly I then dived both hands into my pockets and pulled them outwards, causing pens and tissues to fall on the ground, but this did not help at all.

'Is this yours Arnold?' asked Terry; he was clutching my atlas. 'I found it on the bus.'

I then promptly realised that Dr Terence was holding the key to my tribute. As I ran off to collect the map before sprinting back to the same spot where the reminiscing took place, I violently turned the pages inside the atlas until a double page of Greater London appeared, featuring Orpington. It felt highly difficult trying to concentrate on the starting point of my epic journey from home, infact so difficult that my hands had clamped shut and were busy abusing the atlas. After violently pulling my right hand away, I tried to turn the pages again in order to find more inspiration, but unfortunately the first page that appeared after turning was a bland black and white diagram of the United Kingdom.

And then a quaint thought occurred. I picked up one of my pens off the ground within a split second and pressed it up against England, exactly where Orpington lay. Then suddenly, an assortment of images appeared inside my mind. The first was a large diagram of Milth standing outside my former home followed by the interior of my bedroom, before smaller images of Station Approach appeared where I had performed the "last glance at Orpington". My hand then shifted the pen slowly northwards up the map, which had caused the images inside my head to change, as well as a shiver of discomfort when I had passed Bromley on the train, after the scene where I had vomited. When the pen had finished dissecting London, my experiences of travelling through the capital were strongly highlighted and soon replaced; the pen still continued going further north, this time bypassing Grantham which was close to its halfway point. There a couple of bland images of the flagship train journey appeared, along with the disappointing scenic views outside the windows and the fictional motorway which I almost thought had existed before the train accidentally arrived in Selby. But when the pen dragged itself towards the moors of North Yorkshire, the images then became difficult to create inside my mind and the throwback was promptly finished.

But it shouldn't be finished. In the majority of throwbacks that appear in television programmes, a reference towards the relatives (or the "loved ones") of the main character would appear. I found this very difficult to reminisce because this journey was prompted by my parents wanting to get rid of myself but trying to omit that terrible ordeal out of my head, the only mental images that occurred at the time were myself travelling around Kent with Dad inside one of his vintage cars; and another of the reoccurring Saturdays I had spent with my mother visiting the supermarket.

******

Feeling that the tribute was complete, I placed the items on the ground back into my pocket again and marched slowly towards the reception door, eager to confront Mrs Leslie and begin my new life here. But when my feet landed on the distinctive hedgehog doormat, a familiar pain had suddenly erupted inside my body, almost pushing myself away from the entrance. My stomach ache had returned. It was the same type of stomach ache that occured back when I tried to alter my bi-weekly schedule back at home or whenever an arranged objective does not go as planned. It can detect that something has gone wrong.

To succeed in my finite quest to find Mrs Leslie, I was required to leave Orpington, leave home and worst of all abandon Milth and convince my family that she was dead just to escape. By travelling to the "special village" to lead a peaceful and undisturbed life with my helper, I had to commit something that I had rarely performed since Aaron died from cancer: change.

In order to escape I had to change my schedule, change my objectives, change my actions and most notable of all change my life. But the overall reason for this excessive change; moving the Jobcentre to Bromley, my parents' vile plan to evict myself from the house, the throbbing desire to see Mrs Leslie's aged features once again; ALL CHANGE. The same type of change that would cause a headache every time I saw a shop closing down in the area, or my Dad painting his vintage car to another colour. Even the increasing hoards of disgusting youths smoking around the town square had the same type of change, which alone was another reason to evacuate Orpington.

But the reasons behind disliking these certain types of individual are not entirely known to myself, although my Mother once gave me a thorough lecture on why you should not decide on an individual by the shade of the skin

81

colour, I did not feel any urge to break her promise and disobey her, unlike my Dad who once said to me *"girls from Croydon with orange skin are the ones who sin"*.

And yet it appeared that the specific category of persons, regardless of their skin colour either wore unnecessary jewellery on their own bodies or pointless items, which was an attribute relating to the disgusting youths who would circle town centres like flies circling rabbit droppings. A single glance at one of these hooded creatures was a strong reference to the terrible bullies who would constantly heckle myself and Aaron everyday at school by stealing our sweets, kicking our ankles and writing rude names about ourselves on the classroom walls.

Yet if I had decided not to change my bi-weekly routine back in Orpington, it would have resulted in myself shuffling through the schedule forever until I had pleased the Jobcentre by securing employment, which itself appeared entirely impossible because the recession had closed down several shops and outlets in the area. This included the local *Woolworths* that closed down last year which had depressed me the most because it was another alternative outpost for purchasing Everton mints.

Then a tiny spark ignited inside my head. If the majority of the human race decided to perform short term, satisfactory tasks on a weekly regime (as I originally did) that would loop continuously for a lifetime, then we would end up achieving nothing in life and none of our greatest inventions and discoveries such as railways, computer games and Dad's cars would have existed. This discovery had caused my headache to return, until I instantly recalled a quote from my last day of secondary school, as mentioned by Mrs Leslie which had relieved my headache:

"Change is happening all the time Arnold, it happens anywhere, everywhere and even nowhere. But the one thing that cannot be changed is your soul, your thoughts and your dignity. The only person who has the power to change all of that is you."

Excluding the perfectly minimal task to find Mrs Leslie inside the establishment, now that I had finally succeeded in my quest to find the "special village", the special journey now at an end, what will my next objective be?

14

For someone who was naturally quite irritating for his age, George was quite a patient person as he stood barefoot on the wooden porch on a warm Thursday evening, waiting for a scarlet people carrier to slowly crawl down Repton Avenue. His prayers were finally answered when one happened to turn up three minutes later, reversed onto the block paved driveway and before his eyes the window on the front passenger door slowly lowered itself to reveal the driver.

'Hello mom! Where's me dinner!?' shouted George.

'Same place where it's always been honey!' replied the female voice from inside the vehicle. Once he had heard the car door closing and high heels tapping on the ground, George automatically drew both arms up in front of his face, as if he were ready to catch something. The voice and the high heels actually belonged to his mother Linda Holt, who was clutching a cream handbag with her left arm and swinging a dark anorak with her right hand. She then untidily flung her anorak towards George, landing on his arms like he was a human coat rack. 'In you go you little sausage, we'll put dinner on when Dad gets here,' Linda said to her son as she trotted her way into the hall.

******

Geoffrey Holt had just come out of a dilemma that had lasted a good few weeks. Even when he was pleasantly cruising down the motorway before the rush hour, he still felt the aftermath of those few weeks niggling in his mind. The dilemma centred around his classic Jaguar X, a vintage sports car that he had spent 5 years carefully restoring in the front garage until it finally got in the way of this marriage and he had no choice but to part with it. It made sense to his other half, who saw the idea of maintaining three cars while in the midst of a recession rather farfetched, especially when two cars were reserved for commuting and another reserved for visits to motoring pageants and Sunday drives through deepest Surrey with the family.

For Geoffrey he knew he had to let the Jaguar go at some point and chuckled slightly when he considered selling the Vauxhall or the silver Mazda (the one he was currently driving) instead of his classic motor. Once he left the motorway, he could start mentally preparing to greet his family once he got home, unaware that a new dilemma may be around the corner. The first to greet him was his son.

'Hi honey, you're home!' called George, running into the hall.

'Hey George, you OK?'

'Geoff you're home!' roared Linda 'How was it today?'

'Good, not bad at all. There was some heavy traffic on the A13 earlier but that's about it. Yourself?'

'Not bad either. You remember that elderly couple from Sidcup who had to bring in their own son to make their own decisions? Well they have bit the bullet and finally bought that two bedroom bungalow on Turnpike Drive. Still, like you said better than nothing.'

'Oh well done dear,' smiled Geoff 'I guess it's time to put the dinner on. Is it chicken kievs or escalopes tonight?'

'Escalopes,' replied Linda 'we had kievs last Tuesday night didn't we George?'

'Yeah, the chicken ones!' he shouted.

'OK, Rose gave me a text earlier; she won't be home until nine tonight so there's no point putting anything on for her yet. I'll find out what flavour escalopes the incredible sulk is having so we can get this over and done with,' announced Linda rather calmly 'Arnold!'

There was no reply. Sometimes she wouldn't hear a verbal response from her son and instead hear his feet bashing on the stairs but this wasn't the case either and nothing could be heard from the hallway at all.

'Arnold!'

Silence.

'ARNOLD!'

More silence.

'He might be in the garden instead dear,' said Geoff

'He'll come down whether he'll like it or not. Arnold, Arnold!' shouted Linda but it was no use, the lack of response from upstairs was making her livid. After an easy day at the office that ended with a positive note, the last thing she wanted to do was disrupt the flow of calm by raising her voice. As one last chance she marched straight to the foot of the hallway stairs and at the top of her voice she bellowed out: 'AH-NOOOOOOOOOOOOOOOOOOLLLLDD!'

More silence.

'Right, he must be taking the piss again. George, see if your brother is sulking in his room again.'

'OK,' replied George and he sped up the stairs, leaving his parents behind downstairs where they tried to reassure themselves in the kitchen by talking away from this situation, and wondered if it was just a false alarm.

'Have you checked if he's gone out again Lin?' asked Geoff.

'No, can't be,' protested his wife 'Arnold has always been home on time for dinner, I know it and you know it too. The last time he's been late for dinner was when he was out playing with his friend, the one who had cancer.'

'But that was over two years ago, unless he's found another friend to play with-'

'I doubt it,' interrupted Linda, putting the kettle on. 'You pretty well that boy was never open when it came to making new friends, but when you see the grubby lot that scrounge outside the Jobcentre you can't blame him at all.'

'Well you can't say they're all bad, that's like stating the impossible,'

'I know what you're saying and I agree with it, but let's put it this way. List the number of times our son has been late home for dinner and then add that to the number of times he's been caught outside The Walnuts smelling of booze. Well? I don't need to go any further on this one.'

'I understand dear,' finished Geoff, who had suddenly run out of things to say back.

As they both waited for the kettle to finish boiling, all Geoff and Linda could do was look silently onto the marble floor below like two penguins in mating season, and wait for their son to return from upstairs with the news. Preferably if this was a perfect day George would shoot down the stairs and tell them excitedly that Arnold was hiding inside the wardrobe again, therefore declaring the incident as a false alarm, but to the best of their knowledge the day had been far from perfect.

******

George opened the door into his brother's room and was greeted by a strong odour of antiseptic mixed with the smell of aging cream carpet. He looked at the sunlight shimmering onto the sky blue walls and noticed for the first time that on one of the wall four tiny stubs of blu-tack could be seen where a poster used to be kept. What used to be tacked onto his brother's wall was something George couldn't remember. Putting that aside for a

85

minute George then turned towards the wall and set his sight on the bed. Arnold's bedroom (in comparison to George's own) was minimal and relatively tidy, especially when George realised that he slept on one of those modern bunk beds where instead of another bed at the bottom, he had a desk, an office chair with a matching table lamp and a miniature wardrobe, all painted in the same shade of white except for the ladder which contained smudges of black from fingerprints. He wasn't sitting at his desk underneath the bed reading, nor was he hiding behind the door as George had quickly checked. But he might be hiding underneath the covers, like he used to do sometimes whenever Rose invited her friends around the house. So with much enthusiasm George climbed up the ladder and quickly tore the *Dangermouse* duvet cover off the mattress,

'Gotcha!' he shouted, but was stunned to realise that Arnold wasn't hiding underneath the covers. He let off a childish groan and then smiled again when the sight of his brother's absence made him feel slightly nostalgic.

It reminded him of the half term holidays where thousands of schoolchildren would blissfully jump for joy as schools would close for a week. For George it was heaven but unfortunately for his older brother it was hell because for Arnold it would mean being continually pestered at home by the "Golden Idiot" all week until the new school term began the Monday after. And to avoid being humiliated every day he had to think of a solution. And so for five consecutive days George would naturally wake up around 10am only to find the house completely dead for exactly eight hours until 6pm where Arnold arrives back from his "mystery outing". Upon being asked by George where he had exactly been, he solemnly replies "Out.", which is the only response George can extract out of him. 'Must be around here somewhere,' he said to himself, but then he just had an ingenious thought. He had remembered his brother's book, the one with the picture of the dog with a fork through its chest, looking rather depressed. The one where he enjoyed confiscating out of his bedroom before flouting it around the house and using it as a tool to tease (and sometimes blackmail) his own brother, before repeating the same actions the following day.

Infact he idolised the book so much he would take it along with him every time he left the house, perhaps because he felt insecure about leaving his ex-helper's present alone in the house. Or the book gave him an invisible force that enhanced his own senses as well as shielding him away from the horrors that Orpington had to offer. The book was considered so sacred to

Arnold that he stored it away from the other books that lie on the red bookshelf opposite his high sleeper. In Lehman's terms, if the book wasn't in his room then it meant Arnold wasn't in the house either.

He pulled open the side drawer and was stunned to notice that the blue book wasn't there at all. As George closed it he felt slightly remorseful, and wondered if he should cut out all this book-pinching crap for good. If he did, perhaps Arnold would come home again and be nice towards him. But when he noticed the *Dangermouse* duvet in an untidy heap, George quickly forgot about his wise discovery and climbed up the ladder to make the bed. When he finished hooking the first two corners of duvet around the mattress George leant over to tuck in the last two corners but doing this without touching the rest of the duvet was physically impossible and George eventually lost his balance and slumped straight onto the bed landing face first into an ordinary pillow.

This ordinary pillow managed to jog his memory somehow. The rabbit pillow should be here somewhere in this room, the one that Arnold enjoyed fondling in the dining room every time he was told off. To be precise it was a dark blue pillow which was filled with the fur of his brother's dead pet rabbit Milth. If it wasn't in his room, it would be downstairs in the dining room where it would be utilised, or in the back garden where the pillow casing would be packed with even more black and white fluff. But it can't be in the dining room, besides George was in there earlier before his Mum arrived home from work and he had enough time to get in the garden for a quick game of solo footy but he didn't see a navy pillow lying around in those two places.

It only meant one thing to George, that Arnold wasn't home and he genuinely disappeared.

******

Back in the kitchen Geoff had just finished making the coffee and was just about to add the sugar to his wife's cup when they both turned towards the doorway and heard their son thumping down the stairs with breaking news. When he faced them, they both saw that George had a weak smile on his face which meant to Linda that there was a glimpse of victory and inside she was gleaming with hope and relief. But the reason George was actually

87

smirking was because he had just remembered a joke he heard at school which had something to do with a Scotsman jumping off a cliff after having a row about cheese and pickle sandwiches.

'Well?' asked his mother 'Did you find him?'
George finally stopped smirking and shook his head sideways.
'Are you sure he wasn't hiding anywhere again?'

'No,' said George sadly 'he wasn't hiding I looked everywhere. His books were gone also; you know that big blue one he really likes?'

'No, can't be. Geoff do something!' shouted Linda 'Search the whole house again for god's sake, don't just stand there like a spare part!'

Geoffrey who had been static for the past few minutes sprang into life after hearing his wife's reactions and started the search by rapidly opening the cupboard doors below the kitchen worktop one-by-one, creating a horrible din every time he slammed the doors.

'I really can't believe this is happening,' sobbed Linda, wiping her left eye 'I've been such a negligent mother all this time! If only I could rewind the clocks and be a little more sympathetic, this would never happen at all.' And with much gusto Linda Holt bolted out of the kitchen with her hands cupped on her face to hide the streaming tears and sped upstairs, leaving Geoffrey and George behind who had paused the search party to witness Linda's outburst.
'Should I see if she's alright Dad?' said George, making his way out of the kitchen.
'I think your mother needs some time on her own,' opposed his father.
'Come, we'll go for a quick drive. That should take our minds off this disaster and get out of her hair for a while to say the least.'

As he sluggishly tried to put his trainers on, Geoffrey tried to quickly rack his brains and access his memory banks as he tried to remember the last time one of his children went missing. The closest he could find was the time his daughter Rose went missing in 2000 at a fete in Sussex, back when Rose was hardly a teenager. She thought the idea of carrying old credit cards around in her wallet would make her look more sophisticated and appear grown up in front of the other adults, but when Geoffrey heard his name being called out on the fete tannoy (as well as a poor joke about credit card fraud), he felt embarrassed but most of all relieved that a lifeline had in thrown in at the last minute before he and his wife would've faced an emotional breakdown.

His mind soon returned to normal when George called him again from outside.

     'Dad, do you think Arnold will come home?'

     'I've an inkling that he will come back at one point.'

     'Really? What happens if he doesn't?'

     'Trust me son, I know he'll be back,' finished Geoff as he finally closed the door and swung his arm around the porch, car keys in hand, so he could unlock the doors of his Mazda.

15

The journey had been an adventurous one.

Approximately 7.5 hours before, I was 260 miles away from my designated starting point, which was in Orpington. I had originally decided to leave my home of 11 years after I discovered that my parents were readily planning to evict myself from the house for being unemployed and unworthy; as well as the devastating news that the Jobcentre services were to be relocated to an area presumably worse than Orpington, which weren't part of my original plans to evacuate the area but contributed towards a much greater need to depart from home.

The only person who could guide myself at this sudden turn of events was my former school helper, the infallible Mrs Rita-Ann Leslie. It was nearly two years since I last saw Mrs Leslie, she had previously appeared at the funeral of my late best friend Aaron Lockton who had died from cancer. After a brief discovery of how my life back at home may appear in future, I had decided to organise the fictional death of my beloved pet rabbit Milth, a creature that I had cherished so much for many years and gave purpose, but she had also become a metaphorical obstacle that anchored myself down with Orpington and the dreaded Jobcentre.

But the journey would never happen thanks to the infamous blue book she bought for my 18th birthday. The title of the book was called *The Curious Incident* and it was the first adult book I had ever read with more than 200 pages which sounded illogical because I do not like reading books that solely contain small text. The book had also inspired myself create a foolproof plan to reunite myself with my former helper, although the plan had nearly failed when the train stopped at an alternative station, it could have been part of a deliberate scheme from Mrs Leslie to accelerate our chances of a reunion. And now I was finally at the special village, awaiting her presence and I felt so tremendously excited for the first time in months that my knees were involuntarily moving by themselves.

******

Upon my first appearance at the special village, I had finished reviewing my arduous journey when I was approached by a female staff member with blond hair, wearing glasses above her head. She gratefully carried my suitcase and asked to wait inside the reception until an "induction resident" would appear to show myself around this exciting new place. To be honest the lady did not refer to the guide as an "induction resident". When she spoke I could not understand every single word she were saying because I were distracted by a brass plaque displaying names next to the reception desk, and scanned it to search for any references to Mrs Leslie. When I had finished with the plaque, the only words I could remember were "resident", "you", "snake", "induction" and "buddy" before asking me to take a seat and walking into the room behind the desk.

Eight minutes later, the door on the opposite side of the entrance opened and inside stepped in a man whose clothes appear to be entirely made from denim. I recoiled backwards in my seat as this reminded myself of the dodgy denim man from Orpington with the earring, but when he moved closer he didn't appear to wear an earring nor did he have letters written onto his hands. He also appeared to have several badges on the left side of his denim jacket, the largest of which was blue with yellow and had the letters "ATV" written vertically on it. After gathering these observations, I felt rather relieved, sat upright and waited for him to speak.

'Hi, you Arnold by any chance?'

'Yes,'

'Hi, I'm James,' he replied, holding out his hand, 'they asked me if I could show you around this place.'

'Who?' I replied, before shaking his hand.

'The two doctors, Ian and Terry. They told me you're new and I need to show you the ropes.'

'They told me I was going to visit the special village, not the ropes.'

'Sorry, that was only a saying,' apologised James before punching himself in the arm 'I guess you're part of the literal ones. That's no problem to me though, whatever side of the spectrum you're from you'll get along quite easily here. If you like, you can leave your suitcase down here, they'll look after it while we're doing the tour. Come on, I'll show you.'

As I followed him through the back door of the reception, my mind had tried to object to wandering away from my aim as I gave a final look at the plaque, so I decided to put all plans of searching for Mrs Leslie temporarily on hold while this eccentric host introduces me to this secretive and absurdly sacred place, better known as Welbourne Mills.

******

From the reception we walked down a long slope with a set of wooden steps running parallel towards a notice board which contained a gigantic map as well as a few words and pictures.

'You ought to take a look at this before we start the tour Arnold,' pointed out James with his finger touching the map 'also do you mind being called Arn from now on?'

'Yes.'

'OK, I'll keep it as Arnold.'

This was what the map approximately looked like:

MINI FARM

BRAVO HOUSE

SENSORY ROOM

STAFF HELPPOINT

CHARLIE HOUSE

SOCIAL AREA

CANTEEN

LAKE

LEARNING CENTRE

ALPHA HOUSE

VISITOR CENTRE

DELTA HOUSE

MEDICAL

(under construction)

RECEPTION

KEY

Out of bounds

Steep path, take care

Steps

Car park.

Welbourne Mills XX

93

As we walked forward down the slope I made a double-take when I noticed there actually was a roundabout, decorated with blue arrow signs and black-and-white chevrons as if it were designed for vehicles instead of visitors.

'Why are there road signs in the special village?' I asked.

'We once had a chap called Bryan here, who was obsessed with road signs. The centre helped him get a job as a sign maker and at the same time turned him from a recluse into a proper gentleman. As a thank you to the staff he gave us these unwanted road signs that you see around the place. Livens it up don't you think?'

'Yes,' I replied 'does that mean we have to stay to the left on the roundabout?'

'No you don't have to,' laughed James 'but if you feel comfortable about sticking to the left then that's fine by me. A couple of guys around here do that anyway.'

Out of curiosity we followed the blue signs and walked down the path ahead which logically would have been the second exit. We passed a couple of buildings that resembled primary school classrooms as well as a flower bed to the right and a large lake to our left where a bald man wearing a yellow coat was collecting rubbish around the edge of the lake. We stopped again at another roundabout, albeit this one was marked with a red signpost in the centre and surrounding the roundabout where several buildings, these all had brown wooden walls but the roofs and the drainpipes were all coloured in differently along with ramps in front of every entrance.

Then by taking the third exit and turning right I followed him into the L-shaped building with the green roof. The interior resembled the cafeteria back in secondary school, but it was cleaner and the walls contained posters of people shaking hands and talking in oversized speech bubbles.

'This is the residents' canteen, sitting down over there next to the window is Mark One. If you have any questions to ask about music Mark is your man, for example if you asked what song was No.1 on 17th August 1989 he'll get it right instantly.'

What an unusual surname for a resident.

'Where does he come from?' I asked curiously 'I have never heard such an interesting surname.'

'That's not this last name. We call him that to stop him getting mixed with another Mark at this place, who we call Mark Two. Mark Two is the centre handyman, the one who changes the light bulbs and the locks.'

'Would it be better if you referred to him as "Music Mark" instead of "Mark One?'

'It would Arnold, but everyone here has gotten so used to "Mark One" there's no point changing it at all. And over here is Roger Letts, he doesn't speak much but he does write some terrific poems.'

'Hello Roger.' I replied, before he looked up at ourselves and waved silently.

Before we left the canteen James then walked silently towards a grey cutlery tray which appeared to contain hundreds of food condiment sachets. His head turned side to side and looking down the tray he fished out a sachet of *Heinz* mustard before placing it into one of the lower pockets of his denim jacket. Finished with his task he calmly walked back to myself.

'Sorry about that,' he said 'one of my tics involve collecting huge amounts of sauce sachets, like the ones you get in fish and chip shops for example. It's also affected my diet and my behaviour around others unfortunately, but at the moment I'm fine.'

When we stepped outside again, James introduced myself to the other buildings that were surrounding the miniature roundabout.

******

It was nearly approaching dusk and we were inside the village canteen again eating platefuls of cooked macaroni and cheese which were served on classic canteen trays that were coloured separately. I was sitting next to James but sitting next to him on the other side was a bald individual called Simon. He was wearing a yellow t shirt as well as turquoise rubber gloves because he did not like touching objects with his bare hands, such as cutlery. On closer inspection I noticed he was the same person I saw earlier who was collecting the rubbish around the lake. I assumed by where he was sitting that he was James's best friend.

Feeling confident that the tour would most definitely finish today after dinner, I tried to revive my search for my former helper once again.

'Excuse me, is it now possible to meet Mrs Leslie?' I asked with much excitement.

'Who's that?' asked Simon.

'I think he's talking about Rita Simon, said James 'Rita Leslie. Is that right?'

'Yes,' I replied 'Have you seen her?'

'Yes I have, smiled Simon 'she was here over a week ago.'

'We could try going to the reception,' suggested James 'Dee will be going soon but she would know about it though.'

'You better get there quick,' added Simon, taking off his gloves.

I then exited the canteen, jogged down the pathway, around the roundabout and up the stairs towards the reception which looked much darker than previously. Inside the reception was the same woman that I saw earlier, who now had a name.

'Oh hello there!' shouted Dee 'How are you getting on?'

'Excuse me,' I asked 'could you please find out where Mrs Leslie is?'

'Oh, don't you mean-'

'He would like to know when Rita will be back Dee,' interrupted James, who had just arrived panting.

'I'm sorry but I'm afraid Rita is currently on annual leave at the moment.'

This made me feel suddenly ill and depressed.

'Why is she leaving again?'

'She's not leaving, she's only on holiday for a few weeks so don't be upset. When she's back you'll get to see her again.'

'Yes. OK. Thank you.'

'Don't be sad,' she said 'you shouldn't worry about it, anyway there's plenty of time before she gets back. We could even throw a little party if you want, but you need to get back now because it's almost dark. Do you know where to go tonight Arnold?'

'Yeah, they've sent his stuff to Alpha House.'

'Pardon?' I asked.

'That's what they call the residential areas where we sleep,' said James 'there are four around the centre and new arrivals are usually sent to Alpha House, which is the closest one. I'll introduce you to the other three once you have gotten used to Alpha House, which is where we'll be going shortly.'

'Can you see they're taking good care of you Arnold?' laughed Dee 'I'd like to chat with you longer but I'll be late for Corrie and 'Enders tonight. Bye dearies!'

'Goodbye.'

'Bye Dee, see you tomorrow,' waved James, leaving the reception.

We were outside once again, except that was so dark that I could not view the roundabout properly nor its signs. James beckoned myself to take a left at this junction and walk towards the wide dark hut with the yellow windows until he personally revealed that this building was actually called Alpha House. When we walked closer towards it, I noticed that it was a residential lodge that appeared to be constructed of planks of wood and there were also two floors where the windows sat. Most distinctively, the right hand wall (which contained no doors or windows) was entirely red and on the rest of the building the drainpipes windows and doors were painted red as well. Behind the residential lodge were several more windows; below them were a few bicycles as well as two large wooden containers that were impossible to open without a key.

'What are inside these containers James?' I asked curiously.

'That's just where the rubbish is kept,' he replied 'but don't you want to come in first Arnold?'

'Yes, please.'

Once I was finished looking at the rear, we walked through the red door of the lodge's entrance and wiped our feet on the mat. Inside there were four identical umbrellas hanging off the wall, below them was a large wooden drawer with a number on each drawer and opposite the umbrellas was a white chart containing a list of names written in a variety of colours. Between them was a narrow wooden stairway which appeared to have two sets of railings instead of one. To the left to the umbrellas, the passageway turned into a long corridor where I saw ten doors lined neatly on the right and three of those doors were open with residents walking back-and-forth between them.

'I'll just introduce you to the others before I introduce you to your room,'

We then walked down the thin corridor where James greeted the residents who were walking between the rooms.

'What is your name?' one resident asked rather slowly.

'Arnold.'

'Great name. Please to meet you Arnie.'

'Pardon?'

'He prefers to be called Arnold,' called James 'sorry Ollie, don't want to see that kerfuffle kicking off again do we?'

'No, Jay. Please to meet you Arnold,' replied Ollie before slowly reaching out a hand to shake mine with. When the corridor finished, the passageway expanded and morphed into a generic lounge area with a bulky television screen, two armchairs and coffee table which had a blue office folder glued onto the surface. Apart from the regular lounge furniture, there were five folding chairs lying against the wall next to the television and on the wall behind it was a list of "DO and DON'T" rules relating to the use of the generic

97

lounge. Standing in front of one of the armchairs was a lady with black hair and a red face who was wearing pink nightclothes.

'This is Kim by the way. Why not say hello?'

'Hello Kimberley,' I replied, but Kimberley did not respond back and she walked away from the armchair.

'She's not used to new people,' said James 'but then again neither are we. I'll show you to your room in a few ticks.' We returned to the hallway and walked up the wooden stairway with the four banisters and found another passageway of brown doors which looked identical to the ground floor but there were no individuals racing between the doors like rush hour traffic. I then noticed that at beyond the corridor there was no lounge on the first floor, but a room shaped like a hexagon with windows on all sides and cushions underneath, except for one containing a door that would lead onto a fire exit.

'Hey Jamie!' said Oliver from downstairs 'Kim wants to know where Arnold is staying!'

'Tell her he'll be staying in 8. Right,' he said, looking at myself 'guess you're wondering where they've put your suitcase Arnold. We'll you're going to find out now.' Halfway in the corridor, James turned right and stood in front of a brown door that carried a brass number 8 on it. But instead of the traditional keyhole, above the doorknob were 14 silver buttons with numbers next to each one, it looked similar to the combination safe I found inside my parents' bedroom wardrobe.

'They had these fitted five years ago because the centre was getting fed up of us losing our keys and all that. The code is very simple; all you have to do is press '1111' to open this door, anyone even the older guys can remember that code. If you don't then give the friendly guys near the hub a call, they're happy to help.'

I entered the numbers '1111' on the combination safe on door number 8, but I had to enter them a second time when James reminded myself that you had to turn the doorknob and push the door open after entering the code. Inside the room I first noticed the window straight ahead, revealing nothing but a square of navy. Left of the window, there was a single bed with blue bedcovers and above it was a small picture of a red steam locomotive using a level crossing. Right of the window, there was a yellow drawer with round wooden handles and a plastic chair to its left. I grinned slightly when I noticed that my suitcase was lying on both armrests of the chair, like a bridge. And finally, on the back of the door that I entered was a small map displaying the fire exit on the upper floor of Alpha House.

'You'll get used to it,' said James 'and just to let you know that they lock the doors after 10 o'clock. They do this because they don't want anybody to go out during the night and hurting themselves. We used to have a lady called Marcia who would lock up and stay in the lodge with us but she moved to Delta House where the people over there were more likely to sneak out. Also don't talk about Marcia when Oliver is around because he gets upset about her.'

'Yes. OK. Goodnight James.'

'Good-oh and one more thing Arnold, we usually wake up around 8 o'clock in the mornings. The canteen in the middle of the centre does breakfast until half past nine but we often go down there in groups so you should have no problem finding it tomorrow. And that's it, night Arnold, enjoy your room.'

'Goodnight.' I replied, as James closed the door to my room.

It was extremely difficult trying to fall asleep inside my new bedroom because I simply could not wait to be fully acquainted with the "special village" where my former school helper now worked.

Goodnight everybody.

16

Geoffrey Holt was sitting in a trance like state, slumped onto the living room sofa like a ragdoll with his mobile phone clamped onto one of his hanging limbs. First he had to ring the estate agents where Linda worked to explain why Linda wouldn't be in today; and then he had to call his workplace to explain why *he* wouldn't be in today, which actually turned out to be easier than he thought because his little white lie was that he had to take compassionate leave, but given that the circumstances don't involve bereavement, all Geoff had to do was remember the whole definition back to back until he was certain that what he said on the phone was only a half-lie, therefore cushioning the daunting task of calling the day off work.

As for Linda, she had been staying upstairs the whole time, refusing to leave the bedroom until Geoff had sent for help and called for the authorities or the professionals who would deal with causes relating to missing people to turn up first. At first she was inundated with the myth that one had to wait 24 hours until they could file a report against a missing person but as the day went on this was quickly replaced by depression, remorse and most of all guilt for negligence.

The best that Geoff would do was ask the local police to make a home visit instead of doing the report over the phone but the former was more traditional and he knew that this way would be more reassuring for his sobbing wife. Linda finally left her room and went downstairs once a policeman (a sergeant, not a constable thought Geoff) with a grey beard walked through the front door and straight into the living room, along with a female colleague who followed behind him carrying a black diary. Both of them had followed etiquette by taking their hats and shoes off in the hallway.

'Evening Mrs Holt, it's a pleasure to see you. My name's Clive, Sergeant Fisher and this here is my assistant Brenda,' said the policeman 'I know that you're going through a rough time and would like to make this as least painful as possible but I would need as much information from both of you before I can roll out the report.'

'Yes. I understand,' stuttered Linda.

'It's affected her quite badly,' said Geoff.

'I see. All I'm going to do to ask a series of questions based around your son and my colleague here will note his down before we take it back to the station for processing. Are you ready for this Mr and Mrs Holt?'

'Yes,' said Geoff, who also happened to be saying "yes" on his wife's behalf.

'Right,' paused Clive 'so far I've got his name so I'll start with his age.'

'He's 18 years old, will be 19 in November.'

'OK, now I'll need to take down a description of what he looks like.'

'He has short brown hair, hazel eyes, wears glasses, roughly 5ft 6. I can give you a picture of him, that would be much easier,' advised Geoff.

'If you have any recent photos of him, that would be extremely helpful.'

'We have a few dotted around the house if that helps.'

'Ah good, have you got that all down Brenda?' She turned towards Clive and nodded back 'OK, so when did you last see your son?'

'Yesterday morning,' cried Linda 'he was still lying in bed.'

'Was he about to go to college or work or anything?'

'No neither because he's unemployed. Doesn't really get out much either unfortunately.'

'Oh OK, now do you know where he would frequently go?'

'Just Orpington town centre to sign on, that's about it,' replied Linda.

'No, not quite,' rebutted Geoff 'he does visit the cemetery near Farnborough to see his best friend, but he only does that every Wednesday.'

'I see, but would he go anywhere outside Orpington?'

'Not that I think of, said Linda 'he used to visit his late friend's house near Farnborough but that was a long time ago, a very long time ago.'

Hmm...' said Clive 'Mr Holt may I remind you that even the tiniest bits of information can lead into vital clues that will be beneficial towards finding your son.' He then pauses as Brenda hands the diary over to him to quickly read. After quietly muttering to himself as he read, he handed it back to his colleague before facing the distraught couple again.

'Before I finish is there anything important that we need to add to the report?'

'Errmm...,' slurred Geoffrey whose mind suddenly went blank.

'Yes there is!' screamed Linda. 'Out little boy, he's got something that affects his social skills and understanding of things around him. And now that he's missing, he could be in extreme danger! We need you to help us!'

'I see this is quite serious,' assured Clive 'Could you explain what he suffers from?'

'Asperger's Syndrome,' explained Geoff 'or autism. One or both.'

'Aren't they the same thing?' asked Brenda curiously waving her pen.

'No they're not;' replied Geoff 'things might be different if he didn't have it, but then again that might be contradictory.'

'OK I see. Best thing to do for the time being is to search the places he would normally visit, just to find anything that would lead to him. Hopefully we have enough evidence to produce the report but if you both receive any information in future that is essential for the case, please don't hesitate to contact us.'

'We'll try our best and really thank you, thank you for your help,' said Linda who looked as if she was about to cry again.

'Yes, many thanks indeed,' appeased Geoffrey.

Once the authorities had finally left, Linda then curled onto the sofa and without speaking, gestured Geoff to join her on the sofa for an emotional hug followed by a nap. When she awoke her tears had dried up and felt like she came to her senses when she remembered the harrowing report from the police and had a brainwave. Although regretting her forgetfulness, she now knew that there was at least one person who could actually help in the quest to find her son as well as connections that would remove several obstacles along the way.

Carrie Lockton, Aaron's mother.

102

17

Two days had passed since the Holts had been visited by the police to file a missing persons report and since then, no progress or news concerning the report had been mentioned. Linda's idea was badly timed but she felt that it was entirely relevant to the investigation and she was in the Mazda with Geoff who was blazing up Farnborough Hill during one of the windiest spells in which they couldn't remember the last time they faced this type of weather. All of this driving was part of Linda's big plan and she was actually smiling because of the opportunity to speak to her contact has finally come.

If Linda really had her way she would've spoken to Carrie as soon as the police left and she stopped crying but that wasn't possible because of Carrie's work and voluntary commitments. During that space of two days she had to live with the fear of anxiety and paranoia building up all inside her because of her missing son but now her plan was on the go she could flush these fears out of her system and actually get on with her plan. There was nearly an outbreak of fear when they nearly forgot the house number and drove down two lengths of Tubbenden Lane until Geoff remembered that the number was the same as George's birthday. As soon as they parked up and Carrie showed them inside, this episode was wiped blank from their memories.

Something that wasn't wiped blank from her memory was Linda's inability to keep in touch with contacts from years gone by, and now she felt like kicking herself in the kitchen literally.

Carrie Lockton had first worked as an advisor in the head office of a major bank 9 years ago and she first bumped into Linda by chance during a parent's evening at her children's' secondary school, where after a brief introduction and the mutual fact that both of their sons both came under special educational needs assistance, they soon started chatted to each other more and more often, to the point where Carrie would sometimes deliberately park in a specific spot outside school so she could bump her and have a pointless chat about anything that comes up inside her head.

But a real turning point in her life happened as soon as her soon Aaron left secondary school. His real ambition for a career was to work as a game tester in the gaming industry but sadly his dream never sufficed where after a range of mystery illnesses and weeks confined to a hospital bed, Aaron was diagnosed with an obscure form of cancer and passed away at the age of 17. His mother Carrie was in hysterics for a few weeks and was made no better when the recession took its toll and she was made redundant from her job.

But while she was trying to cope with the loss of her son, Carrie received an unlikely epiphany and realised that the only way she could get over it all would be by taking a charitable approach and helping others who were like her son. So Carrie soon took up a part-time post working for a local company that helped adults with learning disabilities find paid work. And on days where she was off work, she often used up her spare time by volunteering at a charity near Sevenoaks that supported children with dyslexia.

Now, all three were huddled together in her kitchen, Linda standing cross legged. Before Carrie kicked off the conversation they each took a sip of their coffee.

'So tell me, are you with the estate agents Lin?' she asked.

'Yes still good. Is it the same for yourself?'

'Well, I lost my last job to the credit crunch but now I'm helping disabled people find work. You know what they say about cutting back these days, but to be honest leaving the banking crowd has done wonders for me and I've never looked back since. Say, when was the last time we actually had a good chat?'

Linda froze when she heard the last question, it felt like she was being accused guilty of ignorance. The last time they actually had a good discussion was roughly a fortnight after Aaron's funeral where the Holts invited her around for a chat and a few glasses of red to help cover over her loss. It had been a great night and they talked about a great number of things such as fictional tax cuts and TV characters from soaps who were being killed off every five minutes, until Rose sat down and smashed Carrie's wine glass by putting her feet on the table.

'A long time ago,' replied Linda sluggishly 'but that's not the reason why we're here Carrie. I need your help.'

'Oh,' said Carrie, feeling a little offended 'is it a personal thing?'

'Well yes,' said Linda gloomily 'do you remember Arnold?'

'Yeah I do!' she chirped 'Infact I saw him quite a while ago in the cemetery looking at Aaron's headstone. I waved at him but he didn't see me.'

'He's gone I'm afraid,' spoke up Geoff.

'OH NO! You shouldn't tell me that!' cried Carrie as she put her mug down.

'No, what he means is that Arnold has disappeared, he's run away.'

Linda watched her friend hold her chest and draw a sigh of relief.

'You nearly frightened me but that's still awful! But how can I help you find him?'

'We've had the police around to file the missing persons report, but after they left I realised that I knew somebody who saw him from a completely different angle and could possibly have information that I don't know about and that person is you Carrie. All that time he spends playing with your son will help us find him again.'

Carrie paused and took a mouthful of coffee as she tried to absorb the news. She certainly didn't want to let Lin down.

'I'll help you and try to the best of my knowledge, but remember that it's been years since they left school so my knowledge will be a bit hazy. When the coppers came round to do the report, did you tell them everything about Arnold as well as his whereabouts and disability?'

'Yes, yes, yes,' nodded Linda 'told them everywhere we knew such as the places he often visits around Orpington including the cemetery to give his respects to your son.'

'But what about the other places he used to visit with Aaron? You know the, the woods around the borough for example. Sometimes they would come home to mine with their bags filled with berries and plants.'

'Well, never really thought of that Carrie,' shrugged Linda

'They loved going to the woods.'

'But what if he decided to actually leave Orpington?' asked Geoff.

'That's something I can't really help you much with I'm afraid, I can only give places and things that he used to do with my son Geoff. If we're going even further into this, I think Rita Leslie may help. She knows a few extra solutions.'

'You mean Arnold's former school helper? You still keep in contact?' asked Geoff.

As soon she heard his, Linda felt as if she had a massive blind spot vanish inside her head. Mrs Leslie. That was it! Why didn't see think of that before? Instead of sobbing and procrastinating in front of the police she could've bucked up and passed on the teaching assistant's name just before they had wrapped up the report. Besides, how long had she known her for? 10 years on a rough scale. Now all that regret caused from losing touch with old friends over the years was finally catching up with her, albeit in a mentally painful way. First Carrie, then now this. She had to respond to this discovery.

'You're still keeping in touch with her!? But how?'

'Well I've still been talking to her since the funeral Lin. We've also had a few drinks together around the time but infact if it wasn't for her I wouldn't be working for the disabled. You see Linda, since my little Aaron passed away I felt incredibly depressed and with my job on my line, it was something that not even my husband could help with. And then Rita (Mrs Leslie to you) rung me and gave some advice that would soon change my life. She suggested that helping those who had disabilities that relate to your son could help lift the trauma caused from losing a loved one as well as doing greater good on both sides of the situation.'

'And so the only way you could get over your loss was by helping other people who were quite similar to your son?' asked Linda, who was getting confused.

'Well yes and no. Not just that, it's also revealed new bonuses and challenges, infact much more spiritually rewarding than working for a soulless corporation. I was in a fragile state at the time and because of her help, I owe it all to her and that is why I like to keep in good terms with her,' finished Carrie.

'That's incredible. All this time I only saw her as an ordinary teaching assistant. Is she still working up north in that care village?'

'She still is. When I last spoke to her though, she was going on an extended trip to Snowdonia to use up some of her annual leave. If you like I can give you her phone number.'

'Yes please,' smiled Linda 'that would be a massive help.'

Linda and Geoff watched Carrie rise from her seat and collect the black diary that was lying next to the microwave, as if she was trying to collect a priceless and delicate ornament that would shatter if held incorrectly. She opened the diary, wrote down Mrs Leslie's name and mobile phone number in small handwriting, tore the paper out from its perforated margin and handed it to Linda.

'That's the number to call her on. Rita may support you with some vital information on where Arnold may be, but she can't guarantee where he will be exactly like you said earlier, it's all to do with the connections.'

'Yes I know. The sooner we find him, the better things will be for us,' said Linda, folding the paper and placing it into her coat pocket.

'OK, good luck Lin.'

When she finished her coffee and gestured to Geoff that it was time to leave and say their goodbyes, Linda caught an awfully good glimpse of the pictures that were lining the hallway. She could see at least 10 picture frames on a single wall all of different sizes; most of them were portraits of the Lockton family including ones of her deceased son. The rest were still life paintings of fruit bowls and unopened bottles of wine, the latter which caught Linda's eye the most and literally jogged her memory into saying something thoughtful and compassionate.

'Wait, one more thing!' she turned towards Carrie.

'Yes, Lin?'

'Once we find him, when things are back to normal, we'll have a huge party back at mine and share a few glasses in front of the telly like we used to do back then. What do you say?'

'Go for it and good luck.'

'OK. Bye Carrie and once again thank you for all your help.'

'Goodbye Carrie, look after yourself,' concurred Geoff.

Inside the car Linda confidently crossed her hands together and felt a small rush of excitement shiver up her spine, caused by her latest achievement as she waited for Repton Road to come into view. She knew that her personal quest had taken a huge leap forward and she had a powerful contact in her hands that was going to do just that. Someone who can bring her much closer to Arnold than anybody else than her entire family could. Mrs Leslie.

It had been interesting day today, despite it being seen as an average one by the residents. Over 3.5 hours ago, I were visiting the miniature farm located north west of Welbourne Mills with James and Simon (who was wearing a white *Ghostbusters* outfit to protect himself). They were introducing me to the regional farm animals before they introduced myself to Lauren, who was a dark haired girl with no earrings who was capable of telling the pigs apart by staring at their colourful markings. James then told me that Lauren was a volunteer at the "special village" and not a resident, as well as describing her clothes. She was wearing a maroon polo shirt with an orange pattern on her left breast that strangely resembled a television logo.

'That's the new logo for Welbourne Mills,' replied Lauren 'you'll see it more often around the place.'

'Yes, there's a large one just outside the entrance,' continued James 'did you see it Arnold?'

'No,' I replied, before my stomach quietly buckled and felt as if it were consuming itself, which assumedly was my own punishment for failing to notice the huge trademark sign outside the reception.

'Are you alright?' asked Lauren.

'I think he is,' said Simon 'that happens to me sometimes when I get things wrong. The doctors can't cure it but I know it'll go when I leave it alone.'

'Oh OK then,' she replied again 'do you have a medical profile yet?'

'No, what is that?' I asked.

And then without warning James then grabbed Lauren from behind with his arm and pulled her away from the pigs' enclosure and out of sight, leaving myself and Simon alone to watch the pigs grunting and defecating. Simon then gave a long step backward before James and Lauren returned to the pigsty looking rather sad.

'Sorry about that, we just needed a private chat together,' said Lauren 'meanwhile perhaps you could go and meet the other volunteers later Arnold. I know the idea sounds terrifying to you, but I can assure that we'd all be excited to see a new face around here.' She then picked up a shovel and leaned on the handle. 'Anyhow these pigs won't muck themselves out so we'd better get working. Simon I see you're all suited up for the job today!'

Simon nodded before he slowly walked forwards towards the pigsty entrance, I could hear the hay crunching loudly underneath his wellington boots when he did this.

'She has made a great point,' said James 'let's go and explore the rest of the centre Arnold.'

Once he finished his sentence, we said goodbye to Simon and Lauren and left the miniature farm to explore the other side of the "special village".

We walked clockwise around the centre, where along the route I had discovered another residential lodge. This looked identical to the lodge where I had slept overnight in for the past few days, except that the windows and drainpipes were coloured differently and brandished a different name.

'That one we saw back there was called Bravo House and the walls are blue to help it stand out against the other houses,' answered James 'the houses were named after some alphabetical code so the next one we're going to see is Charlie House and the one after that is Delta House. Behind Charlie House there's a secret area that the staff don't know called "the lonely corner". I'll tell you about it another time.'

Along the journey I could see a shallow hedge bordering the centre from the outside that was punctured by two orange gates placed apart by a distance. There appeared to be unlimited squares of green sliding downhill behind the gates and even further than that a small white dot moving from left to right within those green patches. James had stopped a couple of times on the way to the next destination to greet some of the residents; a few of them were giving him tiny milk cartons that he stuffed into his denim jacket before moving again.

'Would you like to take one?' he would ask occasionally. 'When we're finished, we'll go back to the visitor centre where they'll take your photo as part of your "initiation".' And when he said "initiation", James did the bunny sign with his fingers like one of the doctors had done previously before I entered the "special village". But next to one of the allotments there was a dodgy looking individual that sat next to a shed with his hands behind his head. 'Oh and over there we have Stephan Bailey, the village caretaker. He doesn't seem to do much but sometimes he brings his dog around and we play with it while he is working.'

Eventually we managed to pass Charlie House and Delta House before returning once again to the large conspicuous roundabout, where on our right was a small yellow building with a long concrete ramp that appeared to have the word "WELCOME" written vertically in green paint.

The interior of the visitor centre looked like a classroom that had been transformed into a museum; there were pictures of heads on the walls along with vast lines of text next to the images and on the plastic table there appeared to be a miniaturised version of Welbourne Mills, which was a flat image with solid models of the buildings and lodges on top of the map. Quite amusingly there were even more maps of the centre, all of which came from different dates in the past. One of the walls was blank except for a red and purple notice board. Next to it was another volunteer with long brown hair (who looked older and darker than Lauren) and she was sitting down and looking at more images of heads.

'Hello James you OK?'

'Yes, I'm OK. Have you met my friend yet?'

'Hello there, don't be afraid. My name's Emma and I like to do the admin in this place as well as taking the pictures. Are you the new guy that they're all talking about?'

'Yes.'

'Lauren and the others told me about you, was it Arthur?'

'No, Arnold,' I replied, correcting her.

'Sorry Arnold, I'm not good with names. Seeing as you're new could I take a picture so I could hang it on the newbie's wall?'

'Yes. Please.'

'Alright, get ready to say "cheese"!'

'AHHHHH!' I screamed as a dark haired man wearing blue jeans and a white coat appeared out of nowhere behind Emma.

'How's everything?' called Dr Ian Bradbury as he walked towards us waving.

'God,' startled Emma 'you nearly gave us a heart attack Ian.'

'Sorry, should've come through the front,' apologised Ian.

'Arnold, nice to see you again! I bet James has been busy all day showing you around.'

'Yes he has been showing me around,' I said 'except for the ropes.'

'Yes, except for the ropes,' agreed James and nodded.

'Glad to hear that, smiled Ian 'but remember what I had told you back in the minibus Arnold, it was very important that you don't forget.'

'Yes,' I said, looking at Emma's camera.

'OK, let's carry on with the photo shoot,' said Emma, raising the camera 'get ready to smile Arnold!' James then moved slowly around the edge of the room towards the side of the camera before looking back at myself.

'Surely you can do better than that!' he shouted.

'Come on give us a big "cheese"!' said Emma.

'I know,' gleamed Ian 'Arnold just think of anything that you like or something that just makes you laugh! That helps sometimes.' I thought quickly and tried to remember the previous time that I laughed tremendously. Then I remembered a recent event where out of confusion and anger, I had knocked my brother George into a filthy compost heap and lay there helplessly for one minute. I found it so hilarious that I found it difficult to keep my mouth closed.

Then camera flashed and she had taken the photo.

'Cheers, you have such a lovely smile,' replied Emma before she turned to another lady wearing a similar uniform 'do you know where to send the film?'

'If you take them to reception, they should get them scanned, printed and hung up by tomorrow morning. If you don't see anyone around then I'll leave the camera in the office reception if that's OK with you.'

'Yes that's fine, thank you.'

'What are going off to now Arnold?' asked Ian abruptly.

'I am going to the blue lodge with James to play *Countdown* with the other residents in their lounge before returning to the canteen for dinner and then I will watch television inside the red lodge until bedtime,' replied myself.

'That sounds like a good plan to me, well I'd better be off then I've got work to do, see ya all!'

'Goodbye Ian.'

'Bye Ian, it was nice to see you,' called out Emma as the young psychiatrist made his exit and stepped out into the open air where he took a deep breath and shook his coat so that the warm weather wouldn't make it stick to his skin.

'If only he knew how they really felt about him' thought Ian ominously as he walked over to his car in his black loafers with the sun glaring down on him. *'Everything appears to be going well down there but I know that it won't be like that any longer.'*

If only...

19

In regards to long distance driving, they were doing pretty well. That was until Geoffrey thought it would be a sensible idea to fall ill in the car, but in some cases the worst time to suddenly fall ill was when you're behind the wheel on the A1 (M) at 55 mph while having a bereaved wife in the front passenger seat and a cheeky 11 year old who was trying to pick out all the brown grot that lay underneath his fingernails before wiping it on the door handle. And that's what Geoffrey exactly did.

There was an odd and precise manner to how he had decided to declare himself ill while driving at high speed with a Toyota and a removals lorry with two trailers bordering them off to the front and right respectively. And after a very tense minute of frantic shouting, screaming and the odd cry of "Are you OK Dad?" he managed to pull into the nearest motorway service area and neatly put a stop to the car, his passengers both sweating with fear and hoping that he wouldn't pass out while driving and end up parking the car in a ditch.

'Do you really have to choose a better time to start an epidemic!?' shouted Linda sarcastically, while unfastening her seatbelt.

'I really don't feel well,' he protested in a feeble manner 'if you could drive me to the nearest railway station, I'll make my own way back home there; and then I'

'Not a chance at all!' she fumed. 'We've come so far that's there's NO turning back at all, come rain or shine. As a family, we're in this together and I had a go at Rose earlier about the same thing but she had very good reasons not to come. For now, you just have to buy some paracetamols from the garage and stop being so melodramatic for the rest of the trip. Sorry.'

Once Linda jumped out of the Mazda, Geoffrey did the same to take her seat, except that he marched towards the petrol forecourt, and returned to the car with an unsettling pain that had been brewing up in his stomach since he parked up. It was true that he was feeling perfectly well for the first two hours of the car journey; and being a regular user of the motorway the sight of torrential rain or the random gridlock didn't put him off. Even when he faced the local horror that was the queues behind the Dartford Tunnel, he didn't mutter a word at all.

But when he learned the whereabouts of where his wife's emergency contact was for the first time in the car, those two words screeched through his head like an ear splitting racket and Geoffrey felt as if he was driving himself and the family into the jaws of a giant alligator that was ready to snap him up. His palms sweated, his brow sweated and he found the steering harder to grip as a flurry of voices and thoughts floated around the dashboard and past his head. And all of this was because the person who knew where his son may have gone was hiding in a secluded area near two villages in North Yorkshire, one called Kirkby Mills, and the other Welburn where the Holts' destination was a loose combination of the two.

20

Today was an above average day. 5.5 hours ago myself, nine residents and three staff members left the "special village" after 9.30am on one of their white minibuses, which were branded with the Welbourne Mills logo. It arrived at a place called Pickering which had a railway line that was occupied by steam engines similar to one of the books I have read, except that these engines weren't green and didn't have faces. Every resident on the minibus tour (including myself, Oliver and Simon) had to carry an identity card in our pockets and we were not allowed to walk anywhere on our own, unless we were escorted by a member of staff. The weather matched the quality of the day so far which had turned out to be excellent, except for one moment where one of the other residents (a 50 year old man wearing a beard and a blue baseball cap) suddenly vomited on the station platform for no apparent reason.

The minibus tours would occur at least twice a week (or once if there were poor weather conditions) and apart from these occasional trips outside the "special village", there was also a number of brand new list objectives that could be undertaken inside the centre, including the preparation of Mrs Leslie's "welcome back party". Below was a rough example of my brand new schedule:

8.00AM Good Morning Arnold
8.30 Breakfast
9.00 Morning walk across the Dales
10.30 Visit the library
12.30 PM Lunch time
1.30 Woodwork lessons
3.00 Arts and crafts lessons
5.00 General gardening
7.00 Supper time
7.30 Watch television
10.00 Goodnight Arnold.

The new schedule was quite varied and much more exhilarating, in comparison to my previous version that I used to follow back in Orpington. I was currently inside the social room adjoining the library near the centre of the village, where residents from all four lodges would converge and sit against one another at a wooden table and mention their differences and similarities with much enthusiasm as well as relevant news and events. The social room was aso unofficially known as *The Naughty Autie Club* by a few of the residents. I've also noticed that in the social room was the same red and purple notice that I saw in the visitor centre. It read:

Always be kind
Do your best
Say I am sorry
Forgive others
Keep your promises
Try new things
Always share and take turns
Tell the truth
But most importantly, be yourself.

In one corner of the room Oliver was telling James and a group of older residents from Charlie House of today's trip to the steam railway, as well as the vomiting event.

'So. We were on the train platform waiting for our train to show up. Then when Thomas showed up, he blew a big whistle and then Ryan screamed and got sick on the station, and I nearly dropped my camera on the floor. But the train people were jolly nice and they made sure Ryan was better before we got on the train.'

When Oliver finished his sentence, he made a loud breathing noise. He was going to open his mouth and speak when Simon burst inside the social room, wearing a yellow t shirt and a pair of green gloves.

'Good news everyone,' he said, smiling and taking off his gloves 'Rita is back from her holidays! She has just arrived and told me she'll be around the visitor centre, just incase you would like to see her again.'

'Is this correct?' I asked.

'Yes she's here!'

Hooray, how could the day get any more positive? So I left the social room, jumped over the steps beneath the door and ran rapidly towards the direction of the roundabout and the main entrance. After sharply turning left at the roundabout I slowed down when I noticed a lady wearing a green coat was standing on the "E" of the "WELCOME" sign painted on the walkway. She had medium long brown hair had contained thin strips of white, there were wrinkles surrounding her blue eyes, underneath her white blouse she was wearing a belt and underneath that her trousers and shoes were black. Although her clothes had completely changed her face and smile had still remained.

It was Mrs Leslie.

'MRS LESLIE!!!' I screamed, before clasping my arms around her
matured body.
'Arnold! It's really you!' she screamed back in excitement. 'Ooh,
there's a lot that we need to catch up on since we last met face to face, but let's
take a second to get prepared.' When we stopped cuddling, she pulled on her
coat tightly and walked over to the entrance to hold the door open for myself.
'Meanwhile, there is somebody else who has been waiting to see you as well,
she's inside.'
I ran inside the visitor centre and straight into the room where the
photographs of faces were kept, my former helper also followed me inside but
when I saw the mystery guest that she was referencing, I froze in complete and
sudden horror.
'It's your mother,' she finished.
No, no, this was unplanned. This wasn't part of my anticipation at all. My
mother appears to have infiltrated the special village with no advance warning
whatsoever, presumably to give myself a punishment for leaving without
consent. Dad appears to be absent as well as my sister Rose; perhaps they had
absconded to avoid witnessing the punishment bestowed from my mother.
It was a trap. Mrs Leslie had been secretly working with my parents
all that time spent inside the "special village" and now my mother was so
excited at the sight of my capture that she were starting to produce tears. She
then took off her coat, wrapped it around the back of her seat and began
running, but instead of inflicting punishment on myself for leaving home, she
flung her arms around and gave me a painfully tight cuddle, something that
Uncle Tony used to call a "bear hug".
'Huh!?'
'I'm so, so, sorry. I hope you'll forgive me for what I've done!' said
my mother, wiping her tears off her face with her hands.
'?'
'We've missed you so much, we thought you were gone forever!
Please swear that this will never happen again, please!'
'Pardon?'
'We missed you all back home, everyone did!'
'But you wanted to get rid of myself,' I replied, correcting my mother.
'What?'
'One evening inside the kitchen you and Dad wanted to evict myself

117

from the house permanently.'

But instead of replying again, she howled at the top of her voice and continued to cry even further into my left shoulder, she felt heavier the longer she had cried.

'Oh no, I knew this was going to happen!' exclaimed a male voice from the room behind where my mother was sitting. The door from the kitchen area was quickly pulled open and Dr Terry Campbell rushed out of the tiny room, with Ian following behind him.

'Ian, make sure nobody gets into this room until we're finished!' he shouted towards his colleague, who ran straight towards the entrance, closing the door behind him.

'Arnold listen to me!' called Ian, staring at me 'The reason you're mum is crying her eyes out here is because you have been missing from your family for three weeks and everyone back in Orpington has missed you. They were worried about you so much that they've even called the police to do a missing persons search and despite what you think, they have NO intention to get rid of you or throw you into a mental home because that's what mothers don't do. What mothers really do is look after their children and make sure nothing bad happens to them at all! Do you understand?'

'Oh, yes,' I replied.

'Did you really think I was going to kick you out?' said my mother, who had stopped crying.

'Well, you said to my Dad inside the kitchen that I should go because I were draining the resources and driving the family apart.'

'Eh? I wouldn't say that to any of my children!' she said, looking around the room.

'I think we need to sit down and properly address this situation,' said Mrs Leslie, carrying a blue plastic chair with a hole on its back across the room. 'We'll take a break for five minutes, have a cup of tea and carry on from there. How about it?'

'I favour that motion,' said Terry, raising his hand 'I'll go and see if Ian would like a cuppa outside.'

'Is that OK you two?' she asked looking at us 'We've got tea, coffee and squash Mrs Holt, which would you like?'

'I'll have a coffee please, and a coffee for you Arnold?'

'No thank you. Squash please.' I asked.

'Coming up now.'

******

118

Four minutes later, I was sitting down on one of the plastic chairs with a hole on the back drinking the orange squash, with my mother sitting to my right next to the wall of photographs, drinking her coffee. Opposite ourselves was Mrs Leslie and Terry Campbell sitting with their hot drinks, and Ian was standing across the doorway with his coffee, mentioning the time where he used to be an anarchist in secondary school. Apart from that, I noticed that our four plastic chairs were assembled to form a perfect square.

'So let's start again. Arnold, you claim that your mother wanted to get rid of you,' said Terry.

'That is correct.'

'But I'd never say that at all, never!' protested my mother. 'I do have the odd argument now and then with my husband about his hobbies but I swear, we'll never argue about kicking out our kids.'

'Arnold,' asked Terry 'that night when you heard your parents, could you hear *exactly* what they were saying?'

'I could not hear them completely but my mother was stating that an item inside the house had to be removed, but my Dad told my mother that the item was a person and that he'll "be gone by the end of the month".'

'Jesus Christ, oh no,' swore my mother.

'Why what's wrong?' asked Mrs Leslie.

'His cars…' she said silently. Mrs Leslie and Terry both looked at each other in a confused manner, raising their eyebrows together.

'Pardon!?' they both called.

'This was all a misunderstanding caused by my husband's bloody car obsession. You see his hobbies were doing up vintage cars and he loves them so much that he's even given them our cars names.' Terry then placed his hand over his mouth and paused for 5 seconds before speaking again.

'Oh. So you're telling me that your son here accidentally overheard one of your said arguments, misinterpreted the conversation so that to Arnold, he thought that you were both talking about expelling him out of your house, instead of these cars that your husband was coveting about, and because of this he thought you were going to chastise him. Well that just about explains everything that has happened which has lead to this shocking conclusion. And this seems to be all caused by a misheard conversation. It reminds me of how World War I started, with just a single little bullet. You know what I'm talking about Mrs Holt?'

'Yes I know my history very well Doctor, but if that seems the case, where did you get the idea of running away in the first place?' asked my mother looking at myself.

'I received the idea of leaving home after reading this book,' I replied, revealing the infamous blue novel 'the one that Mrs Leslie had sent myself as a birthday present.'

'*The Curious Incident*? The one Rita got you?'

'The very same,' Mrs Leslie said quietly 'but that was only a gift for your 18th birthday. How would that influence you to make it all the way up here?'

'The main character runs away during the story to reunite himself with his mother whom he eventually meets, before living with her as a positive ending.'

'But that's only a story and something that should not be done,' said Terry 'imagine what the author would say if he found out someone tried to mimic his character's goal?'

'…'

'Sorry to cut in Doctor,' said my mother in a strict voice 'but can you please get straight to the point? I've got a son who's gone on a whistle-stop tour of this place and an epidemic going on in my car.'

'OK, I will,' he replied, and he turned his chair so that he faced myself 'Arnold, I know that you and your mother have gone through a traumatic phase, and I can understand the reasons behind your "adventure", but we think that it is all the better that you return back home to Orpington with your loving family.'

I felt my insides squeezing apart when he said Orpington so I wrapped my arms across my chest to keep them together.

'Are you OK Arnold?' asked Mrs Leslie.

'NO!' I shouted 'I will never see you again if I were transported back to that degenerate enclosure!'

'But we will, I promise you won't we Lin?'

'Yes, yes we will, promise!' she replied.

'But I will have to guiltily redeem my disposition back there as unemployed.'

'What is he saying?' I heard Mrs Leslie whisper to Ian.

'No, things will be much different when we get back home I promise. Do you remember Carrie Lockton Arnold?'

The pains inside myself soon vanished and I stopped clenching my body.

'Aaron's mother?' I asked.

'Yes. There is a charity back home where she works that helps special individuals like you find work and she can help you get away from that awful building for good and the better. As soon we get home, I'll phone the Jobcentre, cancel the DEA appointments and sign you up. Think about it, you're doing something you like that gives you even more money, money you can use to get driving lessons so you could buy a car and you could then drive up and see Mrs Leslie as many times as you like! What do you say?'

I thought about this as careful as possible, especially due to the reference of Aaron's mother because Carrie, Mrs Leslie and my mother were the only three female adults I would only listen to and obey (excluding Elaine, the DEA advisor from the Jobcentre who shared similar qualities to Mrs Leslie).

'Yes.'

'That is just superb!' said Mrs Leslie, holding up a thumb.

'Before we pack things up, do you have any other children Mrs Holt?' asked Terry curiously.

'I've got three children. The eldest, my daughter is staying at home to catch up on some work. Anyway my other son George is currently wandering around your centre with one of your staff.'

'Did you both travel here together Mrs Holt?'

'No, my husband drove us here but he's staying in the car because he's feeling sick.'

'Really?' replied Terry, looking intrigued 'We do have a medical hut opposite the visitor centre if that is any help.'

'Thanks,' smiled Linda 'but we tried to get him out of the car earlier but he wouldn't budge at all.'

'Oh, just a quick question. What's your partner's first name?'

'Geoff.'

'With a "J" perhaps?'

'No, with a "G". Why do you ask this Doctor?'

'Just curiosity that is all. It reminds me of someone years ago in my heyday with that name, to come across it again must be pure coincidence, but I won't bide your time with it Mrs Holt.'

Shortly after we finished there was a knock on the door and we saw Ian's head on the distorted glass. Terry waved at him to come inside and Ian opened the door halfway before he spoke.

'Are you all done here? Looks like someone here is having a good time at the moment.' He opened the door fully and holding it open a child with spiked brown hair and a red anorak stepped in, sucking on a lollipop. It was none other than the Golden Idiot.

'Why do you have a roundabout in this place?' asked George 'There aren't any cars here.'

******

After taking a painful last glance at Alpha House and collecting my suitcase, I was inside the reception with George, my mother as well as Mrs Leslie, who were standing in front, talking about the construction site next to the reception. When we stepped outside, I noticed that there were 15 individuals behind us, lined against the wall, waving and shouting "bye". Among the crowd I noticed James, Simon, Kym, Emma and Lauren. The two doctors Ian and Terry were also there smiling and holding their own hands, as well as another "Doctor" wearing a white jacket that I never met before.

'Oh look at this!' yelled my mother 'They're all waving you on like a celebrity, you must be proud of this!'
'They all dress strange,' said George
'Don't be rude, now are you ready to go home Arnold?'
'No,'
'Why?'
'I do not believe that you will allow myself to return to this place.'
'But I will, I promise!'
'That was what you said before Mrs Leslie left Orpington two years ago.'

'I think I know how to resolve this problem,' added Mrs Leslie. She then walked back into the reception and returned ten minutes later waving a white document in the air. 'Have a read of this Arnold,' she said once again. The document read:

I, Mrs L Holt, duly promise that the recipient (Arnold) has and will always have permission to access Welbourne Mills in order to visit Mrs Rita Ann-Leslie, but only if consent is given by his family as well as the appropriate methods of transport; and that the visits are taken on a reoccurring basis on a timescale that the recipient can freely choose.

Signed...

Signed...

'Do you understand what I'm trying to do here?' asked Mrs Leslie towards my mother. 'All I need is a signature from both of you just to make it legit.'

'Yes I understand, if it's for the better,' replied my mother before reaching for a pen and signing the document.

'It's your turn now Arnold,' said Mrs Leslie handing over my mother's pen. I carefully read the document three times to check for any inaccuracies before taking the pen.

I signed it.

'There, with that we can both guarantee that in the form of a special contract that you can keep, so what we've said and promised each other today actually happened and it cannot be broken, all from this little piece of paper that you can take home with yourself and put in a frame if you like.'

'Or you can stick it in the family safe if you want Arnold,' advised my mother 'well we must be going now so I must give my deepest thanks for this emotional reunion.' My mother then gave me the special contract to hold and moved closer towards my former helper before doing something rare and original that I had never seen before in my life. She hugged Mrs Leslie.

'Bye Arnold, take care now!' waved Mrs Leslie.

'Goodbye.'

'Bye Arnold,' waves James 'Do come back soon. Remember we're the naughty autie club!'

'Goodbye. Wait one more thing!'

'What? What is it?' asked my mother.

'Hello Mark One. I have a question for you.'

'Yes,' he replied.

'What was Number 1 on the 17th August 1989?'

'Swing the Mood by Jive Bunny and the Mastermixers!'

'Thank you and goodbye.'

******

At the car park Linda was knocking loudly on the windscreen in order to wake up the guilt ridden recluse hiding inside the car, who had been nestling underneath the green cardigan. She saw a grey tuft emerge very

123

slowly from the cardigan, followed by an eye before a full face quickly surfaced.

'Look who it is Geoffrey! Arnold, he's back!'

'Oh brilliant, that is great, truly fantastic,' he said, half asleep.

'I thought you could be more enthusiastic than that. This is our son we're talking about here.'

Linda jumped onto the passenger seat, picked up the cardigan and threw it back into her husband's lap as if she wanted to say "I know you're ill and all that, but can't you put that aside for a few seconds and at least take the opportunity to savour this moment with a pinch more salt? I don't want to build up another row again, especially at this time in front of the kids." but she couldn't.

'Arnold dear, come and get in. Remember we will see Mrs Leslie again in a few weeks.'

'Yes. OK,' he replied before sitting next to George and strapping in.

As they left the confines of Welbourne Mills and rejoined the dual carriageway for a long journey back to Orpington, Geoffrey took the opportunity to make up for his lack of emotion towards his wife by properly engaging in a full blown conversation with Arnold on all the adventures he had faced at the residential centre as well as all the obstacles he had came across since leaving home, to such great detail. Even George was listening to this discussion and once they had ended the conversation and changed the subject to something vague like electricity pylons and pineapple chunks, they had already reached Peterborough without noticing it.

(Well, except for Arnold of course)

21

I had returned back to my home in Orpington, but with a more positive outlook than previously. Despite my bedroom looking identical since I last visited, the atmosphere looked and smelled extremely different than before, which felt rather unsettling before the smell started to vanish. The only change I had noticed was that my bedcovers were uneven, as if George had been trying to vandalise my bed. I repaired this by pulling the bedcovers with my hands, before lying down on it for the first time since last month.

Today there was going to be a party taking place inside this house. Downstairs my mother had been assembling the decorations and cooking the party food, whilst my Dad had gone to the supermarket along with George to collect more food. I then decided to walk downstairs, content with the knowledge that my mother would then assign myself with a few temporary tasks that related to the party as soon as my foot touched the hall's wooden floor.

'Now tell me Arnold,' she asked, holding a white banner in the hallway 'do you feel comfortable with all this going on?'

'Yes,' I replied.

'Are you sure now?'

'Yes. When is Raymond going to visit?'

'He's coming later with Uncle Tony. They're coming down the M40 right now.'

'Do you mean the M4 motorway?'

'Yes, whatever you say. Do you want to get the napkins out for me?'

'Yes.'

'OK, after that we can get some balloons out and tie them up together if you like.'

'Yes. OK, thank you.'

Raymond Holt was Uncle Tony's son, as well as my main cousin. He was a tremendously funny individual who used to enjoy playing electrical items, such as the video cassette recorder for example. Every time I met him, we would play a variety of silly and exciting games together, over 60% of which would involve humiliating the Golden Idiot which I would find impossible to create if he wasn't around.

I remember when he appeared during Christmas 1998 he grabbed the switches from the Christmas tree lights and connected them to the VCR so that whenever he pressed PLAY on the recorder the Christmas tree lights would switch on and when he pressed STOP they would switch off automatically. He currently worked as an electrician in south west Wales with Uncle Tony; and both of them lived inside a cottage near a town called Tenby (or 10B as Rose once spelt it) that can only be found by travelling on the M25, M4, A48, A40, A477 and A478.

When the party officially begun (at 4.30pm), I stood behind the window inside my bedroom, waiting for the guests to arrive. At least six guests were expected to appear at the party, they were Raymond and Uncle Tony, Mr and Mrs Lockton (Aaron's parents), two next-door neighbours and one of my mother's work colleagues. If Mrs Leslie was at the party, it would've been the perfect occasion.

I continued to stand behind the window for eleven minutes until an apple green vehicle swerved and stopped outside our front garden, which meant that the party was actually going to begin. When the doorbell rung, I ran downstairs and noticed that the first one to reach the house was Uncle Tony, whose wide figure and blue shirt nearly covered the doorway.

'Hi, it's so great to see you lot!' he roared towards my parents, before noticing myself. 'Arnold! Nice to see you back to normal again, ha-ha-ha, just my little joke! We've also brought your birthday present in advance too; Ray is just bringing it in.' Once uncle Tony stepped inside the house, I could clearly see outside again and trembled in sudden excitement when a very tall individual with dark curly hair and a red turtleneck jumper entered my vision, carrying a purple box. This was someone who I genuinely enjoyed visiting.

'Raymond!' I called.

'Arnold, it's you! I've got your present right here, sorry it's too early,' he called back, before I had lunged straight towards him in a playful manner.

'Remember not to open your gift until your big day,' said Uncle Tony 'we were thinking of sending it later through the post but had second thoughts. You can't trust *Royal Mail* these days, eh?' I had no idea what he was trying to say. 'Oh well, I think a nice cup of tea will come in handy after the drive, what do you think Ray?'

'Yes, yes, great idea Dad.'

When attending parties, the guests are normally expected to become overfilled with happiness on the duration of the party but the reason why I wasn't going to complete this task was because the majority of the party was going to take place in the back garden. For the first time since arriving home from Welbourne Mills, I refused to visit the back garden because the reason I used to visit it was to attend to my beloved rabbit Milth, who no longer lived here.

The reason was inevitably this one: Milth's hutch was missing. On the site where her hutch used to lie was a concrete, vacant spot. Apart from that observation the back garden remained as identical as before, except there were four pairs of balloons tied to the garden fence, a plastic garden table with an umbrella through its centre and a rectangular red barbecue which used to belong inside my Dad's garage. I heard the front door open again as well as the distinctive noise that always came from this specific set of keys.

'I've brought the extra sausages and burgers like you've asked, but I really need to use the toilet so I'll light this thing afterwards,' said Dad, clutching an orange plastic bag.

'Well don't be long then, the whole party's depending on you Geoff,' replied my mother as he ran straight inside the kitchen. Once I was actually outside, my mother then immediately turned to the wooden door on the side of the house and once she unlocked it, the remainder of the party guests miraculously poured straight into the back garden. But I was actually more interested in the vacant spot on the concrete tiles, and felt that after realising the misunderstanding over my disposition (which was solved by Dr Campbell), Milth should have never been released from the garden at all.

This called for a remembrance, an honorary silence.

Except that it wouldn't be silent because Rose and George were both outside, playing with the buttons on the purple CD player at the same time.

******

As he heard neighbours and relatives partying and chatting from under his feet, Geoffrey was sat on the bathroom toilet with the lid down, breathing slowly through his mouth while his nose and eyes were deeply buried in his palms. When he did this, he could hear himself think coherently.

'That was a narrow escape,' he thought to himself. 'It may be all over for now, but for how long exactly? I could play the same trick that I did before, but Lin who is already knows my disposition will see straight through me. Then she'll state that it is my turn to make that grave journey back up there and soon enough the past will catch up with me.'

'And if she doesn't catch me out then one thing after another, through an unfair number of coincidences somebody will get wise about my little secret and let it out in front of Rose, George, Arnold and the rest. But will my children really care about that? If we're living in a democratic society they would be indifferent about the news, shrug their shoulders and get back to whatever they were doing. But what would happen if it didn't and it let the past out, before escalating into something much more shambolic, something that I couldn't hide forever from everyone?'

He continued to stay put on the toilet for another ten minutes, until he jumped when he heard a loud banging on the bathroom door. It was someone who actually needed to use the toilet.

'Why the long face?' asked Tony as he looked at his face 'There's no place for a stick-in-the-mud here Geoff! This is a party, you should be forgetting all the bad stuff and enjoying yourself, like our parents did. Now if you don't mind, I really need to go and get little Tony out.'

Without saying anything, Geoffrey yanked himself off the toilet, left Tony to do his own business and crawled downstairs into the firing crowd that was the welcome back party. It wasn't the people who were putting him off celebrating his landmark occasion, but it was the ethos behind the party that was sending him into depression. This reminded him of a mock scenario that would have happened back in the 80s, sometime before he met Linda, except that that instead of his own son being the centre of attraction, it would be him instead.

******

Once Milth's remembrance silence had finished, I decided to walk around the whole length of the back garden between the invited guests and tried to participate in an activity that Raymond called "mingling", where party guests move from one guest to another clutching an alcoholic drink, say hello to them before abruptly leaving to find another party guest to greet.

I tried to listen to the conversations taking place around the back garden and overheard a discussion between Mrs Lockton and Uncle Tony.

'We moved roughly ten years ago and settled near a village on the coast together. I don't mind having Ray around the house at his age but he still keeps me company, especially when the other half passed away a number of years back. That was a very sad time for us.'

128

'I'm so sorry to hear that,' she replied.

'Not to worry, at least we're both sane; luckily Ray has a girlfriend now to help improve his social life and independency outside work, even when I'm gone too. Well, "independency" might not be the right word to use, if you know what I mean!'

They both laughed loudly together with their drinks in hand, which I decided was the right moment to stop listening to them. I walked around the back garden once again and noticed that two of our neighbours were present, including the short blonde woman who threatened to assault myself with a broom when I last visited her house on behalf of the Golden Idiot's "murder mystery". She was wearing a lilac dress and talking to my other neighbour in the white jumper, whose house and back garden I had also visited on that same day. To my horror, the short blonde lady saw me and started waving at herself which meant that she wanted to speak to me, perhaps concerning that particular day. But I refuse to, and do not wish to be assaulted the second time by the broom so I move away and hide behind Raymond and Mrs Lockton, who were standing next to the plastic table.

'Hello Arnold, do you remember me?' It was Aaron's mother Carrie.

'Yes. Hello Mrs Lockton.'

'You can call me Carrie if you like from now on.'

'OK.'

'Your mum and I used to get together often but I must say I'm so glad that you're back home with your family again. What do think my son would've said if he were still around today? He would be shocked and upset.'

'…'

'Anyway I've been speaking to your mum and Mrs Leslie lately, you know, Rita?'

'Yes, I do,' I replied, trying to withstand my excitement.

'Well we've all had a good discussion together and after some careful thinking, come up with a solution to your employment problem. Do you remember the name of that charity I work for that sometimes appears in the newspaper?'

'No,' I replied bluntly.

'I actually work for a branch of that charity that helps people similar to yourself find a paid job, even when going cold turkey in the Jobcentre Plus isn't an option for them. It's called Jobcall, and we're going to put you on their next induction which will take place next week. Your mother told me how much you hate going to the Jobcentre and I think that's one of the reasons why you tried to run away. But the guys who work in the offices are a friendly bunch and I think you'll have a fantastic time working with them, especially when they help you find your dream job! What do you think Arnold?'

'Yes, it is a fabulous idea,' I said, trying to concentrate on Carrie.

'Before I stop, got any questions to ask about Jobcall?'

'No. I'm sorry.'

'Don't be sorry,' she said warmly 'I'll be sticking around for a while so you should have plenty of time to come up with one.'

Then she picked up her wine glass and moved away from the plastic table so she could "mingle" with the other party guests. I then attempted to "mingle" myself by walking around the guests while holding a glass of orangeade but the only individual I managed to talk to was my cousin Raymond, who told myself about his new girlfriend with much detail. When he left to use the toilet, I walked around the garden to continue "mingling" but the music was so loud I could not hear what the crowds were saying, except for their clinking wine glasses. The only conversation I could hear was another one from my uncle and Aaron's mother.

'Oh really!? That's such a surprise,' screamed Mrs Lockton 'when did you find out?'

'Quite a long while ago, he doesn't like to talk about so let's put it that way,' boasted Uncle Tony, taking a drink from a bottle.

'Coming all this way, very brave and lucky indeed. But how did he meet her?'

'Met at a party of mine, of course I was the one who hooked them up.' They must be talking about Raymond again, who was standing close to the back door with my Dad, who was eating a cocktail sausage. Before the party officially finished (around 8pm) I watched the party guests disappear one-by one, at the same time the garden appeared to slowly "expand" to its default size before the party began.

******

Overall this day had been quite a surprising one. What was more surprising was that the party wasn't based on a birthday or any other family landmark, although my birthday was over four weeks away. The most surprising aspect of them all (apart from meeting Raymond again) was the reappearance of Aaron's mother since the funeral happened, except for her split second appearance at Farnborough cemetery which I did not count because it was unofficial. Raymond and Uncle Tony were actually going to sleep

130

overnight in the living room because it would be impossible for themselves to return home to Wales before midnight. They were intending to leave the house tomorrow before 7am so I strongly reminded myself to say goodbye to my uncle and cousin, just incase I were to miss their departure and wait until Christmas to meet them again and apologise for not saying goodbye to them.

I was now lying on my bed in the darkness, trying to recall an important question that I wanted to ask Aaron's mother but was drowned out by mental thoughts of her unchaining myself from the Jobcentre and setting myself free. The question, I that I finally remembered when Carrie left four hours ago was this: what exactly was my dream job?

22

Today was the first day I was going to Jobcall for an induction which should help remove myself from the dreaded Jobcentre permanently. Although I had not visited their new location in Bromley yet since the previous one closed down in Orpington, my mother insisted that I should "sign on" again rightly because their payment is called "Jobseeker's Allowance" and that I was literally a job seeker once again.

But I am not overly anxious. Luckily I discovered that Jobcall was only located outside Bromley, instead of the town centre where swarms of disgusting youths exist. There were also three bus services from Orpington that stopped outside the establishment, although I had planned to take only one of these bus services for specific reasons. That one was called the 358 bus and the reason I favoured that particular bus was because it was single decker.

Traditionally, I do not enjoy travelling on double deckered buses like the 208 for example, because they attract a disturbingly high number of vile teenagers and degenerates; and they remind myself of my years in secondary school when all of the schoolchildren would sit at the rear of the buses and often throw chewing gum into my hair, as well as pour bottles of apple juice onto my school uniform for no apparent reason whatsoever.

I boarded the 358 bus at 9.24am and managed to survive the entire journey without viewing a disgusting teenager or any similar individuals with negative attributes like earrings and tattoos for example. Mrs Lockton also gave myself a close up diagram of where Jobcall was specifically located at the party, as well as the nearest bus stop to alight from. At the entrance of Jobcall, a lady with brown curly hair and a Scottish accent appeared out of nowhere and directed myself to a large room next to an office covered with window blinds.

The induction area resembled a classroom, except that the blackboard was missing as well as the teacher's desk, and every electrical socket inside the room was upside down, as if they were manufactured in Australia. Inside the room were three individuals sitting down, presumably they also travelled here for the induction. One of them was a female with a messy blonde ponytail who was wearing large eyelashes and a grey t shirt. The second was a young man with blonde who looked as if he were the same age as myself. But most alarmingly the other male individual was wearing a pair of animal tattoos on both of his forearms, because of this drastic action had to be taken. I sat as far as I possibly could from this dodgy visitor but at a right angle so that he lay out of my sight.

'Are you here for the induction too?' asked the man without tattoos.

'Yes.'

'That's OK I'm new here too-'

Suddenly a scream was heard from outside and a broad man with spiky brown hair burst into the room wearing a white t shirt that read "I am the Stig" as well as light blue jeans.

'Sorry to keep you all waiting,' he shouted 'my name's Alan and I am your support officer for Jobcall, the place that guarantees a job for all! I know that a couple of you are a bit anxious on the first day, but by the end of the week you'll all be brimming with confidence so let's start by introducing yourself. We'll go with your name first, where you live, the type of job you're after and finish with your last holiday. I'll start with you first young man!'

'OK, name's Frank,' said the dodgy one with the tattoos 'I'm from Locksbottom and used to work as a labourer on several building sites. I have problems with reading and writing since I was small, because of this I've been out of work for two years and would like to get back to building houses again or going into IT.'

'That's excellent Frank, now tell us where you last went on holiday,' asked Alan.

'Hastings a few weeks back, went with the wife and kids.'

'Splendid place, and next we have-' shouted Alan again as he moved left behind Frank and stopped behind the blonde individual who was wearing a polo shirt and two distinctive teeth poking out of his mouth. The support officer then began to tap his fingers on the back of the client's chair until he decided to introduce himself.

'Hi I am Alex; I'm 21 and come from Sidcup. I'm looking for retail work at the moment but I would really like to become a fire-fighter.'

'All good stuff, I can really see you kicking down doors and saving beautiful women,' smiled Alan 'So tell us where you last went on holiday, and don't say Pontypandy if you get my rift!'

'Went to Minorca with my mum and dad back in April, it was smashing.'

'Oh really, I was there a few years back, what part did you stay in?' asked Alan.

'I think it was called Mahon, I'm not good at remembering sorry.'

'Never mind that, we can have a chat about that later. But next we have on the firing line is this little crumpet.' He moved away from behind Alex and was now floating (metaphorically) above the blonde woman who was stroking her own hair.

'I'm Susan, I live near Orpington, and I am looking for work as a carer.'

'Short and sweet Susie, like it. So tell us about your last holiday,' said Alan.

'Well to be fair, I haven't really been on one in years. You see, I can't afford a proper one when I'm stuck on benefits.'

'Then make one up. We do it all the time around here, much better than coming up with nothing.'

'Erm, OK,' sighed Susan 'Last week I went to Cornwall with my family. We loved it.'

'Fantastic Susie, five out of five!' laughed Alan, clapping his own hands. 'And now last but not least…'

He ran around the whole table again, as if he were riding on an invisible merry go round. Then Alan disappeared, I looked left, then I looked right, and finally I looked straight ahead. Then his voice appeared from behind.

'You, my son.'

He had chosen myself.

'Hello. My name is Arnold, I live in Orpington and…'

'Take your time,' said Alan calmly.

'…I do not know what my specified career will be. I am sorry.' For the next five seconds, the room fell silent. I thought Alan was going to shout at myself like most of my secondary school teachers would towards pupils who don't answer questions properly. Instead he patted the wooden desk with his hand and laughed very slowly.

'Never mind that, lots of people don't know what their dream job is. That's really my job trying to find out what their dream job will be. Let's change the subject then, so tell us where you last went on holiday Arnold.' Like Susan, I hadn't actually been on holiday since this year began and the concept of making one up solely to amuse this weird gentleman sounded most vulgar to myself. But defining the word "holiday" as an overnight destination away from home, I had an answer.

'Welbourne Mills, in North Yorkshire.'

'Ooh, that sounds exotic,' he replied 'and who did you go with?'

'Myself.'

'Wow that's brave. How long did you go for?'

'Over four weeks.'

'An extended holiday, how could you afford that?' asked Frank.

'Welbourne Mills, is that like Center Parcs?' said Alex, smiling.

134

'No, it is a "special village" where my former secondary school helper currently resides.' Again the room fell silent and suddenly Alan walked out of the room. I then had an unusual urge to escape out of the window but he returned one minute later and he was actually laughing and waving his arms above his head.

'Wait, ho-ho-ho, it cannot be!' he smiled, touching the back of Susan's chair. 'I swear I saw your face on the back of a milk carton. You're the one that Carrie told me about, the one who ran all the way up to Yorkshire on his own. It's such an honour to meet a celebrity around here.'

'Pardon?'

'You're famous my boy, everyone from Jobcall knows all about your escapades and they've been passing it on to their friends, their friends' friends, and so on. But I must personally say I've never seen any of my candidates go on that kind of journey by myself.'

'Wow, really? Is this true?' asked Alex.

'Yes it is he's a real superstar!' added Alan again, who touched my right shoulder and made myself jump. I did not like how he was portraying my activities from the previous three months. It sounded as if he thought my disastrous journey to find Mrs Leslie was comparable to a fantastic adventure that should be witnessed by everyone, one that might encourage an envious author to write a parody of this adventure before publishing the book around the world and claiming that it was himself who had actually invented my adventure, which was incorrect.

'I should not deserve this,' I said.

'I must say I don't have the balls either to do that by myself,' said Frank 'I can't read any of the signs so the missus has to go everywhere with me.'

'I should not be praised!' I replied again, loud enough for everybody to hear inside the room. Outside the room I could hear footsteps clapping along the corridor and suddenly Alan turned, looked out of the doorway and started to shake his head rapidly and open his mouth, without making a sound. Then he turned around from the doorway and looked at ourselves once again, this time frowning.

'OK, OK, we don't want to get off on the wrong foot now don't we? As most of us are unaware, some people aren't good at being praised because they can't handle it. And for those who can, they enjoy it so much that it all goes to their head so much they have to resort to eating humble pie before starting all over again! But it's true for some people isn't it!?' sighed Alan calmly as we watched Susan and Alex laugh quietly together while Frank crossed his arms and smiled.

'Sorry,' said myself, for making Alan frown.

'Don't say sorry Arnold, but if that feels comfortable with you, we'll accept your apology. We don't want Jobcall to make a poor first impression right? That's something we'll be covering on the programme and believe me it's very, very important. So enough of this, who wants to get started?' As he finished, all of the candidates (except myself) nodded happily and agreed.

'Yes,' I said, taking part.

'Right, on this course we'll be working together for the next eight weeks so to start to get to know each other, we will do some interview practice by shaking hands together. Best hand shake gets a chocolate bar, so I'll start with young Alex here.' We watched as Alan carefully knelt down next to Alex who was still seated, before grabbing his hand and violently tugging it. 'That is what you call a prop-ah handshake, Frankie you can practice with Arnold.' Oh dear.

'No thank you,' I warned.

'Excuse me?' asked Frank.

'No thank you. I do not want to.'

'If there are five of us, who I shake hands with?' asked Susan.

'Why don't you want to shake my hand Arnold?'

'I don't want to touch your hand because you have tattoos on your arms. Sorry.' For the third consecutive time the room fell sinisterly silent and all four were staring back at myself.

'You shouldn't really say those kind of things, they can get you beaten up and put in hospital Arnold,' said Frank calmly without moving his arms.

'Sorry Arnold, but I must agree with Frankie on this one,' responded Alan 'They're not all bad to be honest, besides I've got one of Dennis the Menace on my left leg too.'

Oh. What should I do next? If I were to escape from Jobcall because of discovering these gruesome facts, then I would have no choice but to unwillingly revert back to the Jobcentre by default to continue my infinite jobsearch, where I would be encountered and ridiculed by hoards of disgusting youths and alcoholic adults with untidy facial hair and numerous profanities on their bodies. I had to find a temporary solution for my problem, but I didn't want to offend Aaron or his mother by attacking one of her work colleagues. So I tried to forget the fact that Frank and Alan both possessed tattoos and replaced it with one of Alan's quotes and turned it into an apology.

'Sorry, that was a poor first impression,' I said quietly.

'I've seen racists, homophobes and whatnot, but never anyone who judges them by their tattoos,' commented Frank, who sounded as if he did not accept my apology.

'I've never heard it before either, you could even give it a name like arnophobia for example,' suggested Susan. 'If you invented a new word, then you could make millions and you wouldn't need to find a job. I wish I could do that.'

'Well I don't like saying this,' interrupted Alan 'but my Dad once told me long ago if you can't stand the sight of being around anyone, then pretend that they aren't there at all and that way you don't get into petty arguments about each other. In ten minutes guys, we're going to take five and make do with tea and biscuits, or a coffee and a pain au chocolate if you're French. That should give us enough time to forget about our last hiccup before we move on to the next part.' He quietly stepped out of the room. 'If you could hang on there, I'll get my lovely assistant to put the kettle on!' Hmm... he must be referring to the lady I saw earlier near the entrance.

After the tea break we spent the next 1.5 hours reading through a generic black office file with metal ring binders. It contained ten different chapters about using the special employment services offered by Jobcall, two of them required a signature inside the bottom of a lined rectangle. When I signed both chapters (one of them referred to equal rights conduct), Alex looked at my signature and mentioned that he had seen a copy of my signature before three years ago. After everybody had finished reading the documents, Alan stacked all four of the office files into a neat tower before offering a preview of next week's activities.

'Is everybody alright now?' asked Alan smiling.

'Yep, yeah!' replied Alex, Susan and Frank altogether.

'Right so next week guys we will be talking on our first appearances, why it's important to yourselves and your future employers and most importantly, all the do and don'ts of making first impressions when you're outside work too. So remember chaps, it's the same time next week. If I don't see you next week then I will set your house on fire! Hah, only joking, bye!'

The induction was finished before 2.30pm. Once I had arrived home I tried to play a summary of today's activities inside my head like a video player. Overall I noticed that the most challenging feature of the induction did not belong to Frank, nor his naked tattooed arms, but the behaviour of the Jobcall coordinator Alan which I found too confusing to understand. I never found him funny at all.

23

It was two days ago when I had visited the induction to Jobcall that was patrolled by the friendly but insane individual that was named Alan. I was upstairs inside my bedroom again reading *The Railway Series* while my mother was downstairs because she had arrived home two hours earlier than on an average weekday due to her workplace. This actually reminded me of the classic 'half day' when secondary school used to break up for the holidays by finishing at 1.30pm instead of 3.15pm. At 2.45pm the doorbell rung and inevitably my mother ran to the door to answer it. Out of curiosity I looked outside through the window and saw a police vehicle parked in front of the driveway.

'Arnold, there's someone at the door for you!' shouted my mother from downstairs as I sprinted out of my bedroom, I felt a mixture of excitement and surprise happen inside my own head. Outside the front door, standing on the garden path was a large policeman wearing an open fluorescent coat and standard police helmet. He had neat white hair, lines around his eyes but most amusingly his beard was large and grey.

'Hello, my name is Sergeant Fisher but you can call me Clive,' said the policeman as he held out his hand. I knew from past experience what to do next so I shook his hand to appease him. 'You know I've actually been in close touch with your mum and dad last month since you disappeared, Mrs Holt if you don't mind me mentioning this.'

'Not at all,'

'Although we managed to clear that up, we still need you and your son down at the station to cover two little things, if you don't mind. First is a little paperwork just to close the missing persons report; and the second we just need to have a direct chat with your son concerning a minor issue, which is all.'

'OK, what time shall we get there?'

'Well anytime before six would be suitable Mrs Holt, although I should be back there around four.'

'That's fine, but don't you lot phone first before coming out?'

'Traditionally we do, but sometimes appearing in person does have a positive effect on the community and of course I wanted to see how Arnold is getting on now. See you both at the station.'

'Bye,' concluded my mother as we both watch him climb into his generic police vehicle and drive away from our house.

'We are we going?' I asked my mother curiously.

'We're only going off to the police station for a chat.'

'Which one?'

'The big one in Bromley.'

'Oh.'

'Are you OK? We're only going to leave in an hour, so you'll have plenty of time.'

'Yes,' I said rather uneasily, because my past experiences with visiting police stations had never been positive, especially the previous time when I was escorted to a police station near York while I was trying to find Mrs Leslie.

******

We both arrived at Bromley police station after 4.45pm (instead of 4pm) and waited inside the reception, before we sat down together on a pair of empty chairs facing the toilet. I looked at the yellow wall opposite and saw a large black and white rectangular map of the Bromley borough that featured 22 miniature policeman helmets which included the name of the local police area next to them. I got up from my seat to read the names of these "mini boroughs" more clearly but my vision was spoiled by the sight of a heavily bearded man wearing a filthy brown coat and a large earring, being escorted to the left by two policeman from behind. Luckily Sergeant Fisher appeared next to the reception desk.

'Hello Mrs Holt sorry to keep you waiting, we were just having a quick meeting. If you could just follow me into this room I'll introduce you to Jillian who will sort out all your relevant paperwork.' We followed him as he walked past the reception desk to the right and stopped next to a wooden door containing the distorted glass, just like the doors at York police station. He opened the door and held it from the inside, presumably to let ourselves inside. My mother entered the room first but when I attempted to enter myself, Sergeant Fisher stopped me by placing his right hand in front of my chest.

'Arnold, while your Mum is chatting to Jillian could you please come with me for a brief chat. I just need to talk about something that had happened in Orpington a while ago.'

'OK.' I exited the room and waited for Sergeant Fisher to lead the way towards another room along the long corridor, which was covered in soft, wavy blue carpet. I could even smell the wooden panels that surrounded the doors and the carpet below, the smell was similar to my Dad's current car when he first purchased it. There were also small patches of sweat around my armpits because I weren't expecting to be separated from my mother during the mandatory visit to the police station. At the end of the corridor, Sergeant Fisher faced a grey door to our right and opened it before entering. Inside I could see two parallel doors; between them were a horizontal row of hooks with a red jacket and a black cap hanging off two of the hooks. From the door on the right another policeman appeared, he appeared younger than Fisher, had light brown skin with short curly hair and he was wearing a white shirt with a black waistcoat.

'Ah Arnold, this is Ryan. Ryan, this is Arnold. He'll be taking part in our little chat as well. But first if you could just make your way to this room and hold up this placard, it's just a little exercise that will help with our police research,' suggested Clive as he handed myself a white card that contained a black '5' on it.

Inside the room there were four individuals standing silently together in a line, staring at a huge rectangular mirror and holding a white card each with a different number printed on. Behind them were rows of horizontal black lines painted on the white wall, as well as numbers between the lines.

'You're No5, so you should go down to the end mate,' said the person holding the white card with a '2' on it, who appeared to share the same height and hair colour as myself. Once the correct position was fulfilled (and the numbers in the correct sequence) I looked at the other four individuals again and made some rather interesting observations. Apart from being the same height as No.2, I rapidly noticed that No.1 and No.3 both wore chequered shirts (that were red and green respectively) as well as dark brown trousers which closely resembled the clothes that I often enjoy wearing every day. No.4 wore a blue coat, red and black striped t shirt and dark blue jeans, he but also wore glasses and a similar hairstyle to myself. When I observed him again I felt that he actually didn't resemble myself but a certain comedic character who wore a brown suit, owned a teddy bear and drove a green Mini vehicle around outer London. Three minutes later, the door opened.

'No.5, if you could please stay. As for everyone else, thank you for your cooperation, the Metropolitan Police really appreciate your help.'

I watched the four individuals as they left the white room one by one, still clutching their numbered cards. 'If you could come this way please sir,' said another policeman who congratulated the volunteers. I followed him curiously out of the white room and into the door on my nearest left. There was an orange corridor that appeared to have two blue doors on the other end. On the right there were posters of sleeping children on the wall, below them were five chairs with cushions on the backrests and Ryan was sitting on one of the chairs holding a notepad. But on the left there was an enormous rectangular window which quite horrible revealed the white room with the black horizontal lines where I had been one minute ago. But I could only see a mirror while I was inside that suspicious room! How was that possible? I observed the edges of the window very carefully to look for any clues, before going back into the white room to see if it were possible to look *through* the mirror, but it failed.

6' 6"

6'

5' 6"

5'

4'6"

4'

Once I returned back into the room with the window-mirror I noticed that sitting next to Ryan on one of the cushioned seats, there was an extremely tall man who wore round glasses, curly black hair, red trousers and a blue bag slung around his chest featuring a white bird that said "Hope not hate". But hidden behind him also sat a short, stumpy middle aged woman with grey hair and rings on eight of her fingers, who was pouting heavily like George used to do every time he was punished. The man was then staring at myself and the policeman with his hands held together like a triangle as if he wanted to start a conversation with myself.

'Hello there young man, do you remember me?' asked the gentleman.
'No.'
'We met earlier this year in Orpington, near the Walnuts centre if you remember.'
'No,' I replied again because I did not recognise his face.
'Well I asked you if you could see the light, and you replied with your fist.'
It was when he used the sentence "see the light" that I immediately remembered who this specific gentleman was. He was one of the "dreaded leaflet distributors" who was working in Orpington town centre that day when I discovered that the local Jobcentre was going to close down.

'If you want further proof we've got CCTV footage of the assault taking place in the AV room, and we have no doubts at all that the person carrying out that attack was you,' said the unnamed policeman as he stood next to the window-mirror, holding a white chunk of paper.

'Oh no,' I spoke out loud. Was this another elaborate plan from my parents to confide myself inside a mental institution? And the party, the one with no celebratory milestone? Was that also a highly organised ploy from my mother to cover up her past actions and create another trap for myself in the present? She was missing from this dreadful scenario as well as the hairy PC Fisher, presumably they had worked together to orchestrate this trap so that the chances of escape would be impossible and they both may be watching myself from the miniature mirror located behind the "leaflet distributor". Without speaking I sprinted towards the two doors on the opposite end of the orange room but the blue door on the right was locked but the door on the left was unlocked and when I entered it became another trap. It was a dead end. The room was the same size as the downstairs toilet inside our house and each wall was covered with vast shelves of videotapes that touched the ceiling, except for one wall which contained three small television screens as well as wires underneath. Although there was nowhere to escape I locked the door and saw an outline of the policeman's head through the distorted as he violently shook the door handle.

'Sir, you can't stay in there! We keep valuable police footage in that room, if you open the door we can watch the tape and negotiate this is in a sensible manner.'

'No,'

'Why not?'

'You are going to hurt me.'

'No, I am not. Open the door, I promise not to touch you and we can sit down like gentlemen and talk about the evidence and possibilities of a fair sentence.'

'I don't think that should be necessary officer.' That sounded like the leaflet distributor.

'Eh? Say again please,' gasped the policeman as I watched his head move away from the glass.

'As a follower of Christ our lord, the only justice I'd like to see is forgiveness.'

'Are you crazy Sir?'

'Not at all officer. While I respect the work you all do keeping this country safe I don't think we need to go any deeper and resort to getting the handcuffs out over this little matter. Anyway I can sense that this wasn't done out of spite nor malice.'

'Sorry excuse me, what are you trying to say again?' asked a voice that sounded like Ryan's.

'All I'm saying is the assault wasn't done out of evil and all I'm asking for is an apology, before we make a mountain out of this molehill.'

'Oh, is it possible to do that Matt?' asked Ryan again.

'In certain circumstances when the case is new it's quite normal, but only when the defendant is willing to fully cooperate with the victim,' replied the other policeman before turning his distorted face toward myself 'did you hear that?'

'Yes,' I replied.

'Well, what will it be?'

'Sorry,' I said slowly, 'sorry, once again.'

'That will be all officer,' sighed the leaflet distributor.

'OK, I'll accept that and cross it off our records,' said Matt the policeman 'but Sir, you still have to get out of that room. If you don't cooperate we'll send in the caretaker to open it and believe me, locking yourself in after being let off will not look good on your files.'

'I want to see Clive first,' I asked.

'Who!?'

'PC Fisher. He was the policeman who had sent myself to this place.'

'OK, anything just to get you out of there,' scowled Matt.

Two minutes later, I heard a familiar voice.

'Arnold, are you OK? It's Sergeant Clive Fisher here.' Very slowly, I unlocked the metal latch and opened the door carefully to see Clive's hairy face smiling down at my own, the leaflet distributor still sitting down as well as Ryan and Matt standing up and reading a notepad together. When they looked towards me they began to clap very slowly before Clive joined in.

'I'm sorry for breaking my vow of silence here,' shouted the old woman unexpectedly as she stood up from her seat and marched toward Sergeant Fisher before pointing a finger at myself 'but when are you going to punish that deviant over there?'

'I'm sorry madam but the victim- sorry your nephew has asked for the charges to be dropped; and in these incredibly rare cases we have no choice but to accept these calls at the victims' discretion.'

'But that was far too easy! He even locked himself in your store cupboard when you were about to arrest him and now you're even clapping for him! Where's the justice in that?'

'I'm sorry Pauline but I made my decision and what's done is done, we should thank the cops for making my decision come true,' smiled the leaflet distributor.

'Adam, as much as I admire your work for the church, this does not get my way of bringing justice to these little deviants. We've even got evidence on tape of the attack happening. And what about the notes? Have you two been taking down everything you've seen?' protested the old woman even further. Ryan then stopped reading his notepad and looked at her.

'Well, I have been taking thorough notes of the whole thing but just enough to make a summary and turn it into a police statement. This is the summary:' he coughed before he said out loud. 'Drop the police charges. The suspect is a rather weak case and has had no criminal history in the past. Plus, the suspect had neither motif nor intention to deliberately harm his victim. Also, thanks to my superior over there, we learned that the defendant suffers from a condition called Asperger Syndrome which is a social disorder that affects them differently. This would had put a significant tangent on the police report had it not been mentioned earlier; and the backup we've received is

145

enough to put the whole thing to bed without a court case.'

'I can't believe this is happening,' she moaned.

'I'm sorry madam but it's been done for the second time,' said Clive 'now if you could both follow me to the reception I'll have the form which should close off the case for good.' Then as Clive, Adam (the leaflet distributor) and Pauline left for the reception, I took a last glance at the two sides of the window-mirror before joining the three individuals again at the reception.

'If you just both sign here on the dotted line below, that should be it. Now have a nice day!' said Sergeant Fisher, pointing at the bottom of the form. For courtesy reasons I allowed to let Adam sign the form first which actually looked amusing because he used one of the novelty pens which could write in six different colours. Afterwards I signed the form with an ordinary blue biro. As we turned around to face the entrance the Pauline was standing in the centre, wearing a grey coat and a cream handbag. She looked angry. Then she pointed at me again and then pointed again towards a poster on the wall on my left. The poster featured a blonde child with blue eyes crying behind a pair of bars.

'This is not over, you'll get what's coming to you I swear!' But before I looked back at Pauline she had disappeared from the centre and then somebody touched my shoulder.

'Sorry I must excuse my aunt for her behaviour, she may be old school in her beliefs but I still love her, she's the only family I have left.' It was Adam.

'OK. Sorry for attacking you,' I said, 'I was in a bad mood because the Jobcentre was going to move to Bromley.'

'Heh, that's a funny way to put it,' he laughed, 'but I'm afraid the one in Orpington is already boarded up. I know this because I'm also on the dole there too.' My mind froze when I heard this statement because it sounded illogical. If he was also unemployed (like I were) then why didn't he feel overly depressed? And if he weren't then how did he avoid being absorbed into the hoards of disgusting youths that sat outside the old Jobcentre, spitting on the ground and drinking cans of alcohol? This sounded like a secret I really wanted to know but then I tried to ask him my mouth asked him a different question.

'Why are you so happy?'

'Simple, it's all to do with being positive and having God on your side. If I hadn't seen the light, then I wouldn't be alive to meet you.'

'Oh.'

'Perhaps you could do some charity work for the church one day, or volunteering. That way you're giving something back to the community and realise that being on the dole is not all doom and gloom. Speaking of giving something back, I think you should have this. There's no point of me keeping it because it will just sit on my shelf gathering dust.' Adam then grabbed the blue bag slung over his shoulder and moved the metal latch, he placed his right hand inside and pulled out the CCTV videotape before closing his blue bag.

Before my hand touched the videotape I thought about it very carefully. If my mother were to receive any references to my past incident in Orpington town centre, and/or accidentally watch the CCTV videotape of the attack being operated, it may drastically alter her behaviour towards myself in a negative manner and she may no longer be nice or helpful. I kindly accepted the videotape and placed it inside my shirt. Then he presented a small card with an image of a yellow dove which contained an address and a telephone number. 'This is the name of the church where I hang out, if you change your mind feel free to drop in,' he said. I also accepted the card and watched as his blue bag bounced back and forth around him as he walked out of the police station.

'Ah there you are Arnold!' I turned around and saw Sergeant Fisher again.

'Where is my mother?' I asked

'She'll be with you in a few minutes.'

'OK, thank you.'

'You know the funny thing about earlier is when that chap and his aunt saw that photo of you on the missing persons wall last fortnight, they recognised it as you straight away. They even said the picture was more accurate than the CCTV footage.'

Something did not make sense. If the police already knew that I was the intended culprit when why did they ask myself to participate in an identity test with four strangers who did not take part in the incident and were obviously innocent?

That was illogical so I asked him again.

'It's all for police surveillance records, he said. 'You see, the guys up in Scotland Yard claim that good old police line ups are fading away thanks to modern technology so we sometimes stage one every while or so just to update the records, if you know what I mean?'

'No.'

'Well some people have different opinions, so can't argue with that. But I want to explain something quickly to you before you go, it's about what we've been doing down there with the other officers.'

'Pardon?'

'Well I'm giving you the choice of whether you want to keep this confidential or not. That means you can either tell your Mum about the incident

147

or you can just keep it a secret between us.'

'Yes, confidentiality please.'

'It's your choice, but remember Arnold don't see this as a victory but more like a caution.' His beard moved slightly when he took a deep breath. He then moved an inch closer to myself which I disliked, because it looked as if he were going to become evil and begin shouting at me, which was what my sister Rose would regularly partake. 'Later on in life you may end up being tangled up with the law again and next time you may not be so lucky. Please remember that in future Arnold and enjoy what's left of the afternoon.'

Sergeant Fisher then turned around, placed his hands behind him and returned into the corridor where he presumably disappeared forever. I did not enjoy listening to his sentence because it sounded like I was going to be arrested despite officially apologising to Adam for the incident in Orpington town centre. Six minutes later I saw my mother emerge from the same corridor again, she had her coat slung over her right shoulder and smiled when she looked back at me.

'Ah, there you are Arnold,' Come on let's go home now, you don't want to get arrested for loitering now, do we?'

24

Last Thursday I decided to visit Aaron's gravestone near Farnborough village for the first time since I attempted to leave home over five months away, because I had ran out of activities to complete at home. But once I arrived there, I felt shocked and depressed because all of the dry and rotting flowers that used to adorn his grave were entirely removed as well as all the sweets that would lie around the edge of the marble frame that used to surround all the aging plants. I wanted these flowers to return to Aaron's grave again because they were an original part of his tribute and I was going to walk to adjoining gravestones to check if they had similar flowers that I could borrow until Mrs Lockton appeared out of nowhere and escorted myself to her house.

She asked myself what I were doing with the flowers from other graves so I explained to her before asking why Aaron's flowers had disappeared. She replied that all the flowers were to be replaced exactly with new ones and then she began talking about Mrs Leslie for no apparent reason. She then asked when was the last saw her and I asked her why because it sounded like she could make Mrs Leslie appear from thin air, and then Mrs Lockton said I was being silly and that I should not "borrow" flowers from other graves because they were just as sacred as Aaron's own grave and their relatives would become as upset when I did if they discovered their flowers were missing.

Afterwards my mother had arrived back home early because of her work and when this happened she would sometimes appear in the dining room, writing numbers down on a lined notepad before tearing off a strip of paper and inserting it into an orange folder that reads "DO NOT TOUCH, IMPORTANT!" on the front. She would solely refer to this as "doing her accounts".

'I'll talk to you later Arnold,' she replied back. 'There is some work I have to finish off before the new contract goes through. Besides you're nearly an adult now, you should be making your own decisions anyway.' This gave me an excellent idea, for my mother had reminded myself to do something important, despite not realising that she mentioned it. I ran upstairs to my bedroom, opened the drawer underneath my bed and removed my black jeans from the lowermost drawer where Mrs Leslie's contract was safely concealed. Fifteen minutes later, once she had finished "doing her accounts" I quickly ran downstairs to the kitchen before my mother would have begun her household

149

activities and presented it to her.

'Oh, I can't believe you still got that thing on you,' she replied in a shocking manner 'OK, but you do know we're going to Polhill this weekend for the garden.'

'Oh.' I said.

'But next week will be all yours so I'll ask Dad to drive you up there and back. Sound like a good plan?'

'Yes. Please.'

'Welbourne Mills it is then.'

'Thank you.' And then I left the kitchen and skipped back upstairs to my bedroom with a small grin upon my own face. It appeared that the contract did work after all.

******

It was nearly a quarter to seven when the rest of the family were back home from work or school and the request from earlier crossed Linda's mind while she was carefully putting the cottage pie dish into the oven. Once finished she turned to the living room and felt glad to find Geoffrey sitting slouched on the sofa, with his feet perched on the wicker coffee table and a very heavy blue book resting on his stomach. Perfect, she thought.

'You're not busy this Saturday are you?' she asked him.

'No.' he replied, not taking his eyes off the book.

'It's just that I need you to drive Arnold up to Yorkshire again for the weekend.'

'Oh.'

'What's wrong this time?' she huffed, as she put her hands on her hips.

'It's just that I'm not feeling too good again.'

'But we promised last time that you were going to be the one driving him back up there again.'

'But I just said I'm not feeling well.'

'Well you don't want me passing out on the motorway and killing both of us do you?'

'...'

Silence. She peered down to examine the blue book lying on his front. It was a travel book-slash-encyclopaedia, *1001 Places to Visit Before You Die* to be precise. What kind of foreign and exotic countries was he looking up? Out of all the 1001 places to visit, Linda wondered if Coventry was up there, Nether Wallop, or Pratt's Bottom (which she never found remotely funny), along with any other silly place name she could use to support her counter argument on why he has decided to voluntarily become frail. She may know, but evidence would have to be required first before making a statement. Frustrated that she couldn't find a proper sentence to use, she lifted the blue slab out of his hands and slammed it onto the coffee table without saying a word.

'I'm sorry but can't you take any of my words into consideration dear?' he exclaimed back but these words fell on deaf ears.

Feeling defeated Linda hid in the lobby behind the kitchen, slammed the door shut and suddenly picked up a stack of clean bath towels and hurled them violently across the floor in an act of rage. Then she picked up a smaller pile of hatched tea towels and spread them onto the floor also. Finally she noticed the stacked square of ironed shirts that Geoffrey would typically wear and being crumpling them up into a ball with her tired hands. All of this was just pointless anarchy because three hours Linda would just pick them up and have them washed all over again because she was the only one who did it. If she asked any of the children to pick them up and wash them, they would ask why the towels were scattered like that on the floor, except for George who would have done it for pocket money.

But as she finished undoing the mess on the lobby floor and dumped them into a basket, the door swung open, she turned and realised that it was Arnold again.

'Hello, I have a question Mum.'

'Yes, go on.'

'Where are you going to sleep?'

'Oh, good question. Never mind about that, I'll think of something in the end, besides if it's in Yorkshire your auntie Jen isn't that far anyway.'

She turned around and headed for the kitchen again, secretly cursing under her breath that she can't get away from the terrible two; and that this was the second time the first one went abruptly sick after being asked to do a difficult favour for the second one and then ended up pinning all the tenure on her. *Well he's not going to get away with that again next time*, she thought deviously. And next time, I'll make sure that he does take him there, illness or no illness. Besides I've never taken a day off sick from a headache or a cold and the same goes for school runs. Otherwise if he does that again, I will get sick too.

Sick of him.

25

Since she parked up and ignored the masses of parked cars that took up the gravel driveway, there was one subtle yet huge difference that Linda had yet to notice since her last visit to Welbourne Mills about a month ago, and yet that took place on the weekday. Now this was the weekend, she took a minute after passing through the temporary reception to gawp next to the notice board and look down in astonishment as all the footpaths and tarmac walkways that lay ahead of her field of vision were all occupied and crammed with people. The view from the top of the reception was nearly panoramic with the rising moors in the background. Apart from the unmistakable visitors' centre with its vast "WELCOME" message, Linda could see the cluster of brown buildings with their colourful roofs that made up the hub of this community straight ahead of her, the lake that sat to the left of the "hub" was visible with miniature figures huddling around its rim. Further left she could also make out Alpha House with its red exterior, where her son had been famously staying while she was crying her eyes out, but the overhanging oak tree next to the old reception nearly obscured her vision and made it impossible to see anything further to her left.

'Hi, are you OK there madam?' asked Dee the receptionist as she peered out of the back door.

'Yes I'm fine, just visiting. This building work to the left has caught my eye, do you know by any chance?'

'Yep, that was actually our original reception before we had to move into this gritty portable block. It's been standing like this for over a year or two but funding is getting so difficult these days that we may have to leave it like that for another few years. Quite sorry, I must say to see it behind all that fencing.'

'Yes, I guess the people down there really miss the old building, with change and all that then?' Linda mumbled as she was still looking at the fenced off eyesore.

'Yeah, but then again there are actually a few who will be crying when they see this grey block leave when the new building is complete. It seems that you can't please everyone these days.'

'So when is the building actually going to be complete? To be honest I won't be sad to watch all that construction site bunting pack up and leave.'

'I won't miss that either but like I just said its future lies in the balance. Luckily Carole, our manager and one of our patrons are planning to have some VIPs around to visit so we could hopefully get good public relations and the outside funding we've all been waiting for such as brand new facilities, including a chill out area for people with sensory problems. But I hope it goes better than before.'

'Why, what happened before?' asked Linda as she turned towards Dee, a sign that she was now paying full attention.

'We don't like to talk about it, and neither do the residents.'

'Oh, sorry.'

'Don't be. After all it wasn't us who started it, but it felt like we did,' finished Dee as she turned away before Lin had the chance to respond back to her. Just what she really mean by that? *It wasn't us who started it, it was us.* If she was really desperate to know Lin would've turned back into the reception to ask Dee what she was talking about but decided to respect her privacy instead and leave her alone. After all she didn't want to risk stepping in someone else's business and making a new enemy at this point, besides she shouldn't really be here at all, she should be back home planning an exclusive shopping trip with her daughter.

******

As rightfully planned, I was going to visit Mrs Leslie and the other "special village" staff today before staying one night inside my old dormitory in Alpha House. Tomorrow I was going to eat breakfast, attend a session with the other residents called "Breaking In", visit the pigs and chickens and attend an arts and crafts lesson, before being reunited with my mother again and return home back to Orpington. Back at the reception I asked Denise if Mrs Leslie was available so I could encounter her and fulfil her promise on our previous visit by showing her the contract before making jam sandwiches together, but my stomach churned when I was told Mrs Leslie was currently inside a staff meeting. Instead Denise suggested to myself that I should visit James and the other residents until Mrs Leslie was available because (according to her) they missed me and they were found talking together near a building inside the centre of the village called the social hub.

Inside the social hub there were four crinkled sofas along every wall, rows of classroom tables inside the centre of the room each occupied by a resident, there were a stack of vintage board games stacked 5ft high between

154

two of the sofas where Mark One was sitting alone and examining a classic record, to the far right was another door and a window revealing a kitchen with a blonde haired female staff member who wore a maroon jumper staring towards us. To remove my suspicion, I entered into this kitchen to check if there was a mirror on the reverse side of the window.

'Hi, are you alright?' asked the staff member rather cheerily.

'Yes. Is this actually a window?' I asked.

'Erm, yeah. Strange place to put it don't you think?'

'Yes I agree. I am looking for James Warwicker and Simon Hanley, do you know where they are located?'

'Well, I can tell you where James is,' she replied, pointing at the window 'He's right down over there doing one of his monologues again, bless him.'

'Thank you very much.' At the very far end of the room I found James, Kimberley, Oliver and three unnamed residents were sitting around a brown sofa and a small table shaking their hands at each other. Above Kimberley I saw that particular sign again:

Always be kind
Do your best
Say I am sorry
Forgive others
Keep your promises
Try new things
Always share and take turns
Tell the truth
But most importantly, be yourself.

Then when James saw me, the whole group shaking their hands towards me in a cheerful manner, then I heard each of them say hello one by one next to their table and watched them discuss.

'A few years ago I was at the Metrocentre in Manchester with my parents and I held the door open to let them inside,' said James. 'But before I finished letting them in, three kids on rollerblades flew past and I had to leave the door open for them as if I was a doorman myself. Infact it was so common that they should make a new term for it.'

Suddenly I felt a spark ignite inside my head which had given myself an incredible thought. The idea was called "The Accidental Doorman" and it was a brand new theory that when analysed, was just as intriguing and commonplace as the classic "Three Little Pigs Theory". It was when an individual partakes in a short-term charitable deed (such as holding a door open for somebody else), only to have his services prolonged and abused by individuals taking advantage of his deed, therefore extinguishing the desire to undertake more charitable actions in the future.

'What about the "Accidental Doorman"?' I suggested to James.

'Excuse me?' gasped Oliver.

'What kind of doorman?' asked Kimberly?

I cleared my throat before speaking. 'An accidental doorman. It is an individual who accidentally becomes a doorman due to his excessive kindness towards other individuals.'

'Accidental doorman, I quite like that,' said James clicking his fingers. 'Reminds me of someone we had here called Peter, he liked making up words like that. Say Arnold, do you have any more you'd like to share with us?'

'Once I had created another one called the "Three Little Pigs Theory", but it turned out to be incorrect.'

'Three little pigs!?' asked Oliver 'Is the big bad wolf in it?'

'No, it is a metaphorical theory where three identical objects or events appear in a sequence, but the third event is unexpectedly altered so that it is completely different from the previous two events that it originally followed.' Then the room became silent and James and Oliver looked at the other residents across the table. The female staff member I saw with blonde hair then stopped talking to a pair of elderly resident from another table and began to walk slowly towards myself.

'Is everything alright?' she asked us.

'Yes. We were talking about three little pigs,' answered Kimberly.

'Yeah, what do you actually mean Arnold?' asked James.

'The book about the three little pigs, is there one available inside this place?' I asked.

'I got one under my bed, do you want it?' replied a voice from another table. I turned around to look at the person who could help explain my brilliant theory and saw a middle aged gentleman with light brown curly hair and large cheeks smiling at myself. But before I could response with a "Yes" to his question, he quickly stood up from his seat and left the premises. For the next eight minutes I was waiting with much excitement for this unexpected hero, who held the evidence behind my very own theory under his bed.

'I got the book you are looking for!' shouted the curly haired individual as he returned and slammed the door behind him 'and my name is

Neil, sorry for not mentioning it earlier.'

'Neil, next time be gentle with the door OK?' asked the staff member slowly.

'Sorry Amanda,' replied Neil. He then walked over to our table and pulled out a square brown book with three pink unmistakable animals on the front cover. I picked up the book, opened the greasy pages and read it out loud in front of the group.

'In this book for example, the first little pig's straw house is blown down by the wolf, so he loses. The second little pig's wood house is also blown down by the wolf, so he loses too. But the third little pig's brick house, instead of it being blown down it defeats the wolf and the third little pig wins. Do you understand my theory now?'

'Err, are you trying to mention things that sometimes go similar to that story?'

'Yes!'

Oh, I get what you mean. I saw an advert once featuring blue men playing on a giant keyboard that used your theory Arnold.'

'I've just noticed something too,' said Neil as he pulled out a *Sooty & Co* video from its transparent box and held it towards the group. 'If you look carefully on the holes on the back of this video, it looks like a picture of a steam train puffing towards a pair of buffers over here, look!'

'Heh, looks like you two have something in common,' laughed James.

'It looks like that episode in *Thomas the Tank Engine* where Percy is running away from Gordon,' I replied, by using the first image that appeared inside my mind 'and that looks like the bank of earth where Percy stops,' said myself again, this time pointing to the large oblong hole on the right of the VHS.

'You're funny,' said Kimberley.

'You should meet Gary, he'll like you,' answered one of the unnamed residents.

'Who is Gary?' I asked curiously.

'He is one of the volunteers, he likes telling funny stories. I think he's around today.'

'Last time I heard he's in Charlie House talking to some of the guys there,' said Amanda 'if you like I could give him a call.'

'No, I think we shall see him right now, let's go!' shouted Kimberley before tugging James's and Ollie's arms together.

157

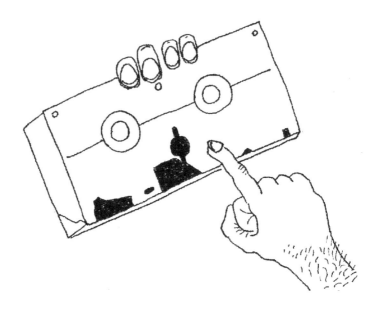

Outside we were briskly walking down the footpath that was leading away from the geographical centre of the "special village", where the social room was placed. Kimberly was wearing a pink anorak and leading the group, which consisted of myself, Ollie, Neil, Simon and two of the unnamed residents I saw from the social room, who were actually called Barry and Meghan. James did not want to help introduce myself to Gary because was too busy talking to Amanda. We continued to travel east along some gravel steps towards Charlie House until Kimberley froze abruptly, which caused Barry to collide with Simon and Neil.

'There he is, let's meet him!' she announced excitedly.

Suddenly Kimberly and everyone else inside the group started to run and I also noticed that the gravel steps were growing steeper as we ran downhill and I felt my legs being kicked by Barry who was running directly behind myself. At the bottom of the steps I saw Charlie House straight ahead, which was identical to Alpha House except that the window frames and gutters were green instead of red, and there was a tall male volunteer leaning on a signpost outside the dormitories.

'Look who it is, hi Gary!'

'We missed you!'

'I have someone for you to meet Gary!'

He had short black hair, a maroon t shirt with the yellow logo but most frightening of all, he was wearing a round silver earring.

As soon as I spotted these profanities, my right hand sunk underneath my left armpit, which according to Rose was one of my trademark gestures. As he drew closer he appeared to grow taller and this caused by left hand to connect with my right armpit again which meant that both of my hands were unavailable to correctly greet him with a simple handshake.

'Hi, you alright? You must be Arnold,' he asked, speaking in a feminine accent.

I ran.

'What's wrong? I'm not THAT ugly am I?' said Gary as the other residents laughed loudly at him.

26

Dr Ian Bradbury was after a cigarette. But he dared not to because it would bring him back to the days when he pretended to be an anarchist punk in his college years when he had little care of life in general and thought lazing around town with a bad haircut and dangling chains on his jacket was the best way to go for the future. But that was over 13 years ago and with his short black hair, clean blue jeans, padded stomach and a 2 year old doctorate in psychology, nobody suspects Ian of hiding a seedy past under his clean cut exterior. Whenever he's not feeling his peppy and lively self he would sneak off for one before dealing with a difficult client but nowadays puts cigarettes as a last resort.

He shouldn't be here at all either. The real reason why he had only discovered Welbourne Mills this year and why he had been persuaded to make repeat visits to the place was because of a dysfunctional 18 year old who ditched his own family back in Kent and tried to start a new life here. And then he had to step in again on behalf of the local police by feeding them info and pictures so it could be passed down to the Met in London, before helping orchestrate the painful and emotional reunion of the family.

But the said mother of this "dysfunctional 18 year old" was now in front of him drinking her coffee, and Ian pretended to cross his fingers inside his head, hoping that she wasn't here to make a sequel to that hysterical scenario, forcing Ian to take the place of his older and more experienced colleague Terry. Mrs Holt was just pleasantly chatting away to another mature care assistant so there should be nothing to worry about and he won't need that cigarette either.

'So what are you planning to do while you're around 'op north?' asked Rita Leslie, in a mock northern accent.

'Well I'm just going to see my sister Jennie, stay the night there and come back here to pick him up tomorrow, simple as that.'

'I never knew you had a sister Linda.'

'Oh don't you remember? But then again I haven't met her for years to be honest, lives near a place called Garforth, you heard of it?'

'Yep, somewhere near Leeds.' She picked up her tea and took a sip.

'We're just going for a quiet meal tonight near the city, perhaps a Chinese or an Italian, don't want to go to a curry house because last time we did I nearly burned my tonsils out and that was only on the starters.' They both took a gulp of their tea together while Ian watched them from the office doorway stroking the back of his neck, as if he wanted to join in on the conversation. It's better to let the ladies finish first before jumping in with your topic, instead of doing it the other way round like most of the people who live in Welbourne Mills do.

'So how's Geoffrey these days? Has he got better since then?' questioned Rita.

'Well, overall we're getting on fine with life in general despite the tough times, the kids are okay too and we've made a bit of money by selling one of our cars, but the only gripe I've had with him is that he keeps going ill at exactly the wrong time.'

'Oh, and what do you mean by that?'

'Well for starters he keeps going funny whenever I ask him to do a little errand like driving my son up to here for example. Infact if he hadn't gone ill yesterday then I wouldn't be here talking to you.'

'What are his symptoms by any chance? Perhaps I could help,' interrupted Dr Bradbury.

'He keeps moaning that he gets migraines, feels weak and suffer from tummy upsets, but you might as well add hypochondriac to it as well.' And then the two women looked at each other and laughed.

'It might not be a laughing matter Mrs Holt, after all when you were last here you did say he wasn't feeling well then. If he's not faking could be the early stages of something much more serious, in which I recommend him going to his local doctor to get a thorough diagnosis.'

'Can't you do a diagnosis yourself?' she asked.

'I'm a psychiatrist, not a GP.'

'Oh.'

'Or else if he is really "faking it" as you may say, it could be because he is trying to deter away from something that may stage a threat or maybe a memory from his past that had been refreshed by a recent event. It's like trying not to face your fear, your first instinct would be to avoid it at all costs, whatever the risks can be.'

'But there was one point where we were on the motorway together and he started swerving all over the place because of his act and that was the only time I thought he really wasn't faking it because it could've killed us all and he would never have done anything that stupid before.

'Hmmm… does he suffer from dyspraxia by any chance?'

'No, no, he doesn't have problems with his reading and writing.'
He froze for a second when he spotted the error. Of course this wasn't the first time Dr Bradbury had encountered somebody who got the names of disorders and syndromes, but instead of correcting them he simply ignored the matter because if he explained the correct term or symptoms they ended up going off course which in the end wasn't worth it. Better not to worry about the littlest things like a certain few do.

'If that's the case then you ought to send him to the doctors then. Where is he now Mrs Holt?'

'He's at home doing god knows what.'

'Is this the first time this has happened to him?'

'Well not in your context no. Other than that we do have the odd tiff, don't get me wrong,' she nodded at Mrs Leslie. 'But sometimes when he cocks up it feels like I'm looking after four children instead of three. I swear if he starts turning into one of those Goths who spend their lives inside their rooms moping around then I'll threaten to chuck him out until he chins up. Also did the same to my daughter back when she wanted to cover herself with studs and chains.'

'Hah, funny you used to say that,' they both turned to Ian who appeared to be smiling, probably because they just mentioned one of his favourite topics 'I used to be a punk in my schooldays, a real genuine punk. If you look closely you can see where I used to keep all the piercings.' He turned his head sideways and edged towards Linda, who noticed the five little pinpricks on his left earlobe. Without making a word, she turned away from Ian and stuck her tongue out at Rita to show distaste while staying mute.

Aahhhh…

'Did you hear something?' he asked.

Aaaaaaahhhh… He spun his head and glared at the window.
Aaaaaaahhhhh….

'There it is again; don't tell you couldn't hear it.'

'I can hear it,' said Mrs Leslie 'it sounds like one of the folks is having a panic attack. I'd better warn the first aiders before it's too late.'

They all rose up from the seats simultaneously and paused, then they tried to track the sound with their ears. The scream escalated very slowly in volume, until Ian pointed to a room at the back of the welcome centre and rushed straight for it with Rita and Linda following behind. The room was only a store cupboard filled with shelves and padlocked filing cabinets. The only window was a filthy square of glass fitted on a fire exit, installed a few years ago to conform to fire regulations. All three wiped the dust of the glass and squinted at the view as the back door gave them a stunning view of the long gravel path, with the miniature lake sitting on the left behind it and the small cluster of buildings in the distance where the path apparently finished. Mrs Leslie scanned the path and couldn't spot any danger out of the groups of visitors, residents and carers who were crisscrossing each other and blocking her. Then suddenly a family of three adults and five children split up and line up on both sides of the path, as if a car was about to whoosh in the middle of the strip, unable to stop. The screaming grew louder. A disabled adult wearing a red cap looks ahead of the family and soon bolts off of the gravel track and out of their sightline. Then Linda and Mrs Leslie gasps in a mixture of shock and embarrassment when they find the source of that horrible noise was coming from a distinctive boy with a green chequered shirt and brown trousers, roaring down the path towards them and waving his arms furiously as if he was being chased by a swarm of angry bees. But Mrs Leslie couldn't see any bees present.

'AHHHHHHHHHHHHHH!'

'Don't tell me this is happening,' mumbled Linda to herself.

'Is that your son running like mad Lin?' said Ian as he glared through the window and saw that it was happening.

'Yes,' she replied through gritted teeth before heading back for her tea. Rita continued to watch Arnold storm down the path until he vanished out of sight on behind the cupboard walls. Her eyes then continued to go left and traced along the wall as if she had x-ray vision until she made a beeline for the front door, leaving Linda on her own as she slumped down on one of the office chairs with her head deep in her hands, as if she realised at the whole of Britain had been burned down to the ground and she had nowhere else to go and exist.

The reality was that her plans had been shattered, well to be precise tonight's plans. She had a night out with Jennie already booked, which for herself would involve taking her out to an Italian restaurant outside Leeds, topping up with a few drinks before sharing childhood memories of eating blancmange out of the mixing bowl as well as other sugary stuff from the 70s that no longer exist. Nothing extreme.

Now she was livid. If Arnold had was standing right in front of her

163

she'd have the urge to grasp his thin neck and pin him against the wall and say every nasty word in the dictionary, but those kind of twisted urges started back when he was eight and now Arnold was almost turning 19. You just couldn't do that to anyone, especially when there was a teaching assistant and a psychiatrist watching you in the same room.

'I can tell this wasn't in your plans,' said Ian as she nodded back in agreement 'Hate to say it but that kind of thing can happen to anybody y' know. Sod's law they call it.'

'I know that.'

'Well when I was small I used to play for my village footy club for over three years, their top striker they used to say and my Dad used to drive me there all the time and cheer me on. But one day I was getting ready for the cup final in our league and I was so excited because I was going to win my very first gold trophy and I couldn't wait for my Dad to get home from work to take me there. But that evening my Dad didn't come home and when he did, he was staggering and tripping over things. He was completely sloshed. And because of that I couldn't play in the cup final and I never got the chance to win a gold trophy. So you see Linda, it can happen to everyone.'

Although he was a very nice doctor (but not a good one in her view) she didn't have the heart to tell him that she didn't give a monkeys about his story because firstly her temper hadn't cooled off yet and secondly she didn't want to put Ian on the receiving end of her anger and therefore undergo another counselling session up north. There was only one way Linda could ease off the stress of having a personal night out ripped to shreds by an antisocial son and that was by locking herself in the toilet for ten minutes.

Once she cooled off, Linda left the toilet and strode off outside and paused when she saw Ian and Rita appeared to be consoling Arnold in front of a small crowd. At the back she saw a very lanky man with a maroon polo shirt and a neat haircut trying to look over the crowd. '*What has he done again this time?*' Lin angrily thought to herself as she peered at the crowd again, wondering if the "culprit" was hiding among them. They had done nothing wrong and she knew that, but from past experiences it was the person who Arnold thinks will most likely be a wrongdoer that she was trying to weed out.

Tired of guessing, she gave up the search and moved toward Rita and Ian who both gave her a summary of what her son had been up today when they arrived, right up to the point where he bolted down to their current location. It turned out that the lanky man in the polo shirt (who also happened to be wearing an earring) was the "wrongdoer".

'Christ, why do these things happen to me?' To top it off, he hasn't even come over and said sorry for ruining his mother's plans. *'Thanks a lot, now I have to wait another frigging blue moon for some private time with Jen once more. A night when I can forget that I even have a family and don't have to put up with the burden of clearing up the problems bought by my three children. Just one night would do. If only there was a bit of luck, just a speck-'*

'Are we going to return home now mother?' asked Arnold curiously as the crowd split up through the centre's many paths.

'Yes,' she said rigidly 'and don't call me mother anymore. I'm your MUM from now on.'

There was an awkward silence as the atmosphere grew tense and Arnold's brow twitched a little after listening to those words as if he understood the message. Rita and Ian who were still watching looked at each other without speaking and both thought that it was best not to say anything for now.

27

I awoke rather quickly, only to have found myself standing on the stage of a television set. The floor was white like bleach but the audience appeared to be dark from the shadows, except for a series of red polka dots that were looking down at myself. Above the audience was a gigantic sign that read "DON'T TRY THIS AT HOME!" I soon remembered this was a programme I used to watch on Channel 3 as a child; and it was hosted by the same woman who presented that disgustingly vile programme known as *Big Brother*. Then I heard a thumping noise that occurred behind my head so I quickly turned around to find the noise.

'Arnold, help! That nasty hostess has locked me inside this thing. You've got to get me out!' It was Mrs Leslie, she was trapped inside a glass box with white edges that matched the floor and she desperately needed my help. I soon noticed another box with a door next to the one Mrs Leslie was imprisoned inside which was completely white, but above the door it read in dark capital letters: FEAR BOOTH. Ignoring it, I entered the "Fear Booth" in order to save my former helper from the terrible hostess. Inside the room was completely white on all six sides as well as a second door to my left where she was being trapped. I opened the door slowly for no apparent reason and then I found myself inside the glass box, with the silent audience staring from the left and Mrs Leslie who was positioned away from myself and oddly silent.

I tried to reach out my left hand in order to touch her and turn her around but something was happening outside the box when I tried to do this. The television set turned red. Then I recoiled my left hand in horror when I realised that the figure wasn't Mrs Leslie at all, it was the goth that I accidently saw back on the train going from Orpington to London Victoria, the one that caused myself to vomit suddenly. I wanted to scream back in horror, but I couldn't.

'Speechless again are you?' cackled the goth, with his hands clasped together. 'Well I've got the solution right here!' He laughed idiotically and then released his hands, revealing something dark and sinister that I would find in nearly every one of my nightmares, a black hole.

'NO!!!'

And then I woke up. It was only a horrific dream, much more horrific than I one I had dreamt before where I was attacked by the BBC2 logo in the back garden while wearing a green swimming costume and an orange rubber

166

ring. The back of my head felt unusually sore and my mouth felt dry so I jumped off my bed and began my journey to the kitchen. But once my hand touched the wooden banister I heard a shuffling noise on the hallway but when I looked down the stairs I could see nobody present. The watch inside my pocket read 4.10pm but it were a Monday afternoon which meant that none of the family should naturally be here. It could have been an audio illusion, which is when I describe a noise that confuses the ears, equivalent to an optical illusion because that confuses the eyes.

But when my feet soon touched the hallway floor my back was struck from behind, I fell forward and crashed face first onto the floorboards. I tried to move my arms in order to stand up but something were gluing my hands to my back so I looked up at the oval shaped mirror on the wall straight ahead but my vision was obscured by my sister Rose who wore a short white shirt with a navy skirt (her career uniform) and appeared to be twirling a piece of her brown hair with her finger.

'George, get off of him now!' she shouted. 'Now that I have your attention, you are a selfish little swine and you know it. You get us into all these buggering problems and yet you don't even bother to help or fix any of them and expect people to pick up after you.'

'Yeah!' said George as he stood beside Rose, shaking his hand.

'Pardon?' I asked.

'Thanks to you this whole family's falling apart!' Rose snarled and pointed a finger at myself 'First you go off on your own without telling me then Mum starts crying her eyes out and getting softer and yet you don't take any notice of it. Then Dad starts going all empty headed and whatnot and I think it's your entire fault. And then Uncle Tony and this huge party comes out of nowhere and all of a sudden those neighbours that Mum hates talking to were at the party as well. Since when did the last time we have a huge party in the back garden? Not even both of us had and we're both higher up the ladder than you will ever be.'

'Sorry, I do not understand-'

'You're not supposed to understand that you can be selfish. Arnold I am giving you a lifeline here, you have enough time to undo all of this mess you've caused and stop breaking Mum and Dad before they have another fall out again. And if you don't you know what happens.'

'What happens?' I asked curiously.

'You know what happens, silly,' replied Rose before she turned left to face the Golden Idiot. George then pulled down the zip of his orange anorak and pulled out a blue square of crumpled paper. There were three lines of distorted pencil writing and below the words was a badly drawn picture of a fox with a giant spoon on his back. Then he pulled out a yellow and black pencil, pressed the sharp end against the drawing of the fox and using his right thumb pressed down on the blunt end of the pencil until it went through the blue paper. Then he held the blunt end of the pencil upright with his fingers and twisted it so that it looked like he had made a helicopter.

'We're watching you Arnie!' laughed George as he dropped his pencil and paper on the floor before running off. It was three minutes later when I fully realised that the Golden Idiot was going to puncture and destroy my favourite book as a result of my alleged failure from "saving the family".

But what had I done wrong to deserve this assault from Rose?

******

After an alluring twist in her plans, Linda Holt's rendezvous with her older sister near Leeds actually got back on track and became a reality where after the plans were thought to be derailed by Arnold's unexpected panic attack. She imagined that there was a speck of luck in the air that triggered the last minute persuasion by Rita Leslie, which managed to reverse polarity of the situation so that instead of her autistic son being better off in the end it was her who got the better part of the deal and that night she was revelling in the royalties that she wished for and sat in a trendy Italian bar with Jennie that night knocking down a few glasses of red wine and recalling the time their uncle Ken finally broke the filthy white deckchair that had been sitting at the back of their childhood home for years.

Overall Linda was quite amazed that Rita's coaxing skills had worked quickly to suit her own needs, only when she realised that her job would involve trying to persuade and dissuade disabled children and adults that it wasn't really that special, after all she had been working in this specific field for over twenty five years. Her son on the other hand hadn't been particularly affected at the fact that Mrs Leslie was actually working against him and calmly agreed that he should give his mother a break from the anarchy of daily life and stay at Welbourne Mills until the next evening when she felt fully rested and content with going back to Orpington to face work once again, but with the added morale she gained after the opportunity of a night out with her sister that she last saw nearly a year ago.

After all the only thing that Amanda Doran (who ran the upkeep of the social hub) noted and passed on to Mrs Leslie was that whenever they saw Arnold hanging around with a group and Gary (the "wrongdoer" according to Lin) was around talking to them, he would behave as if Gary never existed. This sounded rather hard to believe when Rita was first told but it became much clearer when they were playing those classic group activities where everybody would stand in a circle and either play with the space inside the circle or with the circle itself. When it was Arnold's turn to play 'Ask my neighbour' he would unknowingly skip past Gary without realising, as if he was an outsider to the game. Like a squatter.

Or maybe they were just exaggerating?

28

Today I was travelling to visit Jobcall for the third time this week for assistance with searching for a career. Since the induction I had noticed that Alan had become quieter and behaved more like an ordinary adult during our lessons, except for the first ten minutes where he would crash into the classroom and ask everyone a summary of their activities since their last Jobcall lesson. Afterwards the rest of the lesson was dedicated towards genuine job searching, where we passed newspapers, and job vacancies printed from the computer around the table before every current job vacancy had been read by everyone, including Alan who would start jumping up and down whenever he found a career that was applicable to our capabilities. But he still continued to wear his madcap clothes though, this week he was wearing a navy t shirt featuring the *Teenage Mutant Hero Turtles* logo.

Another difference that I noticed were that the lady with brown hair and the strong accent was absent inside the building and there was a younger lady working inside the office adjacent to our classroom with long blonde hair and blue eyes who I had never seen before. When she saw me, she mentioned that she had seen myself before outside the Jobcall building but I don't remember seeing her at all.

'Hello chaps, how has everyone been? I hope you all had a wonderful week and as part of the opening circle we'll be finding out what each other have been doing. It's best not to ask me first because if I did, it may turn your cheeks green!'

'I don't know about that, I used to be a full time rave artist!' laughed Frank, waving his arms above his head.

'As you may remember from last time we're still going on the PSHE topics or personal development if you have already forgotten your schooldays. So today I'll tell you another wacky story from the mind of Alan Coyne.' Susan and Alex smiled towards each other as they sat, shifting their chairs forward. 'One time ago I was helping out at a café next to the salvation army and it was one of those places that was run entirely by older ladies, excuse myself. But one day the place was filled with visitors who were sent from the Jobcentre, and these peaceful mature folk found themselves against a group of young, bossy, underage girls wearing pink lycras, Croydon facelifts and earrings bigger than their own fists.'

'Boo!' I shouted, which caused everybody to laugh.

'Now, now, I haven't finished yet. So these two generations were side

170

at side, terrified of with nothing to say to each other, until the old ladies started to mention The Falklands War.'

'Did they talk about guns and killing people?' asked Susan peacefully.

'Hell no, and watch your language dear. The ladies were telling the teenagers what they were up to when they were their age and soon they discovered they shared a common subject together. Yes, they told all these young ladies how many soldiers they slept with and all the nationalities they bonked in those dark days when war was on everyone's mind. These young ladies were so astounded that none of them wanted to leave and one of them was so opened up by this that she cleaned up her act a bit and got a job as a care worker in Sutton.' The three Jobcall members then turned to view each other without speaking. 'And that's what brings us to today's subject: finding common ground.'

'Sorry but what does this have to do with looking for a job?' asked Alex.

'Well if you find a job and you want to break the ice with your new colleagues, I've met a number of clients from here who have difficulty with doing that so the best way to kick it off is by finding something that you all like doing together, it's perfectly simple my dear Alex. This is something you ought to be paying attention to, especially Arnold because one day it may save your life, seriously.' I was going to put my hand up to ask for an example of what Alan really meant by this when he interrupted again. 'Break time everyone! If you want to pop off for something to eat there's a *Co-op* down the road and you've got half an hour. Don't be late!'

For my lunch break I decided not to spend it inside the classroom as it would result in overexposure to Alan and his tall tales and instead walked outside to the "Smoking Area" which was a tiled garden with an ashtray adjoining the Jobcall car park. It would have been highly illogical for myself to appear in the "Smoking Area" because I had never smoked tobacco but the reason I wanted to appear outside were because there was an upside down "STOP" sign covered in green paint located at the end of the Jobcall car park and I enjoyed looking it at because it was oddly peculiar. Eventually Frank would always appear in front of the ashtray with a cigarette and begin smoking his tobacco.

'Alright?' he asked.

'Yes.'

'He's a right nutcase isn't he?'

'I strongly agree,' I said, believing that he was referring to Alan Coyne.

171

'Sometimes I wonder why they would employ a madman like him in the first place. Some of the stuff he comes out with is nothing but a load of processed bull! Like who would actually follow his advice?'

'I have followed his advice before once,' I said strongly.

'When?'

'On the first day when Alan suggested that if you don't like the look or sound of a certain individual, pretend that they don't exist.'

'What?' shouted Frank 'We've told you before you shouldn't be saying those things.'

'What things might I ask?'

'Don't you get it?'

'What am I trying to get?' I asked again.

'We've told you a million time you shouldn't be saying those kind of things you, you arnophobic git!'

'Pardon?'

'If I catch you doing it again I will bring my relatives around and we will make you change your mind.' Suddenly I had the apparent urge to flee the "Smoking Area" and run straight into the road when the entrance doors into Jobcall swung wide open.

'Break's up guys, it's time to return!' yelled out Alan.

'OK, remember what I said or this might be you one day,' he warned, holding the finished cigarette in front of myself before pushing it slowly into the ashtray on the wall. Finally we returned back to our classroom in Jobcall together (where he kindly held the door open for myself to walk through) but he never spoke to me again until the next lesson.

29

Just incase you didn't know, Geoffrey worked in the HR department for a car showroom somewhere in the backwaters of Essex. He had worked there for over six years and considered it to be his dream job because it combined two of his favourite interests and pastimes together into one career, cars and mental arithmetic. Most of the day would involve sitting behind a computer screen inside a spacious air conditioned office, the type where there would be a massive window behind the desks that would overlook the vast bays of stationary designer vehicles, nearly all of them brand new with a row of tall pine trees to remind him that the lines of cars did not go on infinitely.   Sometimes when it was a nice sunny day and the CEO was really getting on his nerves, he would leave the office via the fire exit so he could be among those endless bays of parked cars and walk very slowly along them until he reached the pines and walk back to the building again. Some of the colleagues that he worked with for years like Rob knew about this and realised that he whenever Geoffrey did this, he would take an exact path inside the parking bays, unless there was a jeep or a limousine blocking his way.

He had just started his lunch break in the common room that overlooked the company car park and despite the stringent company rules where colleagues taking their breaks together would be frowned upon, Geoff found himself accompanied by Chris, one of the younger colleagues who was busy tucking into some kind of salad with a plastic fork. When this happens they normally nod quietly to each other and continue.

'Did you read that story about that guy called Callum Maclean who hacked into MI5's computers?' asked Chris unexpectedly.

'Why yes I have.'

'Well they let him off just because he had learning difficulties. Really, I can't see why the media are giving him all this sympathy.'

'Pardon?' stuttered Geoffrey.

'They pay all this attention to people who are slightly autistic, people who are fully capable of looking after themselves. For example you've got this lad who says he's got Asparagus Syndrome or whatsoever who's written a book and yet he's in uni getting a physics degree and getting praised instead of getting stuck in a care home with a crash helmet stuck to his head.'

'It's not that easy for him I'm afraid.'

'And how do you know? You're not one of them.'

'It's simple, autism is a condition that can affect anyone in a number of ways because it is never the same.

'Yeah right, I still think most of them are self obsessed, pampered gits who try to make themselves famous by saying that they've got the disease.'

'Disease?'

'Yeah, that's what it is right?' asked Chris as he picked up this paper and began to read it again. Then there was a surprise as Geoff then got up from his seat, soup bowl clutched in one hand and without warning he tipped it all over Chris's crotch. Then there was a scream as Chris felt the boiling hot soup sting his groin and sprang up from his chair before trying to mop it up with his tabloid.

'What the hell Geoff!?' screamed Chris 'Have you gone completely wacko or something?'

'No, you are the one who has gone insane with your drivel.'

'Don't call me mental you spas-' Suddenly the atmosphere in the stuffy yet quaint and peaceful room changed dramatically. The CCTV camera in the corner of the room zoomed in as its operator saw two men grappling with each other, the eldest with his hands grasped around the other's neck and the younger of the two was frantically bashing the limbs of the other who was trying to strangle him. When they stopping grasping each other, Chris then picked up the soup bowl and tried to treat to batter his colleague with it but to no avail as the bowl was knocked out of his hand and shattered on the floor.

'What the hell is this!?' boomed a voice inside the doorway. It was the CEO of the showroom, Howard with his distinctive moustache and strong South African accent that would sometimes make the rooms in the building shake and the cars wobble. Both culprits froze immediately and turned to face their superior, who had at least four staff watching from behind.

'He's gone mad sir, he should be locked up,' shouted Chris, who was pointing a hand at his attacker.

'Geoff, this isn't like you at all, are you sure you're feeling okay?'

'I'm just a bit under the weather lately, that is all,' he mumbled sadly.

'He's not under the weather, he's mental,' said Chris angrily.

'Right, I think you and me need a good chat in my office after lunch,' replied Howard with a calm face 'because we can't have this happening again,

And Chris, get yourself cleaned. You look like you've pissed all over yourself.'

'Bah, I hate it when older colleagues stick up for each other,' Chris muttered under his breath.

They left the common room and walked off single file, leaving behind a few puzzled staff as they giggled at Chris with his groin covered in minestrone soup like a child who had just been punished by the father for wetting himself. As the office drew nearer Geoffrey thought to himself once again of how much he had gone downhill over a past few months since he sold the car. His mental state, let alone his patience had taken a battering during this time and it wouldn't be long until everybody starts clocking his behaviour and that would mean being thrown into the world of padded walls and men with white coats holding 4ft long needles.

If he doesn't then that's it. It could never be reversed.

30

'Why are we stopping outside the entrance?' I asked suspiciously to my Dad.

'To drop you off obviously.'

'There is a car park inside the special village, why can't you drop myself off there?'

'Because,' paused my Dad 'I am tired and don't like going on bumpy roads.'

'But it is not a bumpy road.'

'I'm sorry but I'm not feeling that good. And anyway you're out of the car so why are we having this conversation?'

'...'

'I'll explain it to you once we're home, now bye son.'

'Goodbye Dad.'

And then he waved his right arm out of the window before he drove off quickly as if the surrounding area were set on fire. Despite the blunt arrival given out by my father, I had arrived at Welbourne Mills twenty eight minutes ago and because of this it were my third "official" visit to the "special village" (excluding the fact that I had left the centre with the residents eight times to embark on their infamous excursions, which meant that this would actually be my eleventh visit).

At the box shaped reception I noticed that there was a significant change in the staff who were operating the oak desk. Instead of Denise with her unmistakable glasses that stood on top of her forehead, one of the female volunteers were sitting on her chair, as well as wearing her uniform. This was not welcome.

'Hi Arnold, it's me Emma. Did you come all by yourself again?'

'No my Dad drove myself to the entrance and left. Why are you in Dee's place?'

'Oh I'm just filling in her when she's off,' she replied 'I'm actually quite excited because this will be my first paid job in a while and they've even given me new uniform! What do you think?'

'Is Dee going to come back?' I asked.

'Don't worry I'm not replacing her, she'll be back tomorrow.' She then stood up, spun in a circle and waved her arms 'and I'm still the same Emma we all know and love! Anyway they put me on probation so if they'll like me I'll be permanent and if they don't-'

'But if everybody down there likes you why would they hate you on probation?'

'That's how they work I'm afraid Arnold, I can't really describe it to you,' she shrugged her shoulders 'well now that you're here I'll buzz the guys down in the hub to let you know that you're here and while you're doing that could you sign in please?'

After I agreed to this she pushed over a red pen and pointed to a yellow sheet with her left hand while she was holding a telephone with her right hand. Once I finished she put the phone down at the same time.

'Right they know you're here now, most of them are holding an art exhibition near Bravo House but Lauren is at the canteen now if you would like to meet her there.'

'OK Emma thank you, I hope you win on your probation,' I said and then she laughed.

'That's what the others said too. Right, see you later Arnold.'

'Goodbye.'

******

The Naughty Autie Club. I was on my way to find them, but first I needed to recall a brief montage of the entire centre before I was going to engage with them.

Charlie House was identical to Alpha House except that the windows, doors and drainpipes were green instead of red. I asked Lauren previously why the lodges were coloured separately and she said if the lodges were all the same colour then no one would be able to identify them properly. The interior to Charlie House was nearly 100% identical except that all of the building features were reversed as if Alpha House were presented next to a giant mirror. There were also more posters and temporary notices that adorned the hallway. One of the walls featured a poster of that read "Ways to say hello and goodbye" along with an image of a yellow smiling face waving with one hand as well as two lists below the picture of appropriate quotes to say when meeting or leaving individuals. On another wall there was another black and white poster with four squares containing diagrams that gave another set of instructions. It looked like this:

How to make a cup of tea in five easy steps:

1. *Place one teabag into a cup/mug*
2. *Pour boiled water from a kettle into the cup/mug*
3. *Add a drop of milk to the cup*
4. *Then add a teaspoon (or two) of sugar*
5. *Enjoy!*

They were all sitting together inside the communal lounge watching an animated film about a mouse wearing a cowboy hat, except for one individual with glasses who was reading a thick catalogue about drainpipes and hardware. There were a large cluster of residents covering the walls but I soon recognised James, Oliver, Barry, Simon, and Hannah who was still wearing her classic black headphones.

'Hi guys,' waved Lauren 'look who's come to visit!'

'Arnold!'

'Yay it's Mr Holt,' roared Ollie as they watched Lauren leave the lounge.

'Look it's Arnold, are you alright?'

'...'

'Are you alright Arnold?' asked James politely as he paused the film.

'...yes.'

'What's wrong?'

'....'

'You can always tell us what's wrong, we're not going to hurt you if you do, besides playground bullies are in the past so there's nothing to fear.'

'Yeah you can always trust us Arnold, besides we're *The Naughty Autie Club*!'

'OK then. A couple of unfortunate things happened to myself last week.'

'What does unfortunate mean?' asked Hannah.

'Someone referred to myself as an arnophobic git.'

'An arnophobic, what does that mean?'

'No idea. Do you know what it means Arnold?'

'He said it because-'

'Wait I know!' gleamed James 'Perhaps it's someone who has a dislike to none other than our popular friend, the astonishing Arnold Holt!'

And then everybody began laughing for no reason whatsoever.

'No, he mentioned that phrase because I did not agree with himself wearing tattoos, that is all.'

'Oh.'

'Does that mean I will be evicted from this place?' I asked promptly.

'No. What does evicted mean?' replied Barry.

'It means being kicked out,' said James.

The room then fell silent for over ten seconds until the paused film was resumed and Simon cleaned his hands with an antibacterial tissue.

'Some of us wish things can just be the same around here,' spoke John.

'Me also.'

'Yeah I agree. It's never been the same since Marcia left,' said Oliver, holding one of Simon's tissues against his face.

'You know Ollie, Marcia has been in the yellow house the whole time, you can always see her if you like,' replied James.

'Yeah I know. It just won't be the same though.'

'Hear hear!'

Suddenly I heard a distinctive wolf whistle and everybody including myself turned their head around and watched the corridor outside the lounge. It meant that Gary appeared.

'Hey peeps!'

'GARY!'

'Hi Gary, are you alright?'

'Yeah, everyone else too?'

'Yes. Good afternoon Gary.'

'It's the man of the hour, Arnold! How is everything!?'

'I am rather fine, thank you.'

'It's nice to hear you're going strong,' he called out 'let's hope your siblings aren't taking advantage of you again, if they do I'll get Barry to come down there and he'll bounce his belly on them, right?' Everybody was laughing around the room while Gary who was in the centre, rolled up a newspaper and pretended to play the trumpet.

'No,' I replied.

'Hello Gary,' called Ollie 'we were talking about GCSE's earlier, do you have any?'

'Well I don't have any to give away but I've got a degree and a few A levels under my belt from learning different things, but due to working here so long I've also picked up a BTEC in autie-culture!'

Everybody inside the area laughed again except for myself, as if Gary had just mentioned a joke. A few minutes later James explained that the last

179

word was supposed to sound like "horticulture", which was an academic subject and that was when I soon discovered the joke and laughed quietly. Then Gary restarted the conversation. 'Have you heard the news lately? Apparently scientists are trying to find a vaccine to "cure" autism, how stupid does that sound!? You can't cure someone just because they're interested in maps nor have an eccentric lifestyle. There are a lot of naysayers around these days, people who don't want "us".'

'Well I'm in the same boat too Gary but speaking of which, what would happen if someone managed to invent a vaccine that actually causes autism? I know that it would never happen but I know a few ignorant people on TV who could do with the shot themselves.'

'Yeah, like those protestors we met back in Newcastle!' shouted Oliver, who then threw his own fist in the air.

'Protestors?' I asked.

'Oh they're just a nasty bunch of people who think we're just a waste of space. They're the ones who turn up whenever we're out on trips and carry protest boards and call us names. Luckily they don't know where we are but it is better not to talk about them.'

'Oh.' Suddenly there was an abrupt silence. This was quite common throughout the communal lounges where all the residents would run out of anything valuable to say until one of the staff members would appear and manage to ingeniously continue the conversation. This used to happen to myself back in Orpington when my family would invite guests around (which I often disliked), my least favourite occasion was when Uncle Tony told me off for "screaming the place out" even though I never said anything. As expected a familiar member of staff with blonde topped hair would then leap into the group holding a white rectangle and a permanent marker.

'Right, who wants tea or coffee?' asked Amanda

'Coffee please.'

'Tea with sugar, Amanda please.'

'How much would sugar would you like then Barry?' she asked curiously. 'One? Two? Fifteen?'

'I'll have 15 granules please!' shouted John, as he held up a giant mug with his name on the side while everybody laughed.

'Your granules are coming up sir!'

'What are you holding Amanda?' I asked, as she held the white rectangle towards her head.

'That's just the orders for the drinks Arnold. I put them down on a tiny whiteboard because and doing it on a notepad would mean ripping lots of sheets of paper off which a few of the residents dislike, except Barry because he likes recycling. Also it can be rubbed off and used again, here take a look!' She turned the whiteboard over where we saw that she drew a long green crucifix on the board and wrote down "T" on the left and "C" on the right. I could also see the word "Biscuits only" transparently on the rectangle where it had not been erased properly.

'How long have you used that whiteboard?'

'Ooh for a very long time, I think it's over 10 years old but I've only been here for two. The only problem is that everyone is so attached to this system that we just can't throw it away, a bit like my shoe collection you see.'

'OK.'

******

Once the film had finished, *The Naughty Autie Club* split up and returned to their lodges and I promptly departed as well. As part of the routine visits to Welbourne Mills, one of my activities involved "checking in" at one of the classrooms before showing my notebook in the same way my parents used to sign my school journal every week. On the way I passed Hannah who was talking to herself again and a bottle filled with seed that hang off the classroom roof. I entered, closed the door and turned around to see Mrs Leslie who was sitting at the teacher's desk while a mug of coffee was in front of her right arm.

'Are you alright Arnold?'

'Yes, but yesterday I weren't.'

'Why not? Remember you can tell me anything, I used to teach you at school.'

'Well, somebody said I was destroying my family.'

'What? Who would say this to you Arnold?' she asked loudly.

'My sister,' I replied.

'Oh,' she paused and drank some coffee 'I bet Rose really didn't mean that at all Arnold, remember what we talked about last time. She probably had a bad day at work and you got stuck in her crossfire, but as your sister she doesn't really mean to say that and you two will solve your problems eventually. But first go and grab a seat.'

Although she was an extremely supportive and logical person, I could not completely agree with Mrs Leslie's response. She was correct when she stated that I would make up with Rose, I opposed her theory that stated the cause of my sister's negative mood because I felt that my involvement with her was unavoidable, but I did not want to say this towards Mrs Leslie because it

181

may offend her and make herself angry so I took a chair and sat down in front of the desk. 'Well seeing as you're here Arnold, I think it's also time to tell you the truth about your rabbit.'

'Why, what did she do wrong?'

'Nothing, it's just her name I want to talk to you about. You see the truth about her name is this...'

'...'

'Well the name you chose for her, you called her Milth because it was a suggestion you got from your family and you liked how you spelt her name if I remember clearly, is that right?'

I nodded. 'Yes.'

'It turns out that there are a few people in this country who find her name very offensive for a reason because it sounds like an explicit acronym. It is one that people would use in a derogative, I mean negative manner and should be treated just like a swear word. You know what I mean Arnold?'

'Yes.'

'And I'm right in saying that you don't use swear words as well?'

I thought very carefully for an answer. 'No, except inside my head.'

'That's OK because everybody swears inside their head at one point. But there are people less well off than you who can't control their swearing because of a condition called Tourettes Syndrome. Because they can't control what they say, most of them can't get a stable job nor find a soulmate because they end up saying something offensive most of the time, even though it is not their fault. We used to have one resident from Bravo House who had Tourettes but due to our help he now works as a data analyst in Leeds.'

Mrs Leslie paused as she picked up her mug of coffee and drank some. 'But my point is that when you named your rabbit Milth, you had absolutely no idea what her name meant right?'

'Yes.'

'And back when you told everyone in school about her, you said that one of the girls in Year 11 yanked on your tie after that lesson and said that your pet's name was disgusting. And yet that wasn't your fault, right?'

'Yes.'

'I'm sorry if this is a bit late to mention it, but I'd thought it would be nice to tell you because of the misunderstandings you must've had in the past. To be honest I'd only learned that horrible phrase when I overheard my nephew a year ago but if I heard it before back then I still wouldn't have told you because I wouldn't share those nasty words with anyone, you agree?'

'Yes certainly,' I replied.

'And we've also taught ourselves that Tourettes and autism have something in common, and that is they both make the sufferers feel misunderstood. But let's not go any further on that now, have you bought in the diary that I gave you on our last visit?'

'Yes.'

'Good, let's get it out then.'

I picked up the notebook that rested between my shoes and placed it onto her desk so she could read it. It was a sky blue diary with a diagram of a tree inside a black ring and blow it was a horizontal black line where the name would be written above. The diary's pages were held together by small plastic ring binders and the pages had a distinctive red margin like my old primary school books. I would use this diary back home on a daily basis to record interactions between myself and my family as well as social events, which would range from going to the woods for a walk with my mother to going out to Central London to meet several relatives and visit the London Aquarium. The reason why Mrs Leslie wanted myself to record these events were because she said that I should be interacting more often with my family, especially with Rose and my mother because she said there was "too much friction" going on.

'Looks like you've had an interesting week then.'

'What do you mean?' I asked as Mrs Leslie pointed to a page that I wrote.

'You wrote here that last fortnight you went off to Greenwich with the people from Jobcall and you've written down everyone you went with. Later on, you told your family where you went that day and you ended up talking about the market with Rose for nearly half an hour.' For some reason my cheeks felt warm and she turned the page again before resting her finger on it.

'Huh? On this page it says "I LOVE SUSAN FROM JOBCALL POOPALOMPS!" in blue ink.'

'Pardon?' That is absolutely illogical because I never wrote that sentence. Frustrated, I pulled the book toward myself and ripped out the offending page before lowering it into her waste bin.

'Don't worry Arnold, I knew you would never write that. But overall I am impressed at how much you've been communicating because you used to be afraid to do it. If you remember from the lessons the key to maintaining conversations with people is to find common ground and once you do, you'll realise that you'll become more comfortable with that person and less afraid of them. Right, is that everything covered for today?'

'Yes,' I said.

'Good, remember what we spoke about Arnold, and say hello to Mrs

183

Lockton for me once you're back down there.'
    'Yes I will.'
I removed the diary off the desk before I left the classroom.
    'Right, bye now!' she waved.
    'Goodbye.'

******

    Once Arnold left the classroom Rita gave a sigh of relief and too another sip of coffee. All of this was just another little project of hers that ate into her free time but it gave her a little thrill because it reminded her of the days when she used to tick the journals of her candidates back in school to confirm that they followed all their set targets. But this time she was doing the same thing to an 18 year old who cannot communicate with his family properly for reasons unknown. Rita had to tread very carefully when she brought up the idea of using a diary after chatting to Linda Holt, besides this person travelled nearly 200 miles just to see her.

******

    Later on I was travelling back to Alpha House to read Mrs Leslie's book once again when I saw Lauren walking along the gravel path between Delta House and the Social hub.
    'Hello Lauren,' I waved.
    'Oh hi, can't talk now so bye!'
    '......'
    'Bye!'
    She then skipped off rather quickly as if she were trying to escape from somewhere, presumably from one of the genuinely irritating residents that live in Delta House like Christopher Haben who used to talk about mushrooms every day.
    There was something incorrect about Lauren when I looked at her face and arms. She did not look the same since I saw her earlier; it appeared as if her skin complexion had changed slightly for no apparent reason because one of the freckles on her cheek was missing.
    Perhaps I should not think too heavily about that particularly minor observation, like Mrs Leslie had once warned a long time ago.

31

Today was my 19th birthday. I was downstairs in the family kitchen and ate a thick bacon sandwich that was prepared by my mother while George and my Dad (who was wearing a purple dressing gown) sat opposite each other on the wooden table and ate one fried egg and bacon sandwich each. Rose was also inside the kitchen but she was staring at her mobile phone while eating a croissant at the same time, despite appearing uninterested she was actually the first person who gave myself a birthday card, this happened while I was still lying in my bed.

There were three birthday cards that appeared through the post. The first card came from Uncle Tony and Raymond, whom I had met last month at our party. The second birthday card came from my aunt Jennie as well as her husband, but most surprisingly the third card which appeared inside a pink letter, came from people that I were not related to, including someone that I had only known for a few weeks.

'Dear Arnold, Very happy birthday, from Alan, Carrie and the rest from Jobcall. P.S. Keep up the funny stories.' My sister Rose was reading out the text on the card.

'Yes, OK, thank you.'

There were four presents that were stacked together on the pine coffee table inside the living room. The large purple box at the bottom was the present I received from Raymond. At the top was a red rectangular present that had a green card attached to it, this one was from Mrs Leslic. I preferred it whenever she sent letters or items that were red and green because they reminded myself of the jam sandwiches we used to eat back in primary school. After all the wrapping paper was removed I received a notepad, a chequered blue shirt, a DVD box set of *Coast* and an unusual item called a monocular, which looked like a telescope and a pair of binoculars merged together.

'I hope you like that gift Arnold,' said my mother. 'George picked that one out for you. It's like a telescope that you can fit into your pocket, very good when you're out and about.'

'Yes,' then I asked 'May I have another one so I could create some binoculars?'

Everybody laughed, including Rose. 'Haha, we'll do that next year Arnold. In the meantime you'll need to thank Uncle Tony for his gift, don't you think?'

'Yes, OK.' Soon the family members left the kitchen one by one after we made the "thank you phone call" to my relatives. I did not mind my family laughing at myself when I questioned them about the "monocular" because I wanted that to happen. I had told them a joke, which in the past was something that I found virtually impossible.

One and a half hours later I had collected all of the presents and left them underneath my bed apart from the clothing which I had placed on my bedroom desk.

'Arnold, is that you?' It was my mother. I ran downstairs and found her inside the kitchen alone reading the property sub section of the local newspaper.

'You know Mrs Leslie has done an awful lot for you over the years, more than you can probably realise. And I'm not saying that because I'm your mum. But there is going to be a time when you can't rely on both of us for your needs forever.' What is she talking about? 'I think Arnold, for a man of your age and disposition, is time that you needed a girlfriend.'

'Pardon!?' Why is she discussing this illogical concept? She does not realise that I do not prefer to be ridiculed and/or manipulated by a member of the opposite sex, especially by one that who appears to be frighteningly muscular. The best example of this concept came from my favourite television sitcom *Last of the Summer Wine* where every housewife inside the show were dominant, masculine and conniving brutes who regularly abuse their submissive husbands and force them into doing embarrassing chores. But the three main characters don't have wives or girlfriends; instead they were independently single, free to do whatever activities that pleased themselves, from walking across the countryside to drinking unlimited pints of alcohol, as well as watching local husbands being controlled and abused by their wives.

'No? Well if that's your decision then it's OK, but you need to remember that we won't be around forever to look after you and cuddle you, look even your cousin Raymond has a girlfriend too. I'm not forcing you to have one but there are times where you need a someone who can fulfil your needs and you'll soon change your mind one way or another.'

I left her alone in the kitchen and returned to my bedroom where I continued reading the instructions on how to use the monocular properly. Although it was my birthday and I weren't receiving any negative that related to my family nor my "condition", what did she exactly mean by finding somebody to fulfil my needs? Was she referring to my old objectives? Or does she think I spend too much time on my own?

I don't know how to react to her question.

******

The day after my birthday, I went to develop the photographs inside my battered, but trustworthy camera for the first time in nine years. Afterwards I went into my Dad's cars and returned to the special village again to see my friends and acquaintances. But first I visited the sensory room that was located at the rear of the "special village", close to one of the "forbidden exits". It took the appearance of a classroom inside a square wooden hut, except that the walls, the floor and the ceiling was white, except for an orange hollow square where the sole window was removed. The light switch was one that could alter the brightness inside the sensory room instead of turning it on and off; and on one of the corners of the ceiling there was a musical speaker that would play selective music, which would match the emotional disposition of the person that would be inside the sensory room, for example I asked the attendant to play the song "Rush Hour" because it was a song that I would like to listen to whenever I was inside my Dad's car.

Afterwards I returned to *The Naughty Autie Club* where I saw an afternoon discussion taking place with the residents from Alpha House and some of the female staff members. It was actually one of their classic "Show and Tell" sessions where some of the residents would bring one of their possessions into the circle twice a week in order to make a conversation.

'Arnold!' they cried out together.

'Hello all.'

'Hey Arnold, how's everything?' asked Lauren.

'I'm OK, thank you very much,' I said.

'Have you sunning yourself lately Arnold? You look good,' said James.

'Pardon?'

'I think what James means is "have you been outside in the sunshine"?' corrected Lauren.

'Yes,' I replied.

'I've drawn a black cat eating a spicy cucumber and I'm showing everyone,' said Barry. A grey sheet of paper was being passed around the circle and when it landed on the table I looked at it. It was a neatly drawn picture of a cat wearing a grey pinstripe suit and a bowler hat sitting inside a train carriage. The spicy cucumber looked "hot" because it was orange and had steam pouring out of it. There was a signature on the paper. 'Do you like it?'

'Yes, it looks strange.'

'Barry is very good at drawing these things,' said Lauren 'he gets all these quirky ideas in his head and he just draws them as they are. Didn't you draw your dreams as well Barry?'

'Why yeah I did Lauren, this picture was based on the time I went to see the London Underground and I was showing everyone my artwork. On the same day I saw a cucumber market and a cat in Covent Garden so I decided to draw everything I saw at once.'

When Barry had finished portraying his artwork, Julian walked into the centre of the circle to mention the photographs he had taken of a pink letterbox in a local village. Finally, I decided to show everyone the 32 photographs I had taken of my bedroom, starting with Lauren first because she was a female.

'Wow, this is interesting, very interesting,' smiled James.

'That's cool. You should make an art exhibition.'

'I know you can put them up on the wall over there!' said Barry.

'It looks as if your bedroom has passed its best before date Arnold,' said Ollie who walked into the room five minutes ago. Everybody laughed at him and I did as well because he was correct. I picked up six photographs of my bedroom where I had taken the picture towards the window. The earliest picture displayed my school uniform neatly folded on my plastic table with a silver lamp where dark blue walls surrounded the window and the white carpet underneath as well as a banister from my bed that appeared on the right. Then I looked at the photograph I took a few months ago of the same location and the walls appeared brighter, but the carpet was darker and slightly stained from when George spilled hot chocolate on the floor. The chair and the school uniform were gone but the table remained and it was covered with newspapers and brown letters I received from the Jobcentre. But the banister from my bed was gone and it was replaced by a glance of my elevated bed, which underneath was where my chair, lamp, desk and underwear had relocated to.

'Why did you have two drawers Arnold?' asked Lauren.

'I ran out of room for my clothes.' I said.

'Fair enough,' she replied.

Then Julian rose up from his seat. 'I've got an idea!' he picked up the photographs, stacked them in chronological order and then he held them with his left hand and dragged his right thumb across them.

'Please do not ruin my photographs!' I said.

'Don't worry Arnold I'm only making a movie, look!' Myself and the residents watched in curiosity as the image of my bedroom gradually grew paler in colour, the folded up shirts and trousers moved from left to right and the stack of brown envelopes on the table in front of the window increased according to five of the photos. Julian than flicked the photos again, this time backwards so that it looked as if my bedroom was getting younger.

'This is why I love flip books,' said James, eating a sachet of sugar.

'Hear hear!' cried out Ollie. Then I also had something else to show them.

'I remember that book!'

'Yes, I read that book five years ago.'

'*The Curious Incident*? That's my favourite book as well!' replied a female voice. I almost screamed and then turned around and saw Denise standing near the doorway. 'I just love how the whole story revolves around Aspergers and it underlines all the qualities and struggles that the guys who live here face all the time, don't you agree?'

'Yes.'

'It's funny though because nobody else knew about the book when it first came out and the volunteers in the staff room were like the only ones who've read it. But I have never seen anyone who lives on the village actually keep a copy, so you're first for me Arnold. How long have you been reading it?'

'I had been reading this book exactly since the beginning of my eighteenth birthday, Denise.'

'Oh wow, that's quite a formal response Arnold. Of course you don't have to speak like that all the time but if you're more comfortable doing that then it's your choice.'

'Ok then.' Suddenly Barry had thought of an ingenious idea.

'Wouldn't it be strange if someone with autism actually wrote a book instead of some boring neurotypical?' he pondered.

'Neurotypical?' I asked.

'Oh it's a word he says to describe people who don't have ASD like me,' commented Denise.

'Ok then.'

'But if someone actually did, how would they get the book published? I heard there were a lot of authors who had their books rejected hundreds of times.'

'If something like that happened to us, then why would they write a book if it won't get accepted in the first place?' I replied.

'To be honest Arnold I don't know but if someone really wanted to write a book, I suppose they wouldn't give up until it got published. Everyone is different you see; and everybody has their own ambitions as well,' said Lauren.

Then James made a fascinating statement.

'I believe, and this is what I heard from a professor who had Asperger's Syndrome,' he said 'that everyone on the planet has an inside and an outside self. Our inside self is the one that thinks on the inside while the outside self is the part of our body that behaves and can be seen by everyone. This professor said that our inside and outside versions of our body work together all the time.' The residents were listening simultaneously, for example Kevin would often listen from his left ear because he did not enjoy staring at individual's faces. 'but she also said people who have learning difficulties, their inside and outside versions don't get along and this is why many of these people either get frustrated or don't get to follow their dreams.'

'So you're telling that when Charlie flaps his hands around the garden, his brain doesn't want him to do that but he does it by accident?' asked Julian, rubbing his necklace.

'Well yes probably.'

'But when the caretaker spits and swears does that mean his outside self rebelling from his inside self?'

'Er, I don't think what James said has to apply to everyone Kimberley, it's just a speculation, something you think is right but not 100% accurate,' finished Denise.

I spent the remainder of the weekend thinking extra carefully at what James and the staff discussed at the show and tell session until it was time for my exit from Welbourne Mills. I was considering if my internal and external versions of myself were out of sync because most of my vocabulary and desired words (inside self) are never used verbally (outside self). I wondered if this were the same for my Dad, whose outside version appeared to be behaving differently in a negative way from before I visited this place for the first time.

32

It wasn't us who started it, but it felt like we did.

Linda was wondering what the hell did that woman actually meant back in that centre. She wasn't autistic like most of the people there so she shouldn't be twisting her vocabulary like her son would always do. Maybe it was just being cryptic, or logical. Perhaps it was someone in their community who nearly closed down their village unwittingly and Denise was taking a bit of the blame because she had something that some people on the spectrum did not metaphorically have – a heart. But being tired and a little bemused Linda decided to forget about it and prepare for work the next morning by making some lunch.

******

Last night I had a dream. I was inside a classical theatre which had red seats, maroon curtains as well as a trapdoor. Then I heard a drum set play and a man wearing a pink suit and a black top hat appeared in the centre of the stage. He resembled Alan Coyne.

'Ladies and gentlemen thank all you for attending!' he shouted. I looked left to right at the empty seats but I could see nobody else seated except for myself. 'This is what you've been waiting for!' The trapdoor opened underneath the man's feet but he vanished instead of falling down.

At the right of the stage two individuals appeared, one was coloured red completely except for the glasses on its comically large head, while the other individual was yellow but had a large stomach instead of a large head. They were both positioned inside a white circle and they began to attack each other, the yellow character was more violent than the red one.

Then the theatre went dark and a light shined down from the top left corner onto a rough looking individual who wore a green chequered shirt and sharp oversized teeth. He began to levitate around the stage until the theatre went light again.

Two more individuals on the stage appeared, one of them was wearing a black blazer with a grey jumper while the other wore a denim coat and tattoos. They were Adam Langley and Frank from Jobcall respectively. Both of them appeared to be lifting paper mâche bricks and placing them on top of other bricks to build a wall. Above was a sign bordered with lights that read out "COMMUNITY CENTRE". Suddenly I heard terrifying music that sounded like a church organ and the man slowly floated towards Adam while he was "building". The creature opened his mouth and his grew longer until he roared. The noise sounded like an aeroplane and a road works drill combined together and it made Adam run off the stage into the darkness. Then the man's fingers extended outward as he moved until they were long and sharp like daggers and he used them to slash Frank while he still levitated.

It was then I released the man with the green shirt and large teeth were an actor representing myself.

I convulsed because it was nearly accurate. I wanted to scream but unfortunately I could not in my dreams and attempted to run away. There was one door behind the rear seats and it started to shrink rapidly, including the EXIT sign above the door. As I ran toward the door to escape, I turned around and saw the actor flying directly towards myself with his fingers stretched out and making that industrial noise.

And then I woke up.

33

There was no going back, it was time for Geoffrey to man up and face his skeletons once and for all, for his wife and everyone else, no matter what the outcome will be.

******

Today was going to be a positive day because I will be going to Welbourne Mills again in order to meet James, Simon, Gary, Emma, Amanda and the other residents for the weekend; and this day would be a highly significant one because it would be the first time that my Dad will be driving myself up there properly. Previously he only stopped outside the entrance on the main road which meant that I had to walk for fifteen minutes with my heavy blue suitcase, while trying to avoid dirty puddles on the path simultaneously. There was an individual from the Bravo House who would only walk on the grass in the middle of the path and one day he paused for an hour because there was an 8ft long puddle that had covered the grass and blocked his only pathway.

Another reason why this would be highly significant were because three VIPs were going to appear in the special village after 3pm to have their photograph taken with all of the residents, before they present the chairwoman Mrs Hinton with a giant cheque and promptly leave.

I officially said goodbye to my mother but I've noticed since I arrived back home and celebrated the party that I was increasingly going to miss her company or presence for the next few days. So I decided to give her another cuddle instead. Soon we were both situated inside the driveway of our house, ready to depart in Dad's car for North Yorkshire.

'Right, are you ready to leave then?'

'Yes.'

'Before we set off, I've got a treat for you hiding inside the glove box, open it.' He pointed towards his silver car, which he promptly unlocked with his car keys. I opened the front passenger door, pressed the plastic button on the glove compartment door and felt a small bag which I pulled out. It had green and white vertical stripes, a black opening and a transparent window that revealed what was inside. It was a bag of luxury Everton mints. 'I don't think you feel like yourself recently since you stopped eating them,' said my Dad as he climbed into the car and fastened his seatbelt. 'That's only my opinion, but at least we have something to eat along the way.'

'Yes, I agree,' replied myself, which felt strange because my Dad had not been feeling like himself as well.

******

Since we left Orpington we only travelled on the motorways (except for a brief section outside Dartford), until my Dad decided to leave the M1 for no reason despite there being an absence of heavy road works that would sometimes turn the motorway orange because of its excessive signs and highway beacons scattered around the lanes.

We travelled through a suburban area, into a town centre and continued driving down the main road until the houses were replaced with green fields. Then I saw a white road sign with a black stripe and a board below itself that read "Thank you for driving carefully". But instead of passing the sign, my Dad pulled over the car, waited until the road was clear and performed a u-turn before driving back into the town centre again. When we passed the pedestrian crossing again he sharply turned left and continued to turn left and right into several minor roads, so rapidly that I could not read the names of each road properly until he drove alongside a park fenced off by a stone wall. But when he turned left for the last time I could clearly read the name of this road because of the huge plaque on the entrance, it read "Arnot Hill Park & Civic Centre."

The road was actually a car park adjoining the park that was protected by the stone wall and unlike the car parks back in Orpington there were trees standing in front of the parking spaces and I quickly noticed that one of the trees was enclosed by tarmac instead of a square of dry soil. There were eight cars inside the car park, five of them were parked together in a row and my Dad decided to park our silver car away from the group of cars so that both of us could stare at the hedges and the trees.

'You might be wondering why I have driven us here,' he said, removing his glasses and rubbing his right eye 'there is something that your mother and I have forgotten to tell you; and given the circumstances that I may face in future I think this is the best way to get it out.'

'?'

'Do you remember when your teacher told us about your name being

194

forged and ridiculed around your old school so that it read rude words like Arnold Hitler or A.Hole?'

'Yes. Why?'

'And you may have wondered before why you have felt like you're the only "Arnold" at your school?'

'No,' I said honestly. What was so intriguing about my forename?

'Well the reason why you have that name was because you were not named after a person, nor did we use a book of names to help us decide at the hospital, you were named after the place you were born.'

'The hospital?'

'No Arnold you were born here, in a town called Arnold,' finished my Dad in a serious voice. This was illogical, he had postponed the journey to the "special village" and diverted our route off the M1 for over 5 miles to stop inside a suburban car park, so that he could announce the real origin behind my forename. I have watched a couple of American films in the past where the character would perform the same actions as my Dad had done, except that the character would either announce that he was going to commit suicide and die, or that the person inside the car listening to the character was going to commit suicide and die instead.

'Why are we inside a car park?' I asked, trying to change the subject.

'Because I wanted to tell you where you were born. This was the spot where my little Ford at the time broke down just before your mother went into labour while carrying you and she was screaming and grabbing at me for all the wrong reasons. Don't you care about that!?'

'Yes. Was I born in the car park?'

'Well, no. Luckily a local called the ambulance and they arrived just in time to take her to a hospital just outside Nottingham before the pains got worse. But if the ambulance were a minute late, you would have ended up being born here.' Oh.

'If I was born here instead, would my name be Arnot Hill Holt?' I asked.

'Unlikely. I would've called you Bentley instead after my favourite type of car, but your mother would not accept that so I made that your middle name instead,' he replied, winking at myself. As we continued to sit inside the car, I heard my Dad's mobile phone create a noise and while he were trying to pick it out from his pocket (while sitting down) I opened the bag and swallowed another mint. He looked at his phone briefly and inserted it back into his pocket. 'I thought it would be appropriate to tell you this while we're here. You should be lucky were having this conversation because premature babies have a

195

very small chance of surviving.'

'Pardon?'

'There are hundreds of people born prematurely and most of them don't get to live the life that you're having right now. It's like what your Mum said; life is a gift that you must cherish. And sometimes you learn that everything is not necessarily about you and that in reality we're just very small cogs in the colossal contraption that we call civilisation. Well that's how I learned it, but I know your version would be absolutely different. Do you know what I mean by that Arnold?'

I was quite unsure but I believed him. 'Yes,' I replied.

'I also wanted to call your sister Lexus after another brand of car but that's another story. Let's go then shall we?'

'Yes, OK.'

'Actually I have a better idea.' Instead of leaving promptly, my Dad exited the car and walked toward the black metal arches that stood in front of the park. I ran after him and watched as the tarmac path changed into a gravel path and then into a concrete pathway, where it was covered with pigeon defecation. The path expanded and stopped at a filthy stone fountain where I finally found my Dad. He was staring at the coins as well as the crisp packets and bottles that were standing inside the fountain which was half full of water. I asked him why he was staring at them and he replied that the fountain gave him positive memories and that he wanted to forget all the negative ones, until we left the park. Then he said that I should join him as well because I was very good with this exercise and it reminded myself of the hidden places I used to visit in Orpington and Welbourne Mills, like the lonely corner. We stood silently together in front of the fountain with the sun shining between the leaves from above until a very noisy duck emerged from between the bushes.

One minute later we left the car park and eventually we left Nottinghamshire and travelled back on the dual carriageway again. I thought carefully about what my father mentioned to myself.

Apart from my relevance with the fountain and the founding of my very name, what was I supposed to achieve from that discovery?

******

The A1 had been moved, improved and widened since Geoffrey's childhood days, and now the M1 even ran straight into this long historic highway which for himself found rather hard to swallow because he thought that the M1 should have stopped at Leeds instead of bouncing off to the right to become a one hundred and eighty mile bypass of the A1, which was very slowly being converted to becoming a motorway itself. He tried not to think about these conundrums, for they would sometimes affect his driving and have him driving into another ditch.

Quite interestingly they were lucky enough not to come across any road works while driving from the East Midlands, for the first time Geoffrey was praying inside his head that a tailback caused by a closed lane would appear out of nowhere on the dual carriageway because it would give him enough time to relax and prepare for confronting the fear that had been stinging his brain for the last few months and ultimately extinguish it for good without his family knowing. Just time to think, he thought. His eyes stung so he glanced over to the left to Arnold to wonder what he was thinking about. His eyes were fixed on the green and white road signs that passed by but his hand was nestled deep into the bag of Evertons that they bought along and every 6 minutes or so Arnold would pick up a sweet and post it into his mouth without taking his eyes off the window as if he were being fed by a mechanical arm.

The road was rather quiet and the sky was a healthy shade of orange as it reached sunset when they managed to catch up with news of the apparent chaos that had been brewing up north. In normal circumstances they would've steered clear of the trouble by driving away 50 miles and hiding in any backwater retreat but instead they want to plunge right into the eye of the storm for two very contrasting reasons. One wanted to meet his friends and former special needs assistant who appeared to have had an unbroken bond with him since childhood; and the other wanted to overcome his paranoia of bumping into anyone from the epicentre, anyone who would recognise him and expose his difficult secret which could have implications on his family and his job.

Just as they were approaching the turn in there was a mixture of awe and shock when they realised that a purple minibus with orange stripes had lodged itself in the entrance to Welbourne Mills, right between the wooden gates allowing no room for a single person to pass through without touching the coach or the gate. Geoffrey initial thought was *"Well if we can't get in, we'll go home"* so using the space between the blockage and the road he tried to pull off a u-turn but when Arnold realised what his plan was, he wasn't going to take defeat.

Then there was a chorus of blunt banging noises as he heard his son's fists hammer against the side window. Once he had stopped the banging Geoffrey took a deep breath and started to slowly accelerate. He was nearly hitting 40mph when something bright yellow with a gleaming bald head jumped out of a hedge and being dancing on the roadside, waving his arms around like a deranged fitness instructor.

'Stop! Look it is Simon!' Arnold shouted unexpectedly.

'Who?'

'Simon Hanley. He lives in the special village. Stop the car please!' Following his wishes, Geoffrey pulled the car to a complete stop and watched as Arnold yanked the door open and galloped straight towards Simon. When was the last time he actually saw him run in order to greet friends or family? Excluding Raymond of course because the two felt like identical twins whenever they played together. He tried to clear his head of this thought and slowly made his way to meet this yellow guest who was sitting on the verge. On closer inspection he realised that Simon was completely bald to the point where his eyebrows were missing as well, except for neat pencil lines. His yellow jacket was filthy during close up with twigs, nettle thorns and grass stains protruding out of them. His grey tracksuit bottoms, the only part of Simon's body that never stood out was also covered in thorns and there was a small wet patch on Simon's right leg, slightly below his groin.

He was panting and sweating so loudly that he couldn't speak a single clear sentence. They decided to give Simon a minute to relax so that he can stand up and tell them what had happened that made him all flustered, but before he got the chance to recover a humungous trailer with eight wheels screamed past without warning and made the three bystanders jump out of their skin. Geoffrey then ushered Simon into his car so that they can get a proper glimpse of his story without turning into northern road kill.

'Please help, we are in trouble,' panted Simon slowly.

'What is in trouble? Where have you been?' asked my Dad.

'Welbourne Mills. Staff are missing, everything is locked, he's wrecking everything.'

'Why has it gone wrong?' enquired Arnold.

'Arnold give him five minutes to catch his breath for god's sake,' snapped Geoffrey before turning his attention back to Simon. 'Right, when you're ready.' It took two and a half minutes for the chronic breathing to stop before he could speak clearly.

'Mark One.'

'Who?'

'Mark One. Music Mark, lives in the Bravo House.'

'Bravo House? Is that a residential area?'

'Yes. He has gone crazy and no one can stop him.'

'Why has Mark One become insane Simon?' asked Arnold.

'Because someone has stolen one of his records.'

'What!?' exclaimed Geoffrey.

34

Anarchy and complete destruction roared from inside. The socialising room was a far from welcoming place where the most vulnerable of souls would meet up to chat about almost anything. Tables were upturned, sofas had their cushions ripped out of them and strewn across the room, and even a window was cracked. If Simon saw all the mess and destruction that had just took place while retreating, he would've pulled out what was left of his hair before passing out on the floor in shock. Inside one corner of the devastated room there was a pyramid of cushions, plastic school chairs and tables all hastily jumbled together to make a miniature fort. To make it look more like a battlefield, a white paper towel tied to one of the broken table legs was crudely poking out of the makeshift shelter.

Inside Mark's head it sounded like a siren was blaring loudly in red alert, getting louder and louder as time passed because he felt like a stick of dynamite that had been lit and the only way to stop the sirens from blaring is to defuse it before he explodes. But the sirens were also getting faster inside his head and to drown out the pain he lifted up a chair with his adrenalin fuelled arms and smashed it onto the wooden floor, separating the chair from its plastic legs.

The three victims who were hiding behind the pyramid of chairs and cushions also felt their own individual sirens playing inside their own minds; the intensity wasn't as great as the ones rattling through Mark's brain but they could also imagine the atmosphere turning red and revolving around the nightmare of a 16 stone man who also had the audacity attack a fellow resident 20 minutes earlier out of primal anger.

'Mark One just hit me, he hit me, he hit me,' cried a female resident as she crouched down in the kitchenette, wiping the tears off her blemished face. Watching underneath the jumble of furniture was James, Barry and Jonathan, another resident who lived in Bravo House. Out of the three it was actually James who felt the most agitated out of them, because overall he felt that he most the most 'sane' out of all the residents who lived here and had even picked up leadership skills while being here. The exit out of the social room was only three big paces away and if he had all the courage, James would've burst out of the heap, leap over to the door behind Mark's back, lift the latch and go find help. But there was something in the kitchenette that he really needed to pick up first before making that heroic escape, and that was a large sachet of HP Sauce. As most of the staff didn't know, James Kyle Warwicker suffered from OCD and to him, picking up a little sauce sachet was essential to saving himself and his friends from a violent man.

Outside it was an altogether different form of anarchy. Litter bins were pushed over, screams filled the air and all four of the dormitory blocks were mysteriously locked, causing an uproar of yelling and banging from the terrified residents as they found themselves locked from the inside AND the outside. Around the green a small handful of residents walked calmly along and stopped to watch as people of different ages and disabilities ran frantically from building to building around in their colourful garments, some covering their faces with their hands, others even crying.

'What is going on? Why is everybody running around the place? Is this a rehearsal for a play being shown tonight in the recreation room? Should we join them as well? Or not? I don't know but I want to be alone right now,' were a couple of thoughts from the brave but oblivious onlookers who were having trouble figuring out how to respond to this situations because there was nobody around to tell them what had been going on and why everyone had been running around like headless chickens.

And the people who were supposed to be looking after them? Where had all the jolly faced staff with their maroon-coloured clothes been the whole time? And why haven't they flown into the social room to stop Mark Cranley from causing any more destruction?

The answer was quite simple; they were all locked up too, everyone including their boss.

******

We were standing outside my Dad's car now, looking at the minibus that was blocking the entrance. Simon tried to carefully explain to my Dad why the police or the other public authorities had not appeared automatically to remove the minibus and save the village but my Dad only kept asking Simon difficult questions that he could not answer.

'So can you get the paramedics to restrain him or not?' asked my Dad to Simon who was shaking his head in disagreement. He did not have a solution on how to save the "special village" from Mark One and that was why he decided to escape through one of the exits that don't appear on the map. To get outside help, Simon would say because inside help was completely impossible because all the staff and communication devices were locked away. 'Has anyone called the police yet about this?'

'I don't know,' shrugged Simon 'The only reason I came here was to call for help or find a telephone booth.'

'That is because we don't use mobile phones,' I replied helpfully.

'Well is there any way that we could help for now?' asked my Dad again.

'Quick, through here!' pointed Simon as he directed us into a circle cut into a hedge that faced the main road. This was actually one of the secret entrances into the "special village" where none of the staff or the volunteers know of its existence, not even Mrs Leslie. The last time I actually used it was when I went on a classic countryside ramble across the road with James and two other residents whose names I could not remember. The secret footpath ran into a heavily forested area where we were invisible from anybody who used the official entrance to Welbourne Mills. We had to push branches away from our faces and avoid muddied pools to continue but the secret entrance actually lead to the back of the reception, away from the security cameras.

'What's that over there Simon? Is that supposed to be normal?' asked my Dad. I tried to squint between the tree branches and we saw a narrow grey smoke that rose upwards from where the car park would be located.

'No because we do not have chimneys in the reception,' I replied.

'It's a fire! Quick! We must move before we're burned! Haste!' shouted Simon who then jumped up in surprise and ran straight to the end of the footpath as if we were invincible. The footpath finished at a green wire fence that was damaged at the bottom which meant that we had to crouch to cross the fence. But when my Dad tried to crawl through the fence he screamed a little and I heard something tear loudly like fabric.

'Well there goes my no claims bonus,' he said for no reason whatsoever. 'So I am guessing that minibus belongs to that group over there, who are trying to burn down this place?'

'Erm… I could take you to the others. They may know who they are.'

'OK,' replied my Dad, who sounded as if he was going to shout. Instead he silently followed Simon who tiptoed behind the temporary reception where the minibus protestors were unable to see ourselves. We stopped again to view the smoke and ash that was rising upward and then we heard a dog whistle. I turned toward the source of the sound and I felt mildly relieved to see that Neil, Oliver and Kimberley had appeared and were standing inside a circle around Simon. Soon myself and my Dad would join them to increase the circle.

'Help! We can't get back into our rooms!' cried Neil.

'And all the people are locked inside that big building, even Marcia is in there,' said Ollie in his regular voice.

'I can't go and eat my toast,' said Kimberley, who was pointing at my Dad 'Has he come to rescue us Simon?'

'No, he is my father,' I replied innocently to Kimberley. The other residents then all stared at my Dad for no reason, which might had scared him because he walked a step backwards.

'Right, as you already know, the police are utterly incapable right now, so I'm guessing it's our duty to put it right. We can't go out the front right now because we'll be mauled by whatever came from that minibus, but I am quite certain that it was them who locked your friends inside.'

'Yeah!' shouted a few.

'Shush, they may hear us,' warned Ollie. Although I had listened to every word that my Dad had mentioned, I had a negative feeling that his objectives weren't going to work. His overall plan, if it had already finished, would only save 70% of the individuals in Welbourne Mills, instead of the 100% that he would expect. That was because he had forgotten to remember the other disaster that was damaging the "special village".

'So, perhaps if we can open the doors somehow and rescue the staff and then we-'

'We need to retrieve the stolen CD and return it to Mark One!' shouted myself.

'Huh? Pardon?'

'The reason why Mark One is currently insane is because one of his favourite items has been stolen.'

'Oh I see now. But Arnold, how is that supposed to help the situation?'

'If you unlock the doors then Mark One will continue to hurt residents and staff colleagues. If we also find his beloved CD that would be the only way we can prevent him from attacking more individuals.'

'I'm not too sure about that. Arnold you're forgetting that you don't know-'

'Yeah, I agree with Arnold!' cheered Ollie.

'Me too as well!' said Kimberley.

'Well maybe there is a way we could do both of those things,' said my

203

Dad as he wiped his face 'but you all need to work together.'

'Together?' asked Kimberley.

'Yes and I mean it. If any one of you trail off or let your disability get in your way then we're all going to be mauled by that lot. So while Arnold goes off to stop the psycho record collector, we'll figure out a way to break the locks and free the captives. Got it?'

While I agreed with what my Dad mentioned, some of my friends shook hands with each other and decided to split into two teams. Within my Dad's team there was Oliver, Neil, Kimberley, as well as David and Priya who joined them despite not being present to listen to the plan. In my team it was myself, Simon and Roger who decided to help us because he wanted to help in our "adventure". Once we were ready to start our plan, I had a sudden burst of excitement when I realised that for the very first time, I was actually going to lead a small team of individuals which was an activity that I had never followed.

So once I waved goodbye to my Dad I walked down the slope along with my team to finally begin our plan.

35

As Arnold and Simon branched off to start their own mission, Geoffrey felt slightly confused and light headed when he realised that his son had just left him with a couple of vulnerable adults who were either were going to see him as their new temporary leader, or attack him just because they didn't like the colour of his shoes. Nearly everything he saw was virtually new to him, the diagram of the site was an example and yet with a single glance he knew automatically which area they would need to "attack" first in order to carry out their plan.

'OK, am I right in saying that roundabout in the middle of that map is the heart of this place?' asked Geoffrey.

'That is where Emma, Lauren and Marcia and the rest are locked so yeah,' replied Ollie.

'So I'm guessing that there is a caretaker's workshop is down there as well, yes?' Nobody replied back except for a single nod from Neil.

'Well at least we're getting somewhere,' sighed Geoffrey who wiped his brow and put one foot on a wooden stump 'so the plan is this. We go down to the recreational area, find a set of bolt cutters, break off the locks and release the staff before safely evacuating them away from that smoke. Any questions?' There was an awkward silence as Geoff expected them to ask him to go through any word in his speech that they would not traditionally understand like evacuate, but they didn't.

'I know an easier way,' purred Kimberley. She turned and then scurried off behind the temporary wooden fence that surrounded the old Welbourne Mills reception. Between the rickety building and some stinging nettles were a set of metal construction gates that were badly tied together by a blue rope. Geoffrey followed Kimberley who was peering between the bars of the metal gate and joined her along with Ollie, trying to figure out what her "solution" might be. When he finally realised what it was Geoff had a sudden change of mind, surely she must be playing a joke on him but when he remembered the smoke, the bolted up houses and the voices trapped inside them, there was no time to sit down and continue pondering with a group of hapless adults.

So he grabbed his mobile phone out of his pocket, dialled the numbers very carefully and cringed when he saw that the residents were watching him in awe. Everything appeared to focus directly on Geoffrey until the phone finally picked up.

'Hey Geoff, how's it going lately?' roared Tony.

'Great, could I speak to Raymond please?'

'Certainly, why just last week he's-'

'It's quite urgent you see-'

'Ah yes, there was this programme on IT-'

'Raymond NOW PLEASE!' Over the phone a soft fumbling noise that sounded like a gust of wind could be heard and Tony's brash voice was soon replaced by a much younger but less cheerful voice that feel much easier on Geoff's ears.

'Hello?'

'Ray it's your uncle Geoff. I'm in a bit of a pickle at the moment and I know that your specific knowledge can help me.'

'Why, what's going on?'

'I'm going to save a village.'

******

Three minutes ago, the mission to find and return Mark One's missing vinyl record had officially begun. I tried to imagine the map of the "special village" inside my head whilst walking, which I found very difficult. I tried to pretend that there was a single red arrow on the ground that I was assigned to follow around the whole centre, one that would take myself past every building, classroom, shed, bin, allotment, signpost and chicken without repeating or omitting an area by error. The missing record could be anywhere in this establishment, except for Mark One's bedroom which contained eight continuous shelves of classic records inside their covers that were always locked every time he left his room. From the reception we would begin the search from the south-western corner of the map, before moving north toward Alpha House. But first I would need to tell Simon carefully about my plan so that he would understand and support my search.

'Hey you!'

'Pardon?'

'This is all your fault, go away!' I turned my head and noticed that it was Charlie, one of the residents from Delta House whom I saw at the canteen during my introduction. He was wearing a padded blue jacket with a white carrier bag poking out of one of the dirty pockets but what was more disgusting was that he were also drooling heavily from his mouth.

'Pardon?' I asked.

'This place used to be a happy place. Now it is nasty all because of you! Go away!'

Then Charlie placed his left hand inside the carrier bag and pulled out a round brown object. He then shook his arm and dropped the object but it landed on my left shoe instead and the object was so heavy that I could actually feel it pressing down on my foot despite during two layers of appropriate footwear. Suddenly I heard a brief yell come from Simon and between his legs was a similar object to the one that came from Charlie's carrier bag. They were throwing stones.

'Why are they hitting us with stones?' I asked Simon, but before he could answer he turned around and ran away. I looked at Charlie again and all four of his friends had their arms stretched out with a heavy object gripped in each of their hands, including a hole puncher. I stared Simon's attackers and felt genuinely frightened when all five of them were staring at myself with huge eyes and they were all drooling together as well. So I ran.

'Get him!' And I sprinted out of the green as fast as I could, my heart pounded heavily and my lungs scraped themselves as I tried to promptly remember where Simon had ran off to, in the anticipation that he had retreated to a safer part of the "special village" where the other residents and the staff are hiding (I do hope that Gary, Amanda and Mrs Leslie are safe and unhurt).

If only Mrs Leslie was present at that very minute, she would have defeated this horrible situation.

******

Raymond quickly gave him a brief lesson on how to use every button, gear and lever that was inside the filthy, worn out digger with as much detail as he could in as littlest time as possible. He was also about to tell Geoffrey how to break into the cockpit without using a key (which to himself was the most important part of driving a JCB) until Kimberley mindlessly picked up a brick and hurled it straight for the cab window, smashing it in one hit.

He then opened his wallet, pulled out his locker key from work and examined it very closely with his thumb and forefinger.

If this fits in Ray I'm buying you a pint after all this, thought Geoff as his mind wandered briefly. The key was wafer thin and the right size so he wasn't too surprised when the engine roared into life after he plugged it into the ignition slot on his first attempt. For the first four minutes the digger started dancing merrily on the bricks with its front scoop, before twirling rapidly from side to side before lurching backward and forward again, crushing a plastic bucket in the process. Ollie, Neil and Kimberley watched and laughed as the digger splashed into a cement stained puddle and then Neil let out a little yell when he realised Geoffrey was coming straight for him, gesturing with his hands to get out of the way. Luckily Ollie grabbed Neil by his satchel and shoved him face first against the metal construction gate, so that Geoffrey could now leave the confines of the filthy, disorganised and abandoned site of the future reception and head straight onto the clean cut grass and smooth gravel paths that surrounded Welbourne Mills.

As he skirted along the top of the grassy bank Geoffrey treated himself to the stunning view of the buildings and lodges below with its residents walking and running between the houses, and behind them was the unmistakable rolling fields and valleys of the North Yorkshire Dales, just like in that sitcom his son liked to watch sometimes. The one where that pensioner had the same voice as that plasticine man called Gromit, he thought. Along different sections of the grassy bank Neil and Kimberley were running ahead, waving and whistling at him as he drove up to rear of the temporary reception, where the hill is less steep. Before he trundled down the hill to join his new friends, Geoffrey gave a deep breath and made a little honorary thought to himself before clutching the gear that sent him forward.

And the little thought was this: Let the liberation begin.

Soon the residents watched in curiosity and fear as the muddy digger roared down the grassy slope and flattened every daisy and molehill in its path, while its driver bounced around recklessly in the cockpit. Geoffrey now imagined what it must feel like to be the little arrow inside a Geiger counter, the device that flickers left to right as it tries to measure how much radiation there is in the atmosphere but won't bother to stand still and give an exact measurement. Of course he wouldn't pick up radiation poisoning from driving a JCB but he would pick up a very nasty headache. There was also a very nasty smell of white spirit that the last driver left behind in the cockpit. He didn't really mind it but it was distracting his ability to focus on the waving men who appeared to be bouncing in the front window. The persistent hum of the engine was really doing Geoff's head in so he stopped the digger and yanked his head out of the cab window.

'Hey. Turn left,' shouted the young blonde haired one, who was in fact Ollie. Using the right lever (with Ray's help again) Geoffrey steered it to the left towards the lake but was greeted with a chorus of low pitched no's and a lot of angry waving. 'Sorry, I mean to go right.'

'OK, but can you speak a little faster?' growled Geoffrey who was furious towards Oliver and his speech impediment.

'Sor-ry, I'll be faster next time,' apologised Ollie.

'Thank you,' said Geoffrey, who with a frown on his face slammed the door shut and got back to driving the digger again. Once his hands were clamped shut onto the clutches he imagined himself again, this time he imagined jumping out of the JCB before marching over to Ollie and touching a dial that magically appeared on the autistic person's chest that was set to "Tortoise". Then he imagined himself shoving the dial right up to "Hare" which to Geoffrey's eyes magically sped up Ollie's thoughts and reactions.

Back to reality the digger driving felt smoother on the gravel path and the humming noise in the engine seemed to have diminished. Within a few minutes he found himself right in the heart of Welbourne Mills and completely surrounded by shallow buildings. To Geoffrey it reminded him of what *Center Parcs* might look like if it weren't covered in 50ft tall pine trees. Then all of a sudden Neil walked out in front of the digger and began pointing towards a particular building in this unusual village. This building was different to the others because it was silver instead of cream or brown (like all the other buildings) and it carried a long flat roof which had a crude chimney poking from the top like an iron hat. When he steered the JCB closer Geoffrey noticed that there was a thick brass chain and padlock keeping the two doors at its entrance from opening. Looking intrigued, he stopped the JCB to have a look at the people waving from inside. One of them opened a window as far as she could by a few inches so that Geoffrey could speak to her.

'We were called to have a meeting about the upcoming VIP visit with all the staff. But when we tried to leave, we noticed that somebody had locked the front doors as well as the fire exits. We tried to call the staff in the lodges but they were all locked in too. Then we tried to call the police but we don't know long they'll take because we're about over 30 miles from the nearest police station.'

'Well your guys bought me here with this so I'm guessing they have a plan,' said Geoffrey who was trying to be casual by leaning on the digger. He looked over to the individuals who guided him down here for more clues and saw that six of them were lined up on each side of the padlocked doors in a pair of three and were all waving together at him as if the yellow digger was a plane and their specific job was to land that plane into the locked doors. Geoffrey then tasted the fumes from the digger and swallowed bitterly when he realised what their plan really was.

'Oh no, don't tell me you're going to use that to break down the door. No no no, I'm not having it, that's vandalism. I could be charged!'

'We've got no other choice.'

'I say do it,' championed Gary 'there are people who need our help and they need it now.'

There was a nice big wooden ramp in front of the staff HQ that was wide enough for the digger to drive forward and ram open. Pulling the levers as softly as possible Geoffrey dropped the front scoop very slowly so that it went in line with the padlock on the front door. This was it, he thought solemnly. After telling Neil to kindly get out of the way, he revved the engine and at the top speed of 10mph made a running charge for the front doors. Unfortunately the ramp was built for physically impaired residents and not for heavy yellow diggers so there wasn't much surprise when half of the ramp collapsed under the wheels which nearly caused Geoffrey to go off course to career towards the vulnerable people who were shaking with fear behind the windows.

It was too much for senior staff like Denise and Rita Leslie who had their backs turned and faces covered as they heard an almighty crunch, shatter and growl that now crept into the very room they were hiding. Once the noise had stopped Gary and Ryan took their hands off their ears and bravely strode into the reception of the staff HQ to examine the damage that this vigilante had done as well as gaze at the doors which they thought would've been ripped from their hinges.

Well they didn't need to use the door because Geoffrey had cut out a nice new hole for them to use instead.

'You were only supposed to blow the bloody doors off,' shouted Gary quietly but nobody laughed back.

36

'AAAHHHHH!'

'My ears they hurt bad! It sounds like a million crisps being eaten!'

'I don't like the noise too. It hurts my head. I don't wanna be here.'

Once I heard that peculiar sound, I stopped running and turned my head towards the stone throwing residents who sounded like they were screaming. Charlie and one of his friends had vanished but the remaining friends were all kneeling down on the muddy ground, each with their hands covering their own ears and their "weapons" lying on the ground. Andy (one of the attackers) appeared to be suffering badly because I could see that his eyes beneath his glasses were clamped shut and he had mucus flowing down from his nostril, which nearly made myself feel sick.

But instead of confronting Andy for first aid I continuing running further because I feared that if I stopped there Charlie would return with more stones and more people which would result in myself asking for first aid or the hospital. So I decided to run towards the lonely corner instead.

The lonely corner was a secretive place where certain individuals could temporarily detach themselves from staff and other residents from the "special village" and pretend to be alone for a short period of time. It did not appear on the map outside the reception but it was located behind an unused classroom and it contained a gigantic tree that had a distinctive long branch that was longer than the tree trunk itself. To enter the lonely corner one must travel to the north-eastern corner on the map, descend a hill and encounter a dirty wooden hut and a wire fence that was supported by thin wooden planks. That was the official boundary of Welbourne Mills. But the wire fence did not run behind the building and it could be "curled up" so that the lonely corner can be reached without injury.

In order to escape Charlie I ran towards the eastern boundary of the "special village" because it lay at the bottom of a hill and behind the hedges where I would be invisible to himself and his weapons. Then I sprinted alongside the wire fence, gazed at the deep woodland that it held back until a filthy black hut with an overhanging tree behind it broke the fence's pattern. Then I felt slightly dismayed when the fence was already rolled back which meant that somebody had reached the lonely corner first. One of the rules of the lonely corner was that only one individual was allowed inside it at the time, otherwise the existence behind its usage would then be contaminated and destroyed (according to one of the residents at Charlie House). But when I peered between the wooden panels I realised who the culprit was.

It was Simon, he was looking up. Why was he looking up? Then I knew why. Up on the giant tree, lying between two thick branches that rose from the top of the solid main was Mark One's beloved record disc. But collecting the disc was inaccessible because the tree trunk was 9ft high which meant that it cannot be collected alone. It could be possible to stand on top of Simon's shoulders in order to collect it but the tree trunk was covered in a slippery green moss and the last time one of the residents touched Simon he threw a watering can at her head and he was escorted to another remote part of the "special village".

'Sorry Arnold you can't come in,' he called.

'We need to retrieve the record disc at once. Otherwise Mark One will continue his rage.'

And then he turned around, laid both his hands on his head and moaned.

'What is wrong?' I asked.

'I am OK now. But you are right.'

Four minutes later, Roger squeezed through the fence and arrived, followed by Kimberley, Priya, Neville, Christopher, Julian as well as five more residents whose names I had not learnt yet.

'Why are you all in the lonely corner at once?' asked Simon 'What about the rules?'

'Sorry Simon but those guys from the yellow house are throwing stones at us for no reason,' said Julian.

'We need somewhere to hide,' said another resident.

'So we chose this place.'

'Because it is safe.'

'OK then,' moaned Simon 'as this is an emergency for all of us, I'll let the rules be broken. We need to stop those nasty protestors from destroying our home.'

'Hear hear!'

'Yeah!'

'So how can we stop them Simon?' asked Kimberley. Then there was a pause.

'We need to climb up the tree and retrieve the record.' I proclaimed.

'How is that going to stop those evil protestors?'

'If we return the record disc back to Mark One, there would be a high probability that he would cease his terrible rampage and therefore increase our chances of saving the staff as well as Welbourne Mills.' There was another pause that gave me a fright because everybody (including Simon) was looking at myself with sharp stares, which also made my right hand go underneath my left armpit and tremble.

'Can't we leave him in there?' asked one of the unnamed people. Then suddenly there was a dry rustling noise that came from the wire fence and everyone then turned their heads to see the intruder and this positive distraction stopped my heart from beating furiously. It was Ollie.

'Hey guess what everyone? The guys are free!' Everybody apart from myself cheered, hoorayed and began to jump up and down in excitement. The reason why I did not join them was because our mission was still incomplete.

'Should I get Gary and the others to speak to Mark One?' Simon asked myself.

'No,' I said.

'No? But why not Arnold?'

'The "special village" staff and Mrs Leslie cannot stop Mark One from hurting the others. The only way we can save him is by reuniting himself with his precious record disc. I know because a similar event had happened to myself five years ago.'

'Five years ago?' asked Kimberley.

'Ooohhhh, yeah now I remember,' said Ollie 'One time when I was eight my dad snatched my *Power Rangers* toy and I did a mega huge tantrum in front of my aunt until he gave it back to me. So I know what you mean Arnold.'

'Yeah me too, nothing can come between me and my map collection. If they tried to steal one of my maps, I would go crazy unless they bought it back and said sorry to me.'

'Same for my *Thomas the Tank Engine* models too,' continued another resident. 'One time when I was small my brother flushed Toby down the toilet so I ripped his hair out until he got it back.'

Then Kimberly spoke. 'Does this mean you're going to get the record?'

'Yes,' I replied. 'But I may need to stand on top of someone.' When I mentioned that sentence, some of the residents who were sat down then stood up and moved away from the tree, as if I had said something that was incorrect.

'Sorry Arnold,' said Simon 'but some of us don't like the idea of you standing on top of them.'

'I would help you too but I'm only 5 foot 2 and you may break my bones,' said Kimberley who was standing next to the tree. Nobody spoke for the next few seconds because we couldn't find an answer until Julian spoke.

'What about using this? I use it for my climbing.' Everybody turned towards him who then began to unbutton the pocket on his duffel coat and pulled out a thick, grey and untidy rope. I did not like its appearance because there were hundreds of fibres poking out of the rope but Julian said that was normal because it proved how strong it really was. Once Julian prepared the rope, he tied one end of the rope into a cowboy lasso and I placed the loop over myself so that the rope was around my chest. Then Roger grabbed the other end of the rope and tossed it over the branch were the record was placed and watched it hang lightly from the tree. He then grabbed the rope with his left hand and used his right hand to wave for some of the male residents to help him pull the rope. My nose felt sore and my armpits were tense as the rope slowly pulled around my chest and I was being lifted up. I looked down and I saw that Neville and Kimberley were standing below my feet as if they wanted to touch them but Neville said he only wanted to ensure that I was safe.

Two minutes later I was officially on the tree branch. It looked frightening because it looked as if the tree was over 30ft high and if I were to fall off due to my slippery shoes, I would probably land on my head which would mean result in failure to retrieve the record as well as receive terrible nightmares about two headed pigeons. But I was still attached to the rope, which felt like I was immune to falling off because the rope was connected to *The Naughty Autie Club*, except for Kimberley and Priya. As I crawled along the shrinking branch towards the prize I tried to avoid touching the damp green patches of the branch and soon understood how Simon would feel if he had to climb up the tree.

Ahead, the branch felt softer and split into two smaller branches with the record in-between. With my right arm, I very slowly retrieved the record and dropped it onto the grass where three residents then tried to pick up the record at the same time. But I was still up on the tree and I required a way to return to the ground without falling on my head.

'Hey Julian, is your rope normal?' said Ollie curiously.

'I don't know what you mean,' he replied.

'I think he's trying to say the rope is about to break,' shouted Christopher.

Pardon? 'Am I going to fall down?' I asked them below. Nobody replied. The sweat on my hands had increased and spread onto my sleeves as I tried to firmly clutch the branch. The individuals who were pulling the rope then all protested that I should be abseiled down the branch, although the rope contained a small section that looked like a mouse had tried to chew it. I wiped my sweated hands on the rope and held it tightly until I heard a soft snap and I fell out of the tree. But I relieved when I realised that I did not land on my head, nor my feet but I landed on a yellow object that had caught my back as well as the rear of my legs.

It was Simon who had caught myself. Then I heard a small clapping noise that came from the residents. 'Look, Simon had saved Arnold!' claimed an individual in the background.

'It's the first time I saw him touch someone without his gloves,' said Christopher. I turned around to look at Simon and he was rubbing his hands together under the branch after he applied a miniature bottle of hand soap.

'I know I don't like touching people,' he said 'but this was more important than looking after myself, you agree Roger?' Roger nodded and did not make a noise.

'Three cheers and beers for Simon and Arnold!' shouted Ollie, who had stolen one of Gary's quotes. Kimberley was holding the record so I walked over to collect it from her before I returned to the centre of the crowd and spoke.

'We are useless and weak while alone, but together we can all save this village. We do not need to rely on other individuals to motivate ourselves and send ourselves tasks or instructions any more, besides all of you are *The Naughty Autie Club*!'

'Yeah, he's right! When I'm on my own, I feel small. But when we're in a group, we're bigger.'

There was a small applause as I waved the record in front of them with my left hand. And then Julian made a massive cheer and raised his fist into the air as if he was a powerful soldier on a horse.

'Let's return this record back to Mark One before it is too late!' he cheered before we made a massive applause to approve his speech. Then we all left together, while carefully exiting through the wire fence one by one so that it would not become damaged and expose this secret area. One minute later, the lonely corner was officially lonely once again.

37

'I'm sorry, sorry. I am really sorry.'
After battering down the door and rescuing just under 20 staff and volunteers, Geoffrey Holt thought it was still necessary to justify why he had hijacked a JCB and used it to mindlessly crash it into their recreational suite, before parking it next to the canteen with the wooden door frame still hanging off the front scoop as if nothing had happened. But instead of being given a ticking off for rough vandalism, the prisoners were actually applauding and cheering him for setting them free and the autistic residents were doing the same except that a few tried to grab both of his legs and lift him up in the air as if he had scored a goal in the last ten seconds of a football game.

'Our hero!' called out one of the volunteers.

'Get this man a cigar, and perhaps some bricks too,' applauded Gary.

'I'm still sorry, honest,' continued Geoffrey as he tried to calm down the cheering captives one by one with no success before some of the senior staff huddled around him.

'Don't worry about it, what you did really helped and now we can help save the others which is better than nothing,' replied Dee. 'hey Rita, come and meet our knight and shining armour.'

'Well that's not really necessary, you see I'm eh?'

'Ah, nice to meet you again Mr Holt,' smiled Mrs Leslie.

'Huh!? You've met before? Are you-'

'No, no, I used to support his son back when I lived back in London.'

'Oh, they say a little knowledge goes a long way Rita.'
Geoffrey felt a little more disorientated by the ladies nattering away helplessly but he jumped and nearly gave a yell when an exceptionally short woman with a huge brow and chestnut hair, probably in her fifties strode straight in his path and yanked his hand.

'Hi, my name's Carole Hinton and I am the current chairperson of Welbourne Mills residential village. I would like to personally say thank you for rescuing us with your impromptu solution. I must say it is not a solution I would recommend doing again but this is an unexpected emergency which was deliberately planned and must be tackled immediately.' Everybody just looked at the two shaking hands around the rubble. Although shaking hands in this kind of scenario would raise a few eyebrows, some of the curious residents found this very amusing in their own heads and one of them though the man in the centre was going to get a knighthood from the manager.

'So what's the biz going on out there?' asked Gary.

'Well if you ask me,' said Geoffrey, brushing dust off his knee 'somebody has gone and locked all the buildings on this site and we think the culprits are up in the car park making a bonfire or something.'

'And Mark One has gone bananas in the playroom and beaten up Holly and Barry,' replied Neil, who wasn't making eye contact with anyone.

Marcia and Dee opened both of their mouths in horror. 'But Music Mark would never do anything like that, never! We've got to help him before he hurts another soul.'

'But that place is locked up as well,' repeated Geoffrey. 'If you're the head around here, you must know where all the backup keys are kept, right?'

Suddenly all eyes were on Carole. This was quite difficult for her because Carole was the kind of chairwoman who would spend most of her time in the office, either on the phone or holding meetings. Her current new year's resolution was to spend more time around the centre with the residents. Still, she had to deliver. 'Yes, most of the keys in this area are stored here but they appear to be stolen,' said Carole who was gesturing towards a white cubby hole filled with unused hooks. 'The rest of the keys are normally kept back in our reception and in the medical hut but it's too risky going up there at this time with the burning and commotion. Our priority at a time of crisis is to get ever'

'Or I could get the master keys from my workshop and we can open all the dorms at once.'

'And you are?' pointed Geoffrey towards a cocky looking man with five o clock shadow and a toned chest. He looked as if he had been asleep for the whole day.

'Stephan, I'm the site's handyman. If I had my belt on me I could've blown the hinges off the doors but you've done a much better job than I have.'

'But what if they locked the workshop as well?' asked an autistic bystander.

'It's not locked trust me, but like our friend had shown, there's more than one way to open a door.' Soon the whole crowd assembled together as Carole tried to think up a last minute plan.

'Right this is what we'll do. We will split up into three groups; groups A, B and C. Groups A and B will each take a master key and go around each side of the centre, opening any buildings that are locked with people inside. The other group, group C will then go to the social room and calm down Mark Cranley until the paramedics arrive. Once we unlock all the lodges and classrooms we will go into full evacuation procedure and send everyone up to the reception until further notice.'

'Roger that,' cried Gary.

'Haha he said Roger, the one who can't talk,' laughed one of the female residents. As Stephan ran back to the workshop, the crowd was rearranged into two groups with a member of staff playing the designated captain and key holder. Group A was led by Amanda with Rita and Lauren while Group B was going to be captained by Denise with Geoffrey and Emma. The team for Group C had been nominated yet because of its riskiness and the fact the majority of the group don't want to go near Mark Cavendish because he was dangerous. Rita's initial plan was to get a couple of volunteers to enter the social hub and distract him so that the captive residents can safely escape, while keeping physical contact to a minimum. Then he would be safely contained and subject to calming therapy until the paramedics arrive. Marcia, who had experience with controlling children with behavioural problems was selected to be the therapist but everyone nearly took a step back in fear when she asked for a few bodies to "cover" her if Mark were to lash out at her.

So when he arrived back with two silver keys, each tied to a block of wood bigger than his hand, Stephan reluctantly stepped up for the dangerous task, as well as Gary who felt that his amiable charm would help diffuse the situation. Once the master keys were handed over to each group, Gary pulled off a quick salute in front of the desperate crowd before Stephan and Marcia joined him side by side and made their way across the lodges.

'Good luck,' muttered a voice.

******

To outsiders, especially Geoffrey it was mad, surreal and possibly the most unrealistic way to manage a proper evacuation. But to the locals at Welbourne Mills the plan was quite simple. Marcia knew from past fire drills that trying to evacuate over 50 disabled adults, some of which were too oblivious to notice a burning building would be tedious and about as difficult as trying to clean a dirt encrusted oven with an old toothbrush.

And all they used was a 20ft long piece of white string. Whenever a drill was carried out at the centre, once the four houses were fully evacuated the fire marshal would unreel the string and the evacuated residents would then hold onto the string until the crowd changes from an untidy swarm into a neat organised line. Then the fire marshal would lead the crowd, any more evacuees that are found along the way would also hold onto the string until they reach the rendezvous point.

There was once a long running joke that this bizarre method was the only creative thing to come out from Welbourne Mills but to the staff they saw it as a personal achievement because the people who told that joke did not know what it was like to work with tens of disabled adults, especially ones who would get into a fit if someone brushed past them by accident. They had tried other evacuation methods in the past, but the string was much safer and a lot more time efficient, especially because the older staff spent less time guiding them around like lost sheep.

'Right, everybody get into a single line and that means everyone. In a minute Denise here will walk over to the top of the hill with the string and you all have to do is follow her. Do you all understand?'

'I left my video running in the-'

'Just leave the tape alone and please follow the-' said Geoffrey very sternly.

'DO NOT TALK TO ME LIKE THAT STRANGER, I'M GONNA TELL-'

Denise then jumped in and separated the two gentlemen apart. 'Calm down Perry, we're all doing a fire evacuation to the car park. Once we're finished you can go back to your video and rewind it back, OK?'

'But he called me a-'

'He didn't mean to shout at you on purpose. Because this is an emergency we all have to stop what we're doing and leave straight away. Do you understand?

'Yes.'

The passive crowd watched as Perry limped and slowly made his way to the back of the queue that was quickly forming along the string. Once all the residents made a perfect line Geoffrey turned his head to Denise and smiled. 'Thanks,' he said. During an emergency Geoff can't even think straight, let alone keep his temper but when he sees this amiable blonde step over and diffuse an argument just by being lovable and caring during a time of crisis, he wonders how she manages to do it.

Overall the white string was a complete success. As the two lines of evacuees snaked around the perimeter of the centre, Carole bought some of the remaining staff and volunteers to thoroughly check the epicentre of the village, with a walkie-talkie and a spare reel of string just incase they find several more resident who were still aimlessly walking around. There were at least four found minding their own business near the greenhouses while she called through on a walkie-talkie that there were still three more sitting around the pond in the distance. The third conga line was slowly snaking towards the visitor centre near the front to meet the larger two that in comparison were like two giant centipedes on the gravel paths.

When all three of the lines converged, the residents, volunteers, staff, chairperson and finally Geoffrey walked up the stairs and ramp along the grassy incline towards the rear of the reception where they saw a plume of grey smoke fading away in the sky, the smell of ash and burnt firewood that was strong enough to be tasted. One of the senior residents, a ginger haired man with thick rimmed glasses, tried to taste one of the flakes of ash with his tongue but Marcia asked him kindly not to do that. As the reception lobby was too small to take a large crowd, they opened the set of wooden gates that linked the reception building with the construction fence and they were immediately greeted by a group, actually a cluster of tens of angry men and women, young and old with clothes and features that made them look cleaner and more diverse than the residents. A few were even waving picket boards in the air behind a dying bonfire, while the rest appeared to be shouting or sneering, as if every single one of them had a bone to pick with the "special village".

'Who are these people?' asked one of the residents.

'Why are you doing this to us? Why have you burned down our reception?'

'We haven't burned down anything, the bonfire is just a way of letting you all know we're here and we've got serious business to deal with.' A skinny balding man with a full beard, purple sweatshirt and black tracksuit bottoms marched between the picket signs to stand face to face with them. He also had a thick northern accent, which the residents did not find too surprising. 'The reason why we're protesting is this: your establishment, Welbourne Mills is nothing but a white elephant and a waste of taxpayer's money. This place should be converted into a hospital or a centre for people who ARE actually disabled and need support unlike the lot that you're keeping here.'

Carole and Denise both looked defiant as they saw the protestors nodding their heads with the ringleader. Obviously this is not the first time these things have happened to Welbourne Mills and the staff all have immunity to verbal abuse apart from the most senior ones.

'And you think locking us all in will help with your little protest?' asked Carole.

'We're only here to make our point and to make it clear to you, which was why we made this huge bonfire out of your chairs and fences. And if I were you I would take your tacky uniform off and throw it in the bonfire as well'

'Yeah, my sister suffers from cerebral palsy and she can't get any living support from the council because they waste it on trivial things like this,' roared another protestor.

'In such a remote place like this, what this region really need is a hospital or a nursing home for the locals. Like my friend just said you already have your own "village" on the other side of the moors so this whole thing is just a waste of resources,' muttered a female protestor who wore spectacles. Geoffrey could tell by her attire and remark that this lady had a degree education of some sort, but he did not want to ponder it any further.

'You did not answer our question,' hissed Emma whose anger scared a few residents 'WHY would you lock up over 40 disabled and non disabled people in the first place?'

'We have nothing to do with your place being locked, the purple coach and the fire is our doing, that is all.' The lead protestor scratched his chin and yawned. 'We're only here to do a peaceful protest with no violence, but I'm not surprised with your level of security, anyone could walk in there and do anything they like.'

'That's not true! How could you say that when we've been hostage in our own buildings, with vulnerable people who need medical attention?

'Not vulnerable enough!' called out a protestor who had his hands cupped around his mouth.

The protestors laughed and watched as Carole stepped back to confer with Geoffrey and her employees. The laughing went up a notch as the pressure group watched Denise, Emma and Lauren tried to coax the residents back into the reception like runaway cattle, but only a few of them actually obeyed the staff while the rest wandered off on their own. Soon they gave up, it was hopeless so they ushered the ones who did listen into an empty corner of the car park and tried to do a head count to make sure none of them have wandered off. And then something had clocked into Emma's head.

'Wait wait, where's Arnold, James and the others from Group C? Weren't they in the line?'
This caught Geoffrey's eyes unaware and this put him into a small state of shock. Denise had forgotten to make a "string dragon" for his son's group. He must slip back to the village without being seen, otherwise he would cause another commotion. Then suddenly he heard some tinny retro music that was playing quietly in the distance. It sounded like it was coming from the village itself and it was getting louder every second. And the louder it became he noticed that more and more people could hear the sound as well. Curiously he pushed his way between the staff and protestors towards the gap between the two receptions where he could get an overview of the premises and once he did he could see a massive group marching straight towards them, the leader of the group was a man in a chequered shirt holding a massive, old school boom box in the air; and at that point the music was clearly audible.
'Gonna break my stride, nobody's gonna slow me down, oh-no, I got to keep on moving.' Then he thought, is that him? Surely it can't be. Every time I see him in public he's either slouched over solemnly or he's got his hand rammed into his armpit, a bit like that French dictator. Except that instead of planning war on Europe, he's planning to go into a complete strop over something that it entirely little and irrelevant, like people spitting or belly chains because he sees them as dirty and stomach wrenching.
'It can't be...' he murmured.
'And look there's Music Mark at the back!' pointed Denise excitedly 'They've actually done it!'
'B-but they can't do that,' spluttered one of the protestors.
'But they did see!? This proves that in a crisis, we can all work together regardless of all levels of disability or social impairment.'
'I can't believe I'm saying this but they've gone and done something that the rest of us wouldn't have,' replied Emma.
'Marcia, it's you you're back!' screamed Oliver as he waved his arms.
'Silly Ollie, you know you can always come around to the other lodges if you want to say hello.'

'Yeah, I know.'

Then Amanda and Denise burst out of the reception carrying a first aid box, a large bottle of water and a few blankets. Then the staff scanned the crowd and offered relief and water to anyone who was a victim of Mark's rampage. Luckily the only one who was actually injured was Catherine who suffered from a bruised arm when she got too close to Mark. Everyone else like Marcia came out unscathed which meant that Arnold and the others gave the record back on time.

'Everyone stand away please,' commanded Rita 'Mark I know you've got your record back but most importantly are you alright?' Mark nodded back, although he was still oblivious to what he'd done and his face was completely red from earlier.

'What was the name of the record they took?' asked Neil.

'Break my Stride, released in 1983 by Matthew Wilder,' proudly beamed Mark.

'Mark,' asked Rita again 'did you realise that you hit Catherine earlier?'

And then he covered his face and started to cry. Marcia then passed Rita one of the blankets and put it around him. 'Catherine was one of his closest friends,' she said to everyone.

Meanwhile the protestors were still bickering in the background, but with each other. 'Why didn't you did that bloody disc in our van?' wailed a female voice. It sounded like a south London accent, unusual in this region.

'I didn't just incase they found it, because if they did they would've dismantled the whole bus. I've seen their kind before when it comes to technology and solving things, and believe me they're not human at all they're like aliens.' Then the crowd of protestors began to disperse.

'Right that does it,' shouted the lady. 'You, Arnold Holt your time is up!'

'Pardon?' he asked.

38

I nearly screamed when one of the protestors mentioned my name.

'That's the one I was talking about earlier, that git there. Get him!' Then I heard Kimberley scream and saw Neil and Roger being pushed over by two men over 6ft with green anoraks and scarves that covered half of their faces as they marched towards us. Then both men grabbed my arms and tried to pull myself towards the purple coach.

'Heyheyhey! Get the hell away from my son!' screamed my Dad. I could not see him because he was behind myself and the autistic crowd but the man on the left let go of my arm and I looked up and saw that he was lying down on the ground, feeling his stomach. Then I saw a mysterious individual wearing a black hooded coat with blue stripes speed straight to the man holding my right arm and punched his scarf. As he let go of my arm I heard the man collapse onto the gravel. The hooded gentlemen nodded at myself and left before my Dad joined my right side where the protestors retreated and I discovered who the familiar voice belonged to.

'You! You're the one responsible for all of this chaos.' It was the lady from Bromley police station, Adam Langley's aunt. The individual whose fingers were all covered in rings. I presumed her name was Pauline.

'I did say I weren't finished with you back in Bromley and now we're here to give you what you deserve. Everyone listen, this man is a vicious deviant who attacks innocent people and should be kept away from the public. The council should not be giving money to places that support his evil behaviour.' My right hand was trembling in surprise and confusion so I placed it under my arm to prevent anybody from seeing it. The reason I was probably shaking was because I wasn't expecting this specific woman to return, especially in such a quaint location such as this area.

'How did you get here?' I asked her.

'I have been following you boy, to make sure you get fairly punished for what you did to my Adam and with the help of these people, I can finally get it done you arnophobic git!'

'Arnophobic?' asked my Dad.

'Arnophobia!' cried out my friends in unison. 'It is what you call someone who only dislikes Arnold Holt, an arnophobe!'

'Quiet all of you! That's not what it really means. It's a word you call someone who doesn't like other people because of what they wear, like a tattoo or these rings.' She then raised both of the hands in the air so that the staff and residents could see all her jewellery. 'Like I said this kind of discrimination can only come from such a narrow minded person like him!'

And then she pointed directly at myself.

'But Arnold's not like that, never!' shouted Barry.

'Yeah, we can prove it!' Then I felt my shoulder being tapped and it was my Dad. I think he wanted me to leave the crowd for no reason but when I tried to follow him Kimberley tried to pull myself back into the crowd. Suddenly Gary run straight behind us and stood directly in front of Pauline, her head was level with his chest.

'Hi I'm Gary. In an ideal world, we are all entitled to like or dislike anything but what I've learned from working here the key is choosing whether you want to be tolerant of the object or being, or just be plain hateful. I've worked with people who've taken offence to what I wear and who I fancy, these people are no exception but all of them are tolerant souls who like to include me in their daily activities.

Take you lot for example, you come here because you want to express your opinion, fair play to you but the fact you tried to burn down our buildings and hurt our people, you're clearly intolerant and uncivilised. Like I said you have a right to dislike everything but you can't be vile and start a bloody stupid protest about it. And I'm just borrowing words from people who have trouble speaking out against people like you. Is that about right Arnold?'

'Gary is one of my friends from the special villages. Regardless of his jewelled appearance, we have had an excellent time together playing board games, viewing classic sitcoms and he was the person who showed myself how to play blackjack,' I replied before cheering was heard once again.

'I must say he does have a point there, I thought we were all here to wave picket signs in the air but it's gone a little too far for me,' replied a young female protestor.

Then Pauline protested, 'I don't understand why you all like him so much. He's the type of person who wants to burn bridges, put walls up and hates society! Honestly apart from being sat behind a computer, they don't really bother to embrace the 21st century. They hate being around people.'

'That's not true!' said Kimberley 'we do like being around others, it's people like you who put us off from talking to them!'

'Oi! You can't put that fire out, that's essential for our campaign!' shouted the ringleader behind Pauline. The protestors then moved towards us simultaneously and three of the individuals who were holding signs with protest slogans on treated them like spears and tried to push Christopher and the others away with them.

'STOP!' Everyone stopped fighting and froze. I turned my head left to right to find out who that was; then I gave a small smile when I noticed that next to the purple coach there was a small police car accompanied by a larger vehicle with members of the police in yellow high visibility vests who were emerging from their cars.

'Right before you go any further, first of all nearly half of all disputes between large groups are caused by people misunderstanding each other. Also shouting all at once is not a sensible way of solving an argument so please just stop it.'

'Yeah!' shouted Ollie and Kimberley, with their fists above their heads.

'Thank you for the intervention constable,' clapped Mrs Hinton 'we've been trying to call you all day but what's happened is that those people over there tried to instigate a riot in order to try and close down the centre.'

'That's bogus!' replied the ringleader.

'We've actually been working together to undo the mess that these people caused, and we can prove it!' said Simon.

'Ha! But you can't!' shouted Pauline. 'You don't have proof that they've been working together so you can't prove anything.'

'Yes we can, I have recorded the incident.'

******

Everyone turned her heads one at a time and gawped at a calm looking bespectacled man with neat brown hair holding a miniature video camera with his palms.

'It's Roger, he spoke!' shouted the residents.

'But why would you do that Roger?' asked Carole.

'To ensure that this scenario would never happen again I decided to film the whole event for future reference as well as Arnold and his father endeavouring to save this place from ruin for their personal use.'

Roger then walked over to the police, his eyes gazed down on the camera as he tried to switch it on. Sound came from the device and there was a rush as nearly everyone squeezed together behind the policeman as they all tried to watch a glimpse of Arnold hanging off a tree on the tiny portable camera. The film then cut to a scene with Marcia giving Mark Cranley a solid round object at arm's length while he had something running down his t shirt that looked like blood. The film jumped again and this time they saw the car park where they were standing right now, except that the perspective had flipped so that the staff and reception were on the left while the purple bus with the pressure group on the right. The film zoomed in automatically on Pauline and the ringleader as they revealed their motif on a quiet but audible volume.

******

The police constable was writing in his notebook while he spoke to my Dad and the other staff members simultaneously. Mrs Leslie, Gary, Lauren and the others were busy as they prepared cups of orange squash and water to the residents.

'Well part of our undercover job was to track down this group, who allegedly made unrecorded threats against people who suffer from autistic spectrum disorders. Ironically these people claim that what they were doing was for the greater good and had relatives who were disabled themselves. I am guessing from my records that they saw autism as a minor disability that lightly affects sufferers and seen as the least important in comparison to other disabilities such as cerebral palsy or Down's Syndrome. I was lucky enough to run into someone in Selby last year who had this "minor disability" and believe me, he was too dangerous to be left alone and ignored.'

I stepped out of his view because I thought he was referring to myself. 'Unfortunately we couldn't pin any crimes down on this particular group in the past due to a lack of evidence, and you couldn't arrest someone just by holding up a board and protesting, that would be a breach to freedom of speech. But thanks to this guy's recording, Roland I think his name is, and Arnold's detective work here we can now book them down for large scale vandalism and clear intention to start a racket.'

'And Roger, thanks for all your filming, you're a real star,' replied Emma.

Suddenly I had a thought. 'Star?' I said. Then I suddenly realised, that unusual Saturday where I cheerfully greeted Lauren and she responded in a negative manner. I noticed that before she ran off that particular day, apart from her skin changing drastically there was another notable difference when she attempted to wave goodbye at myself. It may explain why during my last visit to the special village, I saw Lauren running between the residential houses and she wore a pair of mineral green mittens, which felt rather odd because she mentioned back in the social hub that green was her least favourite colour because she disliked Brussels sprouts and mucous. Immediately I snatched the master key from Stephan the caretaker, ran through the reception and hurried down the hill back to the village.

The day was approaching sunset and the interior of the care village was deserted, all except for one person who was roaring down the grassy bank, puffing and panting loudly like a runaway train about to crash. He trips over the wooden frame next to the gravel path but soon he picks himself up and continues to run towards one of the dormitories. Two minutes later Arnold runs back up the car park, this time with Lauren in tow behind him, who looked like she had been rolling in cobwebs all day and her brown hair was short and wispy instead of straight. The crowd looked in amusement at what Arnold had just picked up but Geoffrey, standing on the other side of the crowd was the most puzzled because Lauren was also standing next to him.

'This doesn't make sense, how the hell did you find her Arnold?' asked my Dad.

'When you stated that all the doors were locked, I noticed twenty four minutes ago that another door was locked for the very first time since I visited this centre and you had forgotten to unlock this door while you possessed the master keys. There would have been an incentive for this door to become locked because the only valuable items inside this room are the wheels on the bottom of the rubbish bins.'

'Identical twins,' Dr Campbell clapped his hands 'the oldest trick in the book I must say.'

'I'm Lauren!'

'Don't listen to her, that's my sister Kirsty. I'm the real Lauren.'

'Oh no she's not, I am!' It was like watching woman with long brown hair stare into a reflection with a mirror, except that there was not a mirror present and one of them looked dirtier than the other because she were locked inside the bin cupboard.

There was only one attempt at solving the puzzle as to how the "special village" turned into chaos. I felt nervous but certain that my discovery would be correct, but my chest was slightly shaking when I thought what would happen if my finding actually turned out to be incorrect in front of the public. So I pulled out one of my Dad's Everton mints out of the bag, swallowed it and stepped closer towards the identical pair. 'Hello there, can I both see your hands please?'

'Why?' asked the clean looking Lauren.

'Just do it!' shouted her double.

Sweat ran down my forehead and my eyebrows felt wet as I watched the pair exposed two pairs of hands so that I could inspect them. Then as they slowly turned their hands so that their palms were facing up, my heart started to beat furiously and I could taste the swallowed mint in the back of my mouth. Then as I looked at all of Lauren's four palms the beating stopped and I blew some air out of my mouth in relief that I was actually right after all.

'Hey, when did Lauren have a star on her left wrist?' asked Jonathan.

'That is not a star, that is a tattoo,' replied Roger.

'Then that means the one who doesn't have the star on her wrist is the real Lauren.'

This is the real Lauren!

'Is that it? Does this mean the game's over?' There was a brief silence before I heard members of staff whispering and Charlie hiding his face. However behind the purple coach I could see Pauline and two of the protestors each inhaling a cigarette.

'I think I have a logical and sensible way to explain what's going on,' suggested James, who was waving his arms around. 'Those protestors over there who've been bothering us for years, take in a new member who knew the whereabouts of Welbourne Mills due to contacts with Arnold and his local area; and plan their revenge for being arrested by trying to cause a riot so that the centre's funding could be cut and it would close down. But they knew that if they walked in they would be arrested straightaway.

So in order to successfully infiltrate this place they hired a doppelganger to sneak into the centre and steal the keys that help secure our wonderful home. And the best person to do that is none other than Lauren's identical twin so she could pretend to be her sister and take the keys right under their noses. But here's the twist. Why would she want to lock up Lauren in the first place? Perhaps she was anti-Welbourne Mills like those or maybe they gave her a lot of this.'

James then stuck his left hand in the air and rubbed his fingertips with his thumb. 'There are a million reasons but what happens is Kirsty with orders from her boss traps Lauren in the bin cupboard, puts on her uniform, takes one of Mark's records and sneaks into the head building; locks the doors and pretends to be trapped like everyone else.' They clapped their hands at James, who replied by taking a theatrical bow. 'Thank you all!'

Everyone applauded James except for Lauren's sister who looked more confused than guilty.

'Well I actually thought I was taking part in a prank,' shrugged Kirsty. 'That man over there said he'll pay me if I were to impersonate you and give him a bunch of keys. He even paid me £500 a few weeks ago just to check out the site and pretend to be you.'

As the crowd watched the coach finally leave, some of its passengers were arrested and taken to a police van, including the ringleader and Pauline had enough time for one last outburst.

'How can you all keep this place going? They're not vulnerable people. You've got someone who pinches sauce condiments from restaurants, a clean freak who won't even touch his own hand and then you've got that boy over there who stands there all day posing like that person who won the battle of Trafalgar, you know who I'm talking about. They're not disabled it's all in their heads! You shouldn't be keeping such an expensive paradise because here's nothing wrong with any of them, they're all just weird!' Rita watched as the police van shut its doors and pull away towards the exit, one less problem gone she thought.

'I liked the part where Arnold's Dad knocked the staff room down.' laughed Kimberley.

'I say we thank the guy who used the digger to get us free!' yelled one of the staff.

A chorus of hip-hip-hoorays filled the air and the atmosphere grew brighter, as well as a little red due to Geoffrey's blushing. That was when the older, less aware residents began to stare at him awkwardly like a big polka dot elephant that just fell out of the sky.

'Your name, is it Geoff?' stuttered Charlie.

'Yes it is. Why?' asked Geoffrey.

'I think I have seen you before!' he pointed. 'But you used to have brown hair!'

'No!'

'Yes you did, you used to play with your cars here!'

'No I did not! Please!'

'Geoff, is that you? Geoffrey with a J in it?' Dr Campbell called out.

Everybody turned and looked straight at Geoff, or Jeff. That was everyone including the staff, the protestors and the residents, even the ones with short attention spans turned to face this man who appeared out of nowhere earlier and tried to knock down one of their buildings. Then a chill rattled down his spine, his aging legs nearly buckled and he could taste the bitter air as Geoffrey leapt backwards nervously and he tried to find something solid to keep him from falling. The closest thing he could find was a parked hatchback so he sat on the bonnet, rested both hands on the car and gave out the biggest exhale of air that he hadn't done for years.

'Terence, Terence the tractor? It can't be,' he mumbled back.

'The very same,' replied Terry smiling 'but I packed up the driving years ago when I crossed paths with an angry bull and broken my shoulder bone.'

'Hey I remember Terence the tractor as well!' cried out Neil.

'I know a person who called him that first, his name was-'

'NO!' screamed a voice.

That blows it. I knew that stepping foot in this place would be a mistake, thought Geoffrey.

It was as if he was stranded on an iceberg surrounded by sharks and electric eels, that had shrank to the point that it only supported his feet and it was still melting underneath them. And once he inevitably sank into the murky waters below, his secret would be finally out. Not just to Terry the Tractor, but George, Rose, his wife, Rita,   that Carrie lady and even his boss Howard, it felt like they were all watching him as well. Then the penny dropped.

'Do you have autism?' asked Arnold.

To Geoffrey the question sounded even more chilling, as if he was standing naked in front of everyone. 'Yes it is true, I can no longer hide the fact.' He turns around and stoops down slightly to make eye contact with his son. 'Arnold, when I was 14, I used to be a lot like you. I found it difficult to talk to anyone, I got depressed quite a lot and I did not like it when your uncle used to touch me because I used to bite him. At that time I found it hard to control myself and the only thing I used to think about all the time was cars or anything with wheels, a bit similar to how you used to read *The Railway Series* books. But this place back then helped developed me, even if the teaching methods were a bit rough back then compared to today. But I am a lot different now to how I was before and although I regret being like that, I have come to a point where I accept my challenging behaviour back then and it is something you will have to come to terms with as well when you get older Arnold.'

Dr Campbell softly clapped his hands and this turned into a huge applause from the autistic residents. Even someone (could've been Julian) let out a wolf-whistle.

'That was brilliant Geoff,' smiled Terry 'I couldn't have said it better.'

'I have a question,' asked Roger 'if this place made you a better person than before, then why are acting as if you're denying it?'

The applause died down and all eyes back on Geoffrey again.

'I can explain this,' exclaimed Dr Campbell, while adjusting his jacket. 'Back in the sixties and seventies having a diagnosis of Asperger's Syndrome or ASD was like being blacklisted. Society back then had no grasp on what the condition was and what caused it but the public would often misinterpret their condition as if all cases of autism were identical. I believe that the reason why Mr Holt over here did not want people to know that he had the condition was because either he did not want to remember any of the negative fragments from that time or he did not want his family to know because of the ripple effect that these kind of revelations can have. Is that about right Geoffrey?'

'Well, a little bit. My brother is the only living family member who knew and decided to keep it a secret. Of course, the fact that his son was also autistic did help in keeping the secret because he could relate to how difficult life can be just by saying you had it.'

Then they applauded Geoffrey again who replied by nodding his head back, which to him was a less cheesy approach to taking a bow.

'Stop!' Everyone stopped in their tracks again, a couple even turned their heads. 'This is impossible! If he has it then why doesn't his family know about it already?'

'Well logically speaking,' said Terry trying to address the mystery voice, whom he couldn't weed out in the crowd, 'autistic spectrum disorder affects people in a variety of ways. Although you could agree that it does affect individuals who cannot dress themselves or use the toilet on their own, there are also a large number of bright people on the spectrum who have gone on to lead successful lives and even raised families of their own.'

'That is not my point. What I'd like to know is who the bloody hell you are and why you can come along from nowhere and say who is disabled and who's not just by looking at them and why you are focusing on this particular person.' Terry now felt very offended. This ignorant voice coming out of the sky, who did it belong to he thought and why did she think that they were entitled to know Geoffrey more than he did, besides his relationship with Geoff (or Jeff) dated well back into the 80's, whereas this voice (had it also been around this decade) would've been more than a childish croak. Without resorting to swearing, Terry decided to put his foot forward and battle this invisible heckler.

'I'm a professional with over 30 years of counselling and psychology under my belt and I have worked with this dear chap here long before you were probably born so please tell me mystery woman, who are you and why the hell do you think you could challenge a doctor and claim that your knowledge of this gentleman's condition is greater than my own?' He was now getting irate.

'Because I am his daughter.'

39

'What!?'

Rose Holt dropped the megaphone on the ground and snaked along the clusters of crowds that lay between herself and Terry Campbell. Finally they came face to face and there was a bitter silence when a young lady with cropped brown hair and a white blouse under a red parka made eye contact with this gentleman, who looked like a retired university professor with his wispy white hair and wrinkled complexion. 'Rose, what the hell are you doing here?' cried out Geoffrey 'You're supposed to be home with Mum!'

'I'm only out doing the right thing Dad,' she replied.

'I don't get it, has everyone been plotting against me or something?'

'Nobody is plotting against you Geoffrey,' consoled Terry.

'Arnold, did you know anything about this?' he asked.

His son shrugged his shoulders and gave a blank look. Either he was speechless or just didn't care that Rose had come out from nowhere, it was hard to tell.

'Oh, and I have a surprise for you too Arnold.'

Standing beside her was the man in the black hooded coat who saved myself from the protestors. He lowered his hood and I jumped a step backward in surprise and nearly crashed into Neil. It was the policeman whom I encountered in Selby station last year, the one who had tattoos of birds on his arm. But I noticed that his trademark earrings had disappeared which made me feel calmer. Guessing by their presence it appeared that Rose was actually working undercover. This surprised nobody except for me because I thought she would deliberately work against the "special village". There was a brief silence until Denise spoke again.

'Well after all that hubbub that just went on, I think we all need to relax and have a little treat. Simon, we can get you those yellow waders you've been saving up for, and for you James another bottle of HP sauce to add to your collection,' she laughed.

'I'd never turn that down,' he chortled.

'STOP!' shouted Rose. Everyone turned round to look at her as she waved both of her arms in the air 'Can't you understand what we're going on about? Why they were here!?You say this place helps disabled people by transforming them so that they can live normally in the real world, but you are actually making them worse by feeding their obsessions and pampering them.'

'But they are not pampering us,' said a voice.

But Mrs Hinton seemed very angry.

'How can you say that? This is a safe, caring place for disadvantaged adults on the spectrum.'

'Safe!?' she spat violently. 'How can you call it safe? You've got amateurs keeping farm animals down there, ones that could bite and kill any of them. Most of your staff are volunteers who aren't trained with dealing with difficult persons and don't get me started on your boat pond.'

'Whose side are you on anyway lady?' asked Gary.

'I'm the one who tipped off the police about the protests before things went too hairy, slashed that evil cow's car as well.' She paused 'We are on the side of good.'

'Yeah. I didn't feel well when I used to live in Leicester but since I moved to here I feel like a better person than I was 5 years ago,' calmly replied Julian.

'We are quite an intelligent and laid back lot who are well aware of what's going around us, it's just that we don't like to be in sync with those who call themselves "normal", that's all. So why are you giving us the negative feedback?' asked James.

'She wants to kick us all out!' shouted Charlie.

There was a flurry of high pitched screams and objection before sweets and pebbles were thrown at Rose. Suddenly the policeman who saved myself swooped in and stuck his arms wide out in front of the residents in an attempt to halt them.

'Stop and listen, we're on your side, we are here to protect you, not hurt you,' said the policeman. 'She was only explaining why those people were targeting this place.'

'OK, I think I got on the wrong foot there but I'll talk about it later,' apologised Rose. 'What's important is that everyone here is safe but it is hard when they overlook health and safety. Arnold, you remember the time George fell into that river in Scotland?'

'Yes.'

'Well that's my point, I respect you all but your home needs to be more safe to prevent these things from happening.'

Colin the policeman, as I recalled his name was talking on his mobile phone.

'Yep, everything has been sorted. It's safe to park up.' Suddenly a silver Jaguar vehicle appeared in the car park, drove over a puddle and stopped next to the wooden posts. Three individuals stepped out of the car, two females and, a man with a black camera around his neck and another man who appeared to be wearing the same clothes of a traditional mayor.

'Hello! I hope everyone is OK.' One by one the VIPs walked over to the crowd, the mayor leading and shook Carole's hand first before moving onto Geoffrey, Dr Campbell and Marcia; as if they were on a conveyor belt with Emma, Denise, Mark and the curious crowd on the very end. Some of them stuck their hands out at once hoping that the mayor would touch them while a few like Simon didn't like the idea of touching someone they didn't know. But surprisingly Simon actually shook one of the VIP's hands and wasn't seen reaching for his hand soap afterwards. 'I've heard good things come from you lot, especially you sir.' He pointed at Arnold with his walking stick.

'If you can Mr Holt, seeing your heroic actions with Welbourne Mills, would you like to take centre stage in our shoot?'

'Well OK, but I don't think knocking down a wall can be classed as heroic.' Geoffrey felt a jolt of discomfort as he was propelled from behind by Kimberley and placed right in front of the photographer.

Once my Dad stood next to myself the picture was automatically taken. The crowd behind us abruptly spread out like smoke and the photographer picked up his camera and walked over to his vehicle. I watched him load the tripod into his car boot sideways before he started his car, reversed into a brown puddle and drove away from the "special village". I was still looking at the entrance when there was a tap on my shoulder.

'Arnold, hi I'm Carole, I'm the head of Welbourne Mills.'

'Yes, I know who you are.'

'I just wanted to personally give my thanks for what you and your father have done for us today. You have certainly made an impact on some of the people who live here and a couple of them have even done things that they've never done before in their lives before they came here and today's incident is one that nobody will forget. I must admit it had turned my life around a little bit and I feel that I should be working more closely with the residents and even participate with their daily activities. Do you agree with what I'm saying?'

'Yes.'

'So I'm going to ask you this. Arnold Bentley Holt, would you like to stay at Welbourne Mills with your friends as a permanent resident?'

I thought about this very carefully. To help confirm my decision I looked at everybody who were all surrounding and staring at me, except for

Charlie who was instead staring at the black gutters on the reception roof. After two and a half minutes I finished pondering and announced my final decision.

'No thank you. I think it would be beneficial for myself to remain in Orpington in order to support and build relations with my family, especially my sister and my mother.'

'So are you trying to say that you don't want to say here?' said Rose.

'Yes. I do not want to stay here, thank you.' I heard that half of the crowd were cheering quietly but the other half (mainly residents) were groaning sadly for obvious reasons.

Some of the more vulnerable residents began to cry at the news but Rose couldn't believe what she heard and her jaw was wide open. Arnold refusing to join the "special village"? She thought the chances of that happening were a thousand to one.

'But I don't want you to go Arnold!'

'I miss you and your face,' said Kimberley.

'I know that your friends are upset but I think you've made a wise decision Arnold,' said Rose.

'Whether you have autism or not, that was a difficult choice to make and I'm glad with what you've chosen, for that we are proud of you,' consoled Rita as she placed her hand on Arnold's shoulder. There was a small applause that was broken by the growl of the VIP car as it drove over the uneven ground, splashing into a puddle on its way out.

'Looks like it's time for us to head back before it gets too late, we don't want to reach Orpington at midnight,' said Geoffrey, looking at his watch.

'Well we can put you up here for the night, it's not a hotel but at least we're friendly and secure,' said Lauren. 'Normally we watch a film inside one of the lodges or have a traditional campfire when the weather is nice with marshmallows and silly stories like the ones James tells us. Are you up for that Rose?'

'It's not a bad idea, after what we've all gone through.'

'That's a sound plan, let me check if the car is OK,' replied Geoffrey.

'Haha, Dad is his good old self again,' finished Rose.

'So Arnold, what do you say for one last night with us then?' asked Rita.

'One minute please,' he said abruptly.

As we looked up at the sunset that had covered the dales beyond the centre with Rose and my Dad I pulled out Mrs Leslie's contract from my pocket in which I had kept all along. Then I tore it up into four pieces and left them to intentionally float to the ground, reminiscent to those classic films from the 1950s. There was no need at this point to keep promises on fictional pieces of paper, even if some were meant to be broken.

240

Epilogue

One day inside the "special village", a health and safety officer appeared out of nowhere holding a clipboard and wearing a blue hard hat. He was a fat individual with thick white hair, a large stomach that hid behind his white shirt and he looked as if his face had been sunburnt. The district council mentioned that the entire centre had to be checked carefully and given an "audit", otherwise it would be closed down. I volunteered myself to thoroughly check the whole site (as I had done before) but the staff said that somebody else were going to.

They could not keep the pigs and their accommodation anymore because of a rule that concerned general health and safety procedures, the health and safety officer mentioned that pigs were very heavy and had extremely sharp teeth which meant that he thought they were dangerous. But we were happily allowed to keep the chickens but the only individuals who could touch them were the staff and volunteers.

Unfortunately the reception that I saw on my first visit to Welbourne Mills had disappeared. I was initially distraught by this until Mrs Leslie mentioned that it was only temporary and the larger building that stood to its left was the original reception and it had returned to its default position, albeit with a bigger and warmer waiting room, black panels on the roof that absorbed the sun's energy and a balcony that overlooked the entire village. Doctor Terence Campbell, the hairy psychiatrist who revealed my Dad's secret in front of the crowd had decided to retire because he was too old and decided to return to drive a tractor and set up a farm in rural County Durham.

As for myself, I no longer have a desire to automatically create a meticulous schedule of tasks and objectives anymore. Doctor Ian Bradbury believed that the reason I used to make those lists in my head were because my mind wanted to occupy and distract my thoughts from the effects of long term unemployment and writing those lists would have steered myself away from the typical side effects of being traditionally unemployed. Although I do not completely agree with him, my mind feels vastly different before I had first met Ian and I feel obliged to reward him and Terence at once point with a gift.

And as for my Dad, he became what was known as a patron to the "special village" and sometimes we would participate in fundraising events together once every three months. He still works at that building with the endless lines of cars aside it and one time I travelled to his workplace to view any changes as well as to meet his boss, who claimed he saw us inside a national newspaper. My Dad also told me that when he his second car, he felt very upset and distraught in the same way I felt when Mrs Leslie left Orpington or when my friend Aaron died because he had been used to possessing his car for a very long time but he had to adapt and move forward.

But this message when read completely would produce the illusion that I had changed my thoughts and now live permanently at Welbourne Mills instead of Orpington. I am afraid that is incorrect. One month after the incident with the missing record disc, my Mum received a telephone call and we were summoned to the local police station again. Inside I met PC Fisher once again where he presented a newspaper image of myself and my Dad from the special village. I was then introduced to another policeman who mentioned that I had unique abilities and something that the other officers did not have and asked if I would like to begin a work placement with the police force.

Although I dearly missed my mother, I soon began to genuinely miss my sister Rose as well and remembered all the positive thoughts I had of her, such as the time where she used to run a snail farm in our rear garden when we were children and another time when she made "sugar sandwiches" for a picnic that took place near Keston Common.

I was told by my parents and my friends this: never to cling onto the past, for it may only taunt you forever.

Goodbye

This is one of many poems by Roger Letts, a permanent resident at Welbourne Mills, he is happy for me to have it published here:

The lonely corner is where the tree stands
A place where one can think of distant lands
With vast emerald plains where the grass is tall
A haven where they can be never be bothered at all

About the author

Daniel C Betts is an author and illustrator from Bromley, Kent who suffers from Autistic Spectrum Disorder, or ASD. This edition of his book incorporates his first two novels, *The Idiot of Lord Nelson*, and its sequel *The Accidental Doorman*. Part of this story is based on real life experiences from the author and surrounding people regarding autism but the storyline and its characters are entirely fictional.

97063440R00134

Made in the USA
Columbia, SC
08 June 2018